Genghis Khan and Cyrus the Great each had his "pony express" to link a vast empire. But never in history, for speed and distance covered, danger and adventure, has anything approached the Pony Express of Russell, Majors and Waddell.

Daredevil riders, bankrupt owners, political schemers, they all played a part in the legendary but short-lived Pony Express. Armed with bible and shotgun, the riders sped in a night-and-day relay across 1900 miles of wilderness that had been labelled "uninhabitable." At $5.00 a letter (later $1) they established a rapid communications system that made it possible for the North to hold California and Oregon, and win the gold and silver bonanzas of Nevada and Colorado.

"A grass roots view of the men and events of Pony Express Days, and an excellent presentation." Bartlett Boder, President, *Central Overland Pony Express Trail Association*.

HOOFBEATS OF DESTINY

The story of the Pony Express' critical role in holding the West "for the Union" during the intrigues of "Secesh" and the Confederacy's campaign to steal all of the United States of America west of the Mississippi River.

Robert West Howard

and

ROY E. COY
FRANK C. ROBERTSON
AGNES WRIGHT SPRING

BALLANTINE BOOKS • NEW YORK

© 1960 by Robert West Howard

All rights reserved.

SBN 345-23848-6-125

First Printing: April, 1973
Second Printing: March, 1974

Cover painting by Frank C. McCarthy

Printed in the United States of America

BALLANTINE BOOKS, INC.
201 East 50th Street, New York, N.Y. 10022

CONTENTS

FOREWORD *vii*
1. THE IRON FRONTIER *11*
2. WHO WINS THE WEST? *24*
3. THE $5,000,000 TEMPLE NAILS *36*
4. PIKE'S PEAK AND BUSTED *46*
5. ORPHANS PREFERRED *58*
6. MOCHILA'S GLORY *66*
7. AWAKE THE WINDS!
    BY AGNES WRIGHT SPRING *80*
8. THROUGH PAIUTE HELL
    BY FRANK C. ROBERTSON *97*
9. BUT THE DEVIL'S IN WASHINGTON! *107*
10. THE THREAD THAT HELD *119*
11. THE TALKING WIRES *128*
12. GOLD FOR OLD ABE *132*
13. THEY WON THE WEST *138*
14. EXPRESSLY ABOUT PONIES
    BY FRANK C. ROBERTSON *148*
15. WELDED IN STEEL *151*
16. THE KID GROWS UP *155*
17. HALLELUJAH! *160*
18. THE TRAIL TODAY
    BY ROY E. COY *171*
19. HERE THEY RIDE ON *181*
20. THE RECORDERS *186*
    APPENDIX *190*

FOREWORD

"You cannot portray a subject without bias until you are one hundred years away from the happening," the great historian Dr. Charles A. Beard used to tell his students at Columbia University. One of his students was our coauthor Agnes Wright Spring. She passed Dr. Beard's bit of wisdom jubilantly along when, on the threshold of the Pony Express Centennial, we began writing this book.

But, here we are with the book, and, it would seem, possessed of more biases than any of the hundreds of authors who became enamored of the Pony Express saga after "Buffalo Bill" Cody, in 1893, financed the publication of Alexander Majors' *Seventy Years on the Frontier*.

Our post-writing biases are:

1. The Pony Express played a vital role in saving *all* of the American West for the Union during the months of Southern Secession and the first year of the Civil War.

2. The four hundred youngsters "willing to risk death daily" for twenty-five dollars a week are truly among the great American heroes. Their daring and superb horsemanship maintained communications with the Far West via the Central Route, won the gold and silver of Colorado-Nevada and California to bolster Lincoln's war budget, shaped the path that the first transcontinental telegraph, railroad, and highway would follow, and pioneered the greatest revolution in the history of the United States Mails.

3. John Buchanan Floyd, the United States Secretary of War in President Buchanan's Administration (1857-1862), emerges as one of the most despicable traitors in American history—a Benedict Arnold without shame *or* pretreason glory.

4. The names of Alexander Majors, Benjamin Ficklin, William Gilpin, Rev. John Chivington and—yes—perhaps William Russell belong in any Western Hall of Fame, gleaming gold and bestarred.

There are our biases. All we can say for them is that they marched in and settled themselves after years of intensive research by three of America's greatest authorities on the Pony Express, coauthors Roy E. Coy, Mrs. Spring and Frank C.

Robertson. Consequently, our biases are derived from fact. So perhaps we have achieved, on the Pony's one hundredth birthday, the objective portrayal that Dr. Beard recommended a generation ago.

Whatever, *Hoofbeats of Destiny* is the fourth multiauthor "serendipity" in American history that I have had the pleasure of editing. After thirty years of amateur and professional research in Americana, I reached the conviction that teamwork production of popular histories can be as effective as teams have proved in science, medicine, industry and education research. Victor Weybright, editor-in-chief of The New American Library, gave the theory a trial run when he contracted the twenty-six-author *This Is the West* in 1956. The same basic pattern was followed in 1958-59 with *This Is the South* and *The Bench Mark*. Last summer, again, Mr. Weybright gave quick assent to the suggestion that a group of us make an "overview" survey of facts and theories about the Pony Express, from the viewpoint of national politics, the Kansas-Missouri struggle between Slavers and Abolitionists, and the looming Civil War.

Roy E. Coy is director of both the St. Joseph Museum and the Pony Express Museum at St. Joseph, Missouri.

Mrs. Agnes Wright Spring, the official State Historian of Colorado, is internationally respected as an author-authority on Western Americana.

Frank C. Robertson, the 1960 president of Western Writers of America, has devoted a long lifetime to researching and writing the history of his native Utah; his bibliography includes thousands of articles and more than a score of novels, plus the distinguished autobiography *A Ram in the Thicket*.

Obviously, our team functioned superbly in researching data across the two thousand miles of the Pony Trail. Since Mrs. Spring and Mr. Robertson developed the unique—and I mean just that, because you won't find the data elsewhere—detail of Chapters 7 and 8, they have been awarded additional bylines on those chapters. Similarly, Roy Coy deserves a "solo" for his adventure report on The Trail Today (Chapter 18). The balance of the book functioned as a team operation, in the thoroughly sane manner of any newspaper or magazine.

Clem Huniker, the stationmaster at St. Joseph, is *Hoofbeats of Destiny's only* fictional character. Clem, for a variety of reasons, is a composite of several H. & St. J. Railroaders who played such valiant roles in the Pony Express revolution of the United States Mails. Everyone else in our book, from Billy Cody, Jeff Thompson and Alex Majors to Fred Harvey and General John J. Pershing's father, is "as God willed" and as the desperate times of the frontier West shaped them.

We wish to extend thanks for research assistance and authoritative advice to: Bartlett Boder, president, St. Joseph Historical Society, and trustee, State Historical Society of Missouri; Don L. Reynolds, photographer and research assistant, St. Joseph Museum; Dr. Paul Angle and Mrs. Lewis Sawyer of the Chicago Historical Society; Dr. Carl Mapes, Bennet Harvey and Joseph Landes of Rand McNally & Company; Allen Van Cranebrock of the Burlington Lines; Howard B. Blanchard of the Union Pacific Railroad Company; Lyman Anson of Wheaton, Illinois; Miss Rilma Buckman of Woodstock, Vermont, and Chicago; Roderick Turnbull of the *Kansas City Star*; Mrs. Helen Henley and "Headmaster" Paul Deland of *The Christian Science Monitor*; Mrs. Edith Bond Stearns, director of the Peterborough Players, Peterborough, New Hampshire; Arthur Roth of Levi Strauss Company, San Francisco; Louis Lundborg, vice-president of the Bank of America; L. C. Bishop of Cheyenne, Wyoming; the librarians of the State Historical Society of Colorado, the Western History Department of the Denver Public Library, the Wyoming State Archives and, resoundingly, those stalwarts in the Newspaper Reference cubicle of the Chicago Public Library who sleuthed down the obituaries of "Pony Bob" Haslam and Alexander Majors.

Don Russell, Western historian and encyclopedia editor, interrupted work on his own biography of Buffalo Bill Cody (scheduled for publication by the University of Oklahoma Press during 1960) to aid our research. Mrs. Lorraine Brown of Skokie, Illinois, as usual labored nights and weekends to translate editor squiggles into typescript. Walter R. Freeman functioned joyously—even puckishly—as New American Library's editor-with-lasso.

Finally, and humbly, all four of us wish to put large, enduring thanks into the record for the four people who made the largest contributions toward this book—as unpaid researchers, cleaner-uppers, objective critics, temper-soothers, dietitians and best companions. Those four are: Ada M. Coy, Archer T. Spring, Winnie Robertson, Elizabeth Z. Howard.

ROBERT WEST HOWARD

Chicago, Illinois
January 15, 1960

1.
THE IRON FRONTIER

Clem Huniker sighed and added up the bill for the shipment of beaver pelts for the third time. A dollar and sixty cents to Quincy Junction, ten cents for the Mississippi ferry, ninety cents to Springfield City, and from there to Chicago . . . The telegraph key chattered. Clem flipped the pencil across the desk and listened.

B'durn, the Express was through Cameron; only an hour late. And in weather like this, too. He beamed, glanced out the window. Then he felt his hair roots tingle all the way to his shoulders. The chair crashed to the floor as he sprinted through the door. The wind blew his shouts back into the frozen Missouri.

As unconcerned as a prairie dog in June, a figure crouched in the middle of the tracks, one ear pressed against a rail. And ten feet beyond him, back square to the oncoming train, a giant in a striped Mackinaw stared west toward the river.

"Git off'n thim tracks fa-a-a-st." Clem flung the warning again, and lunged on down the platform.

The giant saw him now, swept him with stern, grave eyes, then resumed the stare toward the river. The second figure suddenly bellywhopped full length in the snow and lay with both hands as well as right ear hugging the ice-rimed rail. Clem wigwagged his arms and screamed again. "Train's a-comin'," he bawled. "Git off'n thet track." He flung past the giant, pushing him up toward the platform with an elbow thrust, and grabbed the prone figure by the hair. "Ain't gonna have the likes of you or nobody else givin' this railroad a bad name by gettin' splashed all over the locomotive," he shrilled, then yanked—praying hard that the fool's ear and hands weren't frozen to the iron—breathing thanks that Jim Hanks hadn't tooted his whistle yet to alert his wife that the Express was snortin' into St. Joseph depot and dinner'd best be on the table in ten minutes.

The head jerked back and said, "Ouch." Clem danced away, doubled his fists for defense, and growled, "Git up on that platform." It was just a kid, a big, long-legged kid rigged out in bullwhacker's gear. Butternut breeches tucked into knee-high boots, deerskin jacket and, tumbling down to skinny shoulders from a beat-up porkpie hat, a mass of silky blond hair.

The youngster didn't so much as look at Clem, after the "Ouch" and headshake. He fixed his beaming gaze on the giant and pointed back at the rail. "It sounds kinda like a buffalo stampede," he hollered. "Sortuva cross between that and a cyclone wind. Is that the way the train always sounds?"

"Better stay off the track, Billy." The giant smiled. "Guess I forgot that those things can't turn out around you, like a horse and wagon. Might've got us run over."

"Glory, I'm downright sorry, sir." The boy dipped his shimmering hair and turned back toward Clem. "Wasn't thinkin' on making you all that bother, mister. I never seen a train—yet. Bill Wilson—he's one of our drivers—told me you could lean down onto a rail and hear her hummin' from miles away."

Clem nodded, then shivered and flapped his arms to keep warm. He'd seen that big fellow somewheres. Full face, durned if he didn't look like the picture of Moses in the family Bible. Younger, to be sure, than they made Moses look up there atop Sinai; say—oh—about the time they crossed the Red Sea into the Wilderness—the big, flowing beard still brown; the eyes with a lot of steel in 'em; the nose as pink and firm as a hawk's beak. Yes, sir, Moses about to enter the— That's who he is! That's who.

Clem just nodded to the boy and, slapping his arms again against the cold, walked over to the giant.

"I'm presumin'," Clem gulped, "you're Alexander Majors. If I'm presumin' right, I'm mighty thankful I saw you and the boy in time."

He winced as he held out his hand; there was Jim Hanks spreading the long *boo—hoo—hoo* of his engine whistle to Mrs. Hanks and all of St. Joseph as he slithered past the Patee House into the Eighth Street curve. He'd be lucky, with tracks as slick as this, if the brakemen could keep the train from skating right past the station and into the roundhouse wall.

The hand that took Clem's seemed as big as a beaver pelt, but of woven steel. "It would have been His will, brother, if you hadn't," the giant boomed. "But I should greatly have regretted missing all the excitement that looms over there." He jerked a thumb toward the river. "I stood there wondering how and when your iron horses will cross all the West. Just now, when Billy roared about that noise he heard in the rail, I couldn't help but puzzle whether it really was the Hannibal Express he heard or a mysterious message from Above—a foreboding of things to come." The bearded lips clipped shut then, and the big hand squeezed Clem's. "Sorry. I don't mean to sermonize. I am Alexander Majors. This is my errand boy, Billy Cody. And you, I presume, are the stationmaster."

Clem nodded. "Yes, sir. Clem Huniker. And I wanna tell you somethin' right fast. You're every bit as good a preacher and wagon man as people say you are. All of us here in St. Joe's bettin' three to one that if anybody can put the Pony Express through, you can." He turned as the Hannibal Express clattered into sight, then came up close to Majors. "Russell," he stage-whispered, "may be all right for politickin' and just fine in Washington but—well—I feel like the rest of the boys feel. If the Pony ever gets to Californy, and Hannibal an' St. Joe engines ever follow, it's gonna be the likes of you that do it. Not Russells, nor even Waddells."

Spoke his mind for once. Straight out. Clem tilted his head proudly and hurried back beside the glow of the potbelly stove in the station office. The warmth tingling his backsides, he beamed again out the window. It was still a thrill to see her come in, brass trim gleaming, smoke and sparks billowing from the great funnel. The conductor and his "runner" grunted red-faced against the brake wheels on the open coach platform. Jim Hanks cussed a blue streak and threw the drive rods into reverse.

Almost a year now since Mayor Jeff Thompson handled the engine controls for that first run of the Express across the whole skitter-de-crash, bangity-bump two hundred miles of Missouri from Hannibal to St. Joseph. Still hard to believe that shiny monster out there, its stack so closely patterned after an upside-down starched petticoat that railroaders called it Jenny Lind, its canary-yellow coach not much bigger than one of Mr. Majors' prairie schooners—that, b'dad, was the westernmost train on the whole golblinked continent. St. Joseph was just as important as Chicago. This was the gateway to the West, the terminal place, with eleven thousand rambunctious souls this February day in 1860. Elect a man to the White House who'll keep Kansas gunmen to home and hang a few of those Boston millionaires sending rifles to the Emigrant Aid Society—then, by jing, the railroad could build right on across the Missouri River to the Pike's Peak gold fields and Salt Lake and—yes—to San Francisco. St. Joseph would be bigger than Chicago.

Clem beamed and sighed. Somehow, even on those icy tracks, Jim Hanks was skidding the Express to a stop right at the platform. That lanky Cody kid—hmm! Cody family used to live over near Leavenworth; man of the family died two–three years back; either fever or a bushwhacker bullet. Must be one of his kids. Anyway, there he gawked, mouth wide open as a muskrat trap, ogling from the locomotive to the coaches and back again, until Mr. Majors turned and tapped his shoulder and motioned toward the coach steps.

Yup. There was The Weasel, all right. Clem never said that out loud, not even to Mrs. Huniker. But that's how the great William H. Russell struck him. Suppose, maybe, the fact that he looked like a weasel had something to do with it—a pompous little prig in a tall hat; whiskers coming down either side of his face to meet in sort of a point below his nose; two big eyes popped out, rollin' this way and rollin' that way, takin' you and everything else in. Oh, for a struttin' general-store bumpkin from Vermont, he'd built himself a kingship, all right. Russell, Majors & Waddell—the greatest freighting outfit in the West. Russell first, mind you. And Waddell traipsing along in the rear, glum and fat and squinting to see if the other two had dropped anything. But Majors in the middle because he had the broadest shoulders and liked a wagon seat better than a swivel chair and could preach two-hour sermons to a warehouse jammed with five hundred stinkin', adobe-hard wagon men, without so much as a belch or mumble out of a one of 'em.

Clem slid into his buffalo greatcoat this time and pushed back through the crowd to collect the train reports. The Cody kid was hiking Russell's two shiny portmanteaus down the platform. Russell glowered after him, popeyes a-wobble. Clem climbed into the cab with Jim Hanks, pried trip information from the big fellow in a series of grunts and monosyllables. Young Cody rode off on a pinto, a portmanteau slung on a rawhide strap, down each side of the pony's neck. Smart kid.

On the way back to the station, Clem passed Russell and Majors again and lifted his cap and bowed. Backsides rewarmed, he sat down, opened the telegraph circuit and tapped Hannibal's call signal. Hannibal boomed a reply against the tin can Clem had rigged to amplify the rat-a-tat. He pounded out his report, idly watching the long, proud stride of

Majors, the slinky trot of Russell, as they crossed the street and turned south. Not going straight to the Patee House, eh? Hmm. He finished the report, then signaled again. "Majors met Russell at train," he tapped. "Heading now for Holladay's. Looks like fix-up for Pony Express. All here pray Kansans and them so-and-sos back East let 'em alone." Clackety-clack. Hannibal signaled. "Amen, brother," the tin can banged out. Hannibal signed off.

Heading up toward the black bulk of Ben Holladay's Pike's Peak Stables, Alexander Majors rumbled similar thoughts. And William H. Russell's gullet jumped as he reached for answers.

That scalawag preacher James Montgomery had skulked back into Kansas after failing to rescue John Brown or stir up a slave rebellion. Now, again, Montgomery and Senator Lane were urging open warfare. They'd brought back a new song, something about John Brown's body moldering in the grave and his soul marching on. It could be dangerous—more dangerous even than John Brown's trigger finger and mad brain. "I think it disturbs me even more," Majors said, "because they have set those words to a lovely old campmeeting tune we used to sing in Kentucky. 'Say, brothers, will you meet us on Jordan's golden shore.' And now, John Brown the martyr has captured it."

"Passing fancy." Russell's throat muscles relaxed. He might have known it would be something like this. "If we haven't got more problems than Montgomery and Lane turned into song-leaders, we're made." He even forced a laugh on that one.

"Music is an expression of the soul." Majors stopped in the middle of the road, scuffed a boot toe in the slush and began fingering his beard with his right hand.

The gullet jumped again. Dammit. This fellow and Brown looked alike and thought alike. Moralists and philosophers, both of them. If only the bullwhackers would hate him just a little bit.

"That song," the big man mused on, "is a sign of what men believe. There is, as you must have heard in Washington, also the rumor that the Republicans will include a homestead law in their 1860 platform. And there is much talk about this fellow Lincoln at Springfield. Add these up; stand them against our financial distress and the corner that cat Floyd has pushed us into. What's our future? What do you hear on all this?"

"Floyd's all right." The little man spat the words, in his

eagerness to defend the Secretary of War. "I hope you're not parading those thoughts publicly?"

"I'm not parading anything publicly." Majors stared at his boot toe. "There are just too many things to think through. This is an age of opportunity. If we fail, we can start again. But I need a clear conscience. If now, or in the future, that conscience dictates that I can't continue these dealings with Mr. Floyd, you will be the first to know. Has he signed more notes?"

"Of course he's signed more notes," Russell snapped again. "How else would I be getting the money? Butterfield and the Postmaster General are as cozy as bundling lovers about that mail contract over the Southern Route. Congress goes along with 'em. There's been a lot of criticism, mind you, about Floyd repeatedly giving us supply contracts. That's really why the Mormon War bill can't be paid. Good heavens, man, how can you suspect a secretary of war who not only offers to sign notes against our next contracts but uses his influence in New York and Philadelphia to raise cash on them?"

Majors grinned. "Any bear who sees a pot of honey set out atop a mound of fresh earth has the right to sniff around the edges of that mound. Floyd was governor of Virginia, wasn't he? And so slippery that not even Jefferson Davis or Edmund Ruffin trust him? When he signs those notes, he signs away our good name at the same time, too, doesn't he? Where would we stand with Lincoln elected and Floyd exposed as— Well, perhaps I shouldn't prejudge the man. But he is reputed to be one of the leaders in this insane Knights of the Golden Circle."

Russell clenched his fists tight against his hips and glowered up into Majors' face. "Do you want out right now?" he gritted. "Throw the whole business?"

Majors stared gravely back. It wouldn't do to laugh at this bantam. Just plain gall. That's what got Russell where he was—the gall to bluff through a crisis. It was one reason for not laughing at him. Russell was gutty. Then there was a second reason—but he couldn't explain that even to himself. It was somewhere in that loneliness that swept him like a black fog out there on the railroad track. No. He had made a promise. And beyond that . . . He heard himself say out loud, still staring gravely into Russell's eyes, "I gave you my promise when we took over your stage line—and its debts. I shan't back out."

"Fine. Fine. You won't regret this, Alex." Russell was all smiles, and held out a hand. "We'll shake on it and let that be an end to it. I'll handle Floyd and the Congress; you handle the men and horses. We'll come out of this wealthy."

"No need to shake." Majors' hands stayed in his pockets. "A pledge is a pledge. Yes. We will come out of this wealthy. But then, there is wealth and wealth." He paused, cleared his throat. "Have you ever thought, as you rode the trains, what they mean to slavery and our whole way of life out here? We were brought up to believe that the black man's slavery is natural and right. But the steam train can change that. It pulls more than coaches. It pulls homesteaders and new tools and new ideas. It pulls cities and farms to be sown, like seed, from the Missouri to the Pacific. This, too, is wealth, as well as Mr. Buchanan's stumbling currency and Mr. Floyd's sly notes." He shook his leonine head as though to clear it and strode off.

"My God," Russell muttered to the snowdrifts. "He's gone Abolitionist." He trotted along behind.

All business again, Majors led the way to the stables and introduced Bill Richardson, the head hostler. Bill guided them through the harness room, heady with perfumes of neat's-foot oil, lard and gleaming leather, then on to the great cavern of the pony stalls. Ben Holladay built on a scale with his mountainous, hickory-supple self. The chestnut beams soared six hundred feet from front doors to rear wall. Down each side, cavalry-precise and Amish-neat, stood stalls for one hundred horses, each with a set of hardwood pegs on which to hang bridles and individual gear. The Pike's Peak Stables were built in 1858 when, in the very months that track gangs raced to finish the Hannibal & St. Joseph Railroad, horsemen ferried the Missouri with news of gold nuggets picked up in the wilderness behind Zebulon Pike's towering mountain on the west edge of Kansas Territory. Gold fever plus train service. There could be as much profit in a big livery stable at St. Joe as there had been in San Francisco mule rentals during the 1849 Gold Rush. So agile Ben rushed in. His stables were as splendiferous to a horse as Mr. Patee's new hotel was to a human being. Now, thoroughly briefed on the havoc that William Russell's dreams and political shenanigans had brought to Russell, Majors & Waddell finances, Holladay waved his big hands, laughed and offered the stables as home base for the Pony Express. Of course, business being business, he accepted some promissory notes—properly discounted.

Majors, Russell and Richardson were deep in plans for pony deliveries and feed supplies when Billy Cody tiptoed through the door, the floppy, wind-burned hat clutched across his chest. Majors saw him and beckoned. Billy dipped his head, then stared at Russell and gulped. "Mister Russell's bags is all up in his room," he shrilled. "Not even a scratch. But, that ain't why I come. There's a fellow up there been waiting for you almost an hour, pacin' back and forth and chewin' seegars. I guess he's th' mayor here, or sump'n. Kinda thought I oughta—" His voice trailed off. He squished the hat tighter against his chest and scowled.

"Jeff Thompson. Why, yes. I wired him to have dinner with us." Russell snapped open his watch. "My gracious. It's past bedtime in Washington now. Good boy, Cody. Mr. Richardson, you will receive adequate and—uh—obviously most competent instructions from Mr. Majors. We bid you good evening, sir."

Bill Richardson stared after the strutting little man. His lips pursed and, with a *ting*, tobacco juice hit a stall stanchion at eye level ten feet away. Billy Cody stood like a cigar-store Indian until Russell was out the door. Then his head turned an inch; his lips pursed. A splat of saliva hit the center of the tobacco juice, and seeped down over it. Richardson nodded congratulations, pulled out his bandanna and walked toward the stanchion. Holladay would raise unholy, if he ever spotted that stain.

Alexander Majors, hands in pockets, had to swallow to keep the laughter out of his voice. "See you in the morning, Bill," he said, and beckoned to Cody to come along. Bill Richardson couldn't quite decide whether Mr. Majors pursed his lips and considered the distance to that stanchion when he turned again at the front door. Anyway, he didn't.

The Patee House gleamed like a gold mountain at the head of the little valley that formed St. Joseph's south boundary. John Patee, a Southerner and slaveowner like most of Buchanan County's leading citizens, had spent $130,000 on construction of his hotel when it became evident that the railroad would finally get through. Experienced travelers, including the noted English adventurer-author Sir Richard Burton, claimed the Patee House was the finest hostelry in the West; some called it the "Waldorf-Astoria of the frontier." Patee, like Holladay, built for durability. The brick-and-cutstone walls soared four stories above the prairie, bulked the width of a city block and were topped by an octagonal tower where guests could stare across the twisting brown torrent of the Missouri River to the savanna and bluffs of Kansas Territory. The Patee House, too, was a gamble on St. Joe as gateway to the West and, above all, on an era of peace. The steamboat wharves and the city's center were more than a mile to the northwest. Patee, the railroaders, Ben Holladay, were all betting that the new, greater city would spread south toward them. With the prospects of a transcontinental Pony Express, the odds seemed excellent that this area would be the terminal for the first transcontinental railroad by 1865 or 1870.

The lanky figure striding between the lobby windows paused when Russell's stylish Eastern shoes clattered against the walk, then beckoned and hurried toward the door. Jeff Thompson was as tall as Majors, and as skinny as Billy Cody. His hair, black and curly as a buffalo calf's, accentuated the swarthiness of his lean face. Even his mustache seemed to exude the furious energy that had turned the railroad from an 1846 daydream in Justice of the Peace Clemens' Hannibal office to an 1859 reality, and now drove to install river dikes above the city that would enable development of the Kansas-side savannas into the booming suburb of Elwood.

John Patee hurried up, smiling and bowing; Thompson shook Majors' hand, then turned toward Russell. Thompson had seen the little Vermonter now and again in train-time bustles at the station. But they had never met; not even—uh, alas—in those devil-ridden days of 1856 when Russell, Majors & Waddell warehouses at Leavenworth were used to store some of the horses, plows and guns taken from the Kansans in the raids against Brown, Lane, Montgomery and other skulking Abolitionist dogs. Jeff pumped Russell's hand as Majors made the introduction. Anybody who could parlay a harum-scarum Kansas general store into the largest freighting business on the continent, come Indians, Hell, or Mormons, was a man worth knowing. If the Lord willed him to have popeyes and be knee-high to a mule, that was the Lord's business—even in Vermont.

John Patee was next. Dinner, he burbled, would be served immediately in Mr. Russell's suite; roast wild goose, spiced buffalo tongue, antelope steaks and that rarity of Patee rarities, a pecan pie. The gentlemen would have coffee, of course? There would be no other refreshments?

Nobody blinked. Alexander Majors' attitude toward whisky and rum was as well known, from Weston clear through to Salt Lake City, as Senator Atchison's Kickapoo Rangers and Brigham Young's Avenging Angels. Jeff Thompson had quoted lyrically from the new *Rubáiyát* of Omar Khayyám while sampling French cognac during the hour's wait. One of Mr. Russell's portmanteaus, if shaken gently, gurgled; he would indulge at bedtime. "Coffee for three. And please see that young Cody has a hearty meal."

Small talk resolved quickly over the steaming entrees. Russell was as eager as Jeff Thompson to hear Majors' report on progress. He agreed that Major Howard Egan, the grand Indian fighter and cattleman, was the logical superintendent on the Salt Lake division. After all, Egan had time and again driven herds of cattle from Salt Lake to the California Mother Lode country, almost as casually as Russell rode Washington-Hannibal trains. Ben Ficklin, superintendent of their Leavenworth & Pike's Peak stage line, was off rounding up ponies and riders in Nebraska and the Rockies. Egan's appointment and letters of instruction would go by the next stage.

Majors had also held conferences with Israel Landis, the local leather craftsman. They had adapted, for Pony Express use, a kind of saddlebag sometimes used by the Mexicans to carry government dispatches. Called a *mochila*, it was a supple leather pad that fitted over and alongside the saddle. Oblong leather boxes would be whipstitched front and rear on each side of the pad, so that the rider's legs could fit snugly between. Each box would have a flap top fitting over a steel staple, and thus could be padlocked. Sets of keys would be delivered to the superintendents in Salt Lake City and Sacramento. A third set remained in St. Joseph. And each rider would carry a time card to be filled out with the exact moment of arrival at each remount station across the continent. The *mochila*, capable of ten-second transfer from one horse to another, would permit a time limit of two minutes for the station stop.

Obviously, Russell hastened to point out, such a gigantic enterprise could not hope to make a profit. The greatest benefits would accrue to St. Joseph, the new village of Denver, Salt Lake and, of course, the Californians. Not only would the Pony cut down transcontinental mail deliveries from Butterfield's stumbling thirty days to a miraculous ten days, it would for all time end the snide talk by Butterfield, Postmaster General Brown and—uh—other interested parties that this Central Route was impassable and foredoomed by nature to remain wilderness throughout eternity. In view of this vast promise for St. Joseph, it was to be hoped that the citizens . . .

Mayor Thompson had already smelled the bait, and liked it. The citizens, he pledged, would do their share to support this great enterprise. Indeed, a committee was now soliciting funds to assure Russell, Majors & Waddell of gifts of splendid land tracts within the city limits. And there would be more.

He hoped the Kansans would be one-tenth as patriotic—and co-operative.

Mr. Russell beamed and patted his pocket. The Kansas charter for the enterprise was drawn up. He was heading for Kansas in the morning and had assurance it would pass the territorial legislature.

"At a price?" Jeff beamed.

The little man flushed, then nodded. "At a price," he said.

"Good enough." Thompson pushed back his chair. "The glorious adventure is begun. I shall keep friend Alex informed of local matters and should have a complete report, sir, before you return to Washington."

"There is one matter, Jefferson." Majors stared, bleak and grave again. "We might as well be clear on it. Too much is at stake. Where will St. Joseph stand if, our Lord forbid, this Kansas-Missouri war spreads, if the Republicans win in 1860, and such states as South Carolina renew the old threat and secede?"

Thompson's face flushed. "We stand right here," he said, and smashed a fist against the table. "This is our destiny. We do not belong to Washington or South Carolina any more than we belong to those Kansas jayhawkers. I was born a Virginian. You were born a Kentuckian. But now we are both Missourians. There I stand. There, if need be, I die. And most Missourians stand as I do. Never fear, sir, of national intrigue, or insurrection, in this city. Our future lies with yours—in the great West."

Majors nodded. There was more small talk, then good nights. A quarter-hour later, the giant climbed the stairs slowly to his room. Billy Cody sprawled, snoring, on a blanket at the foot of his bed. Majors tiptoed across the room, sank into a Boston rocker and tapped his index fingers gently on the arms. Somehow, they began to beat out that childhood tune, the one that had made his neck hair tingle every time he heard a camp-meeting crowd chant its noble cadence. "Glory, glory, hallelujah," they used to sing. "Glory, glory, hallelujah." And now, over there beyond the river, it was something about John Brown's soul marching on. Marching where? To the Majors' home up in Nebraska City? To Jeff Thompson's dream of Missouri destiny? To Pike's Peak and California? Was this the cyclone wind Billy had heard in the frozen rails that afternoon? Was this the great sorrow that swept him as he stared from iron's frontier out to the frontier of the Pony's challenge?

All the intricate planning he had lavished on the Russell, Majors & Waddell wagon-train empire trembled on the verge of ruin. The Pony Express might save them. Yet, if his fears of John Buchanan Floyd were justified, the Pony Express, too, would fail. Ben Ficklin and Egan and Finney would build masterfully. Tough, bright youngsters, like Billy Cody, and tougher Western ponies would disprove the stupid testimony by General Frémont, Senator Jefferson Davis, Postmaster General Brown and others that the Colorado-Utah Route was impossible for year-round travel.

Yet that song kept chanting. Behind it loomed the desperation of both Southern politician and Northern Abolitionist. Weren't Davis and his Southern friends fighting for something more than a mail monopoly over that weary El Paso-Los Angeles Route? Was the five-hundred-thousand-dollar loss Russell, Majors & Waddell had suffered in that silly Mormon War part of a larger, bloodier plot to bring all the American West into Slavery's domain? Was the Pony Express doomed because Southern politicians dared not let it succeed?

"Glory, glory, hallelujah." There had always been a ring of prophecy in that chorus. There was now. The great Senator Benton, Frémont's father-in-law, urged that the transcontinental railroad be built west across the Pike's Peak country and Utah. Pony Express must be the pioneer to prove it. Then the telegraph line and the railroad could follow.

Chorpenning . . . Woodward . . . Woodson . . . Hockaday . . . Liggett—the list of Central Route pioneers was already long. Major George Chorpenning and Absalom Woodward had faced sandstorms, floods, Indians and blizzards to launch a California-Salt Lake mail route in 1851; Egan helped them pilot it. Woodward and four others had been murdered by Indians and robbed of the ten thousand dollars' worth of bullion in their saddlebags. Chorpenning saved the contract by torturing a wagon train across the Sierra from Sutter's Fort to Carson Valley in forty days. Thirteen of the horses and mules froze to death. The drivers and guards cut filets from the mules and ate them during the two-hundred-mile walk into Salt Lake City.

And now—Pony Express' turn was coming up. Perhaps, despite his fears, success on the route would shame Congress into mail subsidies to Fort Kearny, Lodge Pole Creek, Chimney Rock, Laramie, South Pass, Salt Lake, Carson Sink and Lake Tahoe. But weather, mountains, desert, wild animals, Indians—all teamed, unknowingly, with Senator Davis, Secretary Floyd, Postmaster General Brown and the frightened old man in the White House. Despite them, somebody must do it. Would it be Pony Express?

These churning hopes and fears about the future would not

let him sleep. The memories paraded like witches of foreboding around and around the seething cauldron of the Slavery Issue. The great West would be conquered. The railroad and the telegraph would finally weld the peoples of the Atlantic Coast, the heartland sierra, the Pacific Coast into an economic whole. But what would their social beliefs and laws shape toward? Was Slavery even imaginable for the great plains of Nebraska and West Kansas? Were the plaintive echoes of the plantation's sad songs meant to mourn from the proud, wildly free crags of the Rockies?

West!!! West!!! West!!! The word even sounded like freedom. The lungs pushed it out with a rushing, *We-e-e-e-e*. It frisked across tongue and lips with the exhilaration of a colt on a spring morning. And this is the way the American had always regarded it. West to freedom!! West to liberty that could be wrested by your own skills and daring!!! Was there, in the very formation and sibilant lilt of these four letters, a sign of the Almighty's will? Were the heady hope and freedom-vision inspired just by saying "West" some kind of God-warning that it must be a land where laws and social practice would guarantee full opportunity of freedom for all men?

His own life story pointed toward such a conviction. So did the careers of Russell and Waddell, Jeff Thompson and Ben Holladay. All had marched penniless to the banks of the Missouri River. All had found freedom-to-do and freedom-to-succeed on that vast grassy sea beyond the river. A mere fifteen years before, he had first ventured up the Kaw with a shabby wagonload of trade goods to peddle among the Indians. Now the wagon lots and warehouses of Russell, Majors & Waddell behind Fort Leavenworth were a veritable city. This is what the West offered. This was "the land of Canaan" come true.

And tonight the whole great area trembled on the precipice of final destiny. The promise of the new gold and silver mines in the Pike's Peak and Nevada wilderness pointed toward it as surely as that eerie *boo hoo* whistle of the locomotive and the magical *clackety clack* of Clem Huniker's telegraph key.

The Pony Express would be an advance courier of the huge changes to come. The pompous bravado of The Mormon War, the rashness of Russell's Central Overland and Pike's Peak stageline were both, in their way, symbols of these things-to-be. Perhaps the politicians of North and South would interfere in ways that could not be foreseen. Perhaps the faint-hearted were right, and Pony Express would fail to get through.

But it was coming. Somebody would do it. Why not the Pony Express? If they did win through and Congress could be

23

shamed into underwriting mail deliveries across their Central Route, new opportunities in The West would be almost limitless. How, then, could anything but full human freedom prevail?

Alexander Majors reached, cat quiet, for the Bible that always lay on his bedside table. There was enough light from the Franklin stove to read a few passages. He needed its strength and faith.

2.
WHO WINS THE WEST?

Historians of the Pony Express may differ in answering the question: Who won the West? But the ultimate conclusion points, among others, to the dream of Alexander Majors. He thought in terms of human destiny, and inevitably in terms of the destiny of the American people.

President Buchanan's Postmaster General, Aaron V. Brown, had favored the Southern Route. Senators William M. Gwin and John C. Frémont insisted on the Central Route and suggested it to Russell, who promoted it with all his nervous enthusiasm. He was a volatile New Englander, confident of his schemes, reckless about debts, which he believed he could pay. His partner, Missourian William B. Waddell, was always cautious. But in 1854 they agreed to take into their business plainsman Majors, who showed them how to dominate the freight business. It was his experience that inspired Russell to say in Washington: "I can put the mail through from Missouri to California in ten days." Furthermore, according to the story, he bet ten thousand dollars he could do it. This was the decision that shaped the destiny of the West.

Historians have only rarely agreed on the details of the Pony Express and its significance to every American. Like the romantic novelists of the 1890's, they examined the two thousand miles of buffalo grass, desert, and tortured mountain, with the raw hamlet of Denver and the town of Salt Lake as the only communities between the Missouri River and the Pacific Slope. Here, it would seem, was another world. The West of 1860, they concluded, was separate and distinct from the rest of the nation. They treated it that way and then, imbued by the idealism of Russell, Majors & Waddell in launching the Pony, went on to flaunt the derring-do.

But look to the records. Politics, economics, sociology were as tightly woven into the Pony Express story as they are in today's space missiles and postal-rate increases. Russell, Majors and Waddell were neither sentimental nor naïve. They had more than four million dollars invested in their freighting operations. They were willing to take the expensive risk of the Pony Express because they desperately needed a United States Mail contract to save their business. And that business was in jeopardy because political, economic and social forces in the "Yankeeland" Northeast and the slavery Southeast were fighting a desperate battle for control of the national government. The huge question confronting the United States in 1860 really was *Who wins the West?* This was as apparent to Massachusetts millowners and to Memphis cotton-factors as it was to Alexander Majors. These warring forces are in the West's story, too.

From New York's swarming four million through South Dakota's 4,837 to California's 380,000, the citizens of the United States pondered a decision in an issue that had been shaping for 250 years. Could America survive that decision? When the gauntlet was finally flung in fatal crash against the war drums, would the dream of New World freedom die? Who would win the Great West and, by the act, shape all America's future?

Accepting the Republicans' nomination for United States Senator from Illinois on June 16, 1858, Kentucky-born Abraham Lincoln drawled, " 'A house divided against itself cannot stand.' I believe this government cannot endure permanently half slave and half free." Yet, in truth, Abolition was a new name for an old feud. It was as Johnny-come-lately as the gawky frontier lawyer.

The real issue was there for anyone to see, on all the waterways west of the Hudson and the James.

Albany, New York, developed on the west bank of the Hudson for the same reason that Chicago and Milwaukee developed on the west shore of Lake Michigan, and Davenport, St. Louis and Minneapolis developed on the west shore of the Mississippi. The same pattern still unfolded for the new communities of Kansas City, Des Moines, Little Rock, Mobile and Jackson. It was simply and plainly a product of American instinct. The human urge was toward the west. The largest cities developed on the western banks of rivers and lakes.

Southerners had reached the prairie and High Plains

decades before the New Englanders and New Yorkers. A Northerner was responsible. In 1793 the Yankee schoolteacher Eli Whitney invented a gin that tore short-staple, upland cotton from its tenacious seeds. That doomed the southern Appalachians, Gulf Coast and lower Mississippi Valley to be cotton plantations. And it saved the slave system. The factories and diversified farming developing in Virginia, Georgia and the Carolinas had proved that slavery was too expensive for their kinds of labor; in 1795, it was on the way out. But Whitney's gin enabled cotton fields to push through the Gaps and down into the lush "bottoms" of Alabama and Mississippi. The absence of field machines re-established the Negro slave as an essential to cotton profits for the planters, the factors, the merchants.

During this melee, disinherited upland farmers and cattlemen pushed west, urged along a Glory Road by saddle-sore preachers, paced by the land agents prowling Arkansas, Louisiana and eastern Texas for more and more cotton land.

Meanwhile, the Northerners sampled the wilderness virginities of Vermont, upstate New York, Ohio and Michigan. They sauntered west, and quickened their pace only during periods of mercantile depression. Typically, the ministers and Home Missions Societies of Connecticut and Massachusetts directed prayers—and second-hand clothing—to the "heathen red man" of Vermont, Maine, and Ohio until the 1830's.

The South's preachers had hungered out on Wilderness Road by 1785, invented the emotional orgy of the camp meeting in the 1790's, extended circuit rides to Louisiana Territory in 1804, and in 1825 operated schools, missions, and camp-meeting grounds on the Texas and Missouri frontiers.

Southern Indians, too, were swept across Old Man River in this flood of King Cotton's henchmen. Just as the Northerners hacked the Iroquois, Delaware, Miami and other Indian nations out of the Allegheny passes to Ohio, the Southerner bushwhacked across the fatherlands of the Tuscarora, Cherokee, Creek and Chickasaw, and finally exiled tribal remnants to a western desert named "Red Man," or, as the Choctaw called it, "Oklahoma." The grimmest of these exoduses was the march of ten thousand Cherokee under military escort, during the winter of 1838, from the Georgia-Carolina highlands to unknown lands beyond Arkansas.

For two reasons, these deportations of the Five Civilized Tribes from the South to the Far West were as ominous to the United States' future, and to prospects of civil war, as

Whitney's slapdash invention of the cotton gin. The Cherokee, Creek and Chickasaw, particularly, were excellent farmers and stockmen; the Chickasaw pony, bred up from Spanish wild-horse herds before 1700, was the "best piece of horseflesh" in the colonial South; the Cherokee had pioneered contour plowing, crop rotation and semiannual cattle round-ups. But, as assiduously as any savanna or piedmont planter, the Five Civilized Tribes held to the ancient Indian system of slavery. Thousands of Negro slaves were among the "farm equipment" taken to Oklahoma. Cotton fields, livestock ranches and slave cabins sprang up in this newest Far West. Thus, the Southern Indian—himself a victim of the westward sweep of cotton gin and slave—carried the tradition of "slaves for fieldwork" across both the Mississippi and the Missouri rivers to perpetuate—and dominate—in midcontinent.

The second war fuse to be lit in the Cherokee fatherland glowed from yellow pebbles discovered in the vicinity of Dahlonega, Georgia, in 1833. The Dahlonega gold rush was the first in the nation's history; it was a realization of the legends that drew Cabeza de Vaca, De Soto and Coronado west before 1550, a snarling prelude to the California Gold Rush in 1849. Some Cherokees learned the tricks of gold prospecting before they set out on the "Trail of Tears." A few ventured on to California a decade later, failed to "make a strike," and jogged home through the bleak passes of the Rockies. There, near a snowy peak named for Lieutenant Zebulon Pike of Trenton, New Jersey, a Cherokee spotted gold flecks, panned out enough to fill a goose quill and carried them home. The whisper filtered into Missouri and the South.

When the Virginia explorers Lewis and Clark turned in their 1805 report on Louisiana Territory, geographers had labeled the area west of the Missouri River "uninhabitable desert." Nevertheless, with disdain and desperation, Southerners established slave plantations all across Missouri before 1835, slashed the Santa Fe Trail into New Mexico before 1840, took firm possession of Texas before 1850, then thoroughly convinced Congress and the White House that the only usable land routes to California ran due west from New Orleans or willy-nilly southwest from St. Louis through Santa Fe to sleepy El Pueblo de Nuestra Señora la Reina de los Angeles de Porciuncula, thence up the great valley to San Francisco.

(Advice to forty-niners heading overland for the California gold fields came graciously and copiously from Hon. Jefferson Davis, United States senator from Mississippi. A distinguished veteran of the Mexican War and son-in-law of Zachary Taylor, Senator Davis warned all comers that the Southern routes were safest and best. Then, in substantiation of the desert theory, he initiated an expedition to Africa to collect camels for a United States Army Camel Corps soon after his 1853 appointment as secretary of war. The animals would be used, of course, *exclusively* on the Southern routes.)

The Northerners, dazzled by their sea industries and the ravishments of Ohio—they still blissfully referred to Ohio as the Northwest—went along with this Southerner's geography lesson. Indeed, the first large group of Northerners to attempt settlements west of the Mississippi were, like the Tennessee cattlemen and Five Civilized Tribes, social outcasts.

Joseph Smith, a Vermonter, developed the *Book of Mormon* from revelations he said were dictated to him in upstate New York. Around this, in a period and area aflame with prophecies and visions, he developed the Church of Jesus Christ of Later-day Saints. The bumptious Methodists, Calvinists, Baptists and Presbyterians around Syracuse and Rochester were as resentful toward Mormon concepts of family life as they were toward the "no sex" dictums of the Shakers and would be toward the "selective sex" rules of the Oneida Community. (Banned from polite discussion, sex found escape into politics, had a whiz-bang across upstate New York all through the nineteenth century.)

Smith led his converts to Ohio. The Methodists and Baptists there were as vigorous as the Syracuse-Rochester brethren. The Mormons trekked southwest across the Mississippi, to run headlong into circuit-ridden hard-shell slaveowners from the South. Both the Missourians and the Mormons were of British stock, with smoldering contingents of Scotch-Irish and Welsh. Barns and outhouses burned; gunsmoke billowed from underbrush. Only the derring-do friendship of Alexander Doniphan, the soldier-lawyer who would lead the epochal 1846–47 battle march across Mexico, prevented a North-South war in Missouri that summer of 1838.

So, during the months when survivors of the Cherokees' Trail of Tears floated west across the Mississippi, the Mormons retired grudgingly east across the river, and secured a peninsula of prairie facing Iowa Territory. There they built temple-centered Nauvoo, largest city in Illinois. Joseph Smith had already prophesied a civil war between North and South. In 1844, he announced his candidacy for President of the United States. Then his leadership was challenged. A series of threats and counterthreats landed him in the brownstone jail at Carthage, Illinois. An armed mob of two hundred men, with faces carefully corked black, murdered the prophet and his brother in their cells. Nauvoo was sacked during the terror that followed.

Brigham Young, a man of brusque, steely genius, assumed Mormon leadership, then planned and brilliantly executed a fifteen-hundred-mile exodus across the High Plains and over the Continental Divide to a bleak desert beside Great Salt Lake, 750 miles from the Pacific. The haunting melodies of "The Handcart Song," "Come, Come Ye Saints" and other hymns fashioned during that march echoed back across the South's Arkansas and Missouri frontiers to the fat pastures of Yankeedom. It created a hairline crack in the South-fostered theories about "uninhabitable desert" and that meandering Southwest route to California. Reports sent back by wagon trains that used the same passes to create the Oregon Trail widened the crack.

Meanwhile, machine-age economics had shaped a bitter political feud between North and South—and spawned the Abolitionist. Eli Whitney had a hand in that, too. Sputtering home to New Haven after the planters refused to honor patents on his gin, Whitney refocused his tinkerer genius on rifles that could be assembled from interchangeable parts. This marked the birth of assembly-line techniques and the machine tool. It transformed the Northeast's industry as radically as the gin transformed the South's.

Neither down-East Yankee nor New Yorker had ever been conscience-smitten about slavery. Somehow, from the austere beauty of his church pew, the proper Bostonian managed a bleak smile for the masts of slave ships framed by the vestry doors. The "three-legged journeys"—to Africa, with Old Pilgrim rum; to the West Indies, with slaves; then back to Boston, Salem and Portland, with sugar and profits—built lovely homes and endowed spinster daughters who, gripping freedom of conscience carefully above the hips, endowed taller, lovelier churches and busier Home Missions Societies. New Yorkers and Jerseymen pursued a similar course but, not endowed with Unitarian subtlety, sometimes required the preachers to marry their spinster daughters before opening the strongboxes.

Adaptation to Whitney's assembly-line technique, and assiduous development of immigration, enabled the Northeast to hire day laborers at cheaper rates than the food-medicine-shelter costs of slavery. Thus, over and beyond England's Victorian rash of humanitarianism (*outside* Great Britain, of course), slavery became a bad business risk. New York briskly followed Yankee lead, and abolished the system in 1827.

This economic realism soon showed up in Washington to clash, with classic echo, against the South's increasing dependence on cotton. When the Tariff Act of 1816 reached the Senate floor, John Calhoun of South Carolina had been eloquent in praise of its measures—and Massachusetts' Daniel Webster was equally eloquent in condemnation of "restrictive tariffs."

Then—"bow to your lady and we'll all change sides"—when the Tariff Act of 1828 reached the Senate, Calhoun screamed against it with the fury of a wounded Abbeville bobcat. But Webster, pious as a Salem slaver discoursing on original sin, now favored a tariff.

Politics is politics is politics. Both Webster and Calhoun were exquisite trial lawyers, blessed with Blarney-stone glibness. And devil take the truth. The Northeast had switched to manufacturing because of its new factories and assembly-line developments. It needed tariff protection. But the South, committed to belligerent dependence on Whitney's cotton gin *plus* slavery, saw tariff-free exchanges with Europe essential to her raw-cotton market.

It was a simple, short step, then, for shrewd lawyers to orate "States' rights" and "the pusillating barbarism of slavery" at each other. The South was weaned to individualism by the nature of her isolated plantations and up-country herdsmen. The Northeast, dedicated to urbanism and factory-dependent tenements, nestled toward collective securities, union, central government. Nevertheless, the real issues in the Webster-Calhoun clashes between 1828 and 1850 were (1) cotton vs. factory and (2) factory wages vs. slave costs. Obviously, these were too blunt for Congressional oratory. But States' rights and evils of slavery offered lavish opportunity for torch parades, campaign issues, and adrenal surges throughout the citizenry. And sincere preachers in both North and South could locate Bible quotations to support either "cause."

So the breach was created. The ever-present sprinkle of crackpots, idealists, and power-plotters began to react. William Lloyd Garrison, unmindful of the "Jim Crow" cars hitched onto New England passenger trains, established *The Liberator* a few blocks from Boston's segregated North Station and began a thirty-five-year rant for "immediate abolition of slavery." John Brown, brooding neurotic and business failure, discovered the excitement in smuggling refugee slaves across the Northeast to Canada.

The South responded "in kind." South Carolina voted for Secession—the first time—in 1833. From Richmond, Governor John Floyd promptly announced that any attempt to cross Virginia's territory with Federal troops would be met with armed resistance. (In 1831, after the hopeless fury of Nat Turner's slave rebellion, Governor Floyd had urged the state legislature to revise all laws in order "to preserve in due subordination the slave population.") Southern congressmen lock-stepped into belligerent proslavery, pro-State unison. Southerners appointed to Cabinet posts held to the same goal, prejudging departmental budgets and staff appointments accordingly. There were secret societies and furtive political teamships. The Knights of the Golden Circle, assumedly formed to incite another war against Mexico and so extend cotton-slave territory south of the Rio Grande, was one of numerous "hypochondriac" organizations. President Polk in 1845 urged purchase of Cuba from Spain so that Southern slaveholdings might be extended, and proslavery votes added to the congressional roster.

Andrew Jackson saw the bloody road ahead and, on his deathbed, growled, "I should have shot Clay and hung Calhoun." Few paid heed then, as they had failed to do when Joseph Smith prophesied civil war. Southern leaders, scanning the prevalence of kinfolk and former neighbors in Missouri, Arkansas, and Iowa Territory, assumed that the South would continue to dominate that vast wilderness beyond the Mississippi. Moreover, the Negro had demonstrated his skill as a horseman and cowhand. Many of the South's best masons, carpenters, iron-workers and craftsmen were Negroes. And, they reasoned, slavery offered sounder year-round security to these workers than the New England system of seasonal layoff, six-day work weeks, that ran from dawn to dusk, and the blood-spitting pallor of four- and five-story tenements.

Thus a confederation of South and West seemed sound. The secession plotters of the 1850's took it for granted that their frontiers against the Northeast would extend the full length of the Mississippi Valley, with Illinois and Wisconsin as western outposts of the United States. Moreover, what with the Texas War for Independence, the Mexican War, the Florida and Navajo and Apache campaigns, weren't the best officers in the Army proslave, States'-rights Southerners?

Then, North Europe and the machine began to tip the balance. Railroads from New York, Philadelphia, and Baltimore pushed through the Allegheny gaps toward the new Yankee village of Chicago. The telegraph chattered in, too. Revolutions in Hungary, Denmark, Schleswig-Holstein, Ireland brought millions of refugees to New York, Boston, and Philadelphia; railroads and land agents convinced many that glorious opportunities waited in the Wisconsin and Minnesota wilderness. Chicago and Milwaukee boomed. Relentlessly, the railroads clanged on toward the Mississippi shore. German liberals, fleeing the *Junkers'* purge after the Revolution of 1848, joined the surge of Scandinavians toward the Midwest. Cincinnati, Milwaukee, Chicago and then St. Louis beckoned them in. All these refugees were fresh from revolts against monarchies. They had bitter prejudices against slavery.

In the same years, Yankee initiative won California as a free state. While Germans and Scandinavians pushed across the Mississippi into St. Louis, drovers from Ohio and Maine herded thousands of sheep and cattle across the Rockies, the "uninhabitable desert" and the Sierras to provision mother lode mining towns and restock the old Spanish ranges around Los Angeles Pueblo.

Finally, just as Tom Paine's pamphlets had bellowed smoldering resentment to blazing revolt in 1776, a Maine professor's wife fueled Abolition. Harriet Beecher was a preacher's daughter, ardently spreading good works of temperance and suffrage as she followed her father from Connecticut to Cincinnati. There she married Calvin Ellis Stowe, Professor of Sacred Literature at Papa's theological seminary. The Stowes joined the groups smuggling slaves north into Canada. Dr. Stowe transferred east to Bowdoin College, Maine. Despite six childbirths, housekeeping and temperance lectures, Mrs. Stowe seethed her indignations against slavery into a melodramatic novel. *Uncle Tom's Cabin, Or Life Among the Lowly* appeared serially in *The National Era*, an Abolitionist magazine, between June 5, 1851, and April 1, 1852, and was promptly published in two volumes by a Boston house. It sold three hundred thousand copies the first year. In 1853, Little Eva flapped cheesecloth wings up to the catwalks of a score of theaters; even Methodists by-passed Wesleyan dictum against play-going to join in hissing Simon Legree.

Coincidentally, the Abolitionists mounted a full offensive against the South's West. Textile factories in Massachusetts earned millions for A. A. Lawrence and his nephew, Amos. The Lawrences' sadness about Little Eva may have been conditioned by the West's safety-valve potentials as a population dump during future business recessions. Whatever their motive, they financed the New England Emigrant Aid Society. The Society, in turn, outfitted Free-Soil settlers in Kansas Territory—and included Sharps rifles and bullet molds in the provisions. John Brown was among those who responded.

Lawrence, Kansas—named for Amos—became the capital of the Free-Soilers. Leavenworth, founded by Southerners who had pioneered the Santa Fe Trail and perfected the prairie schooner and wagon train for High Plains travel, developed as command post for proslavery strategy.

Here civil war finally began in 1855. Senator Robert Toombs of Georgia addressed a mass meeting held at Columbus to raise funds for a Southern wagon train of settlers to Kansas. Boatloads came up the Mississippi, flying the state flags of South Carolina and Alabama; the cannons were parked aft. Lawrence was sacked.

A Chicago saloonkeeper led a regiment of water-front bully-boys in through Iowa, then down to the Emigrant Aid Society's strongholds; John Brown, Reverend Montgomery and the Abolitionists used them on murderous raids into Missouri.

Franklin Pierce was in the White House, with Jefferson Davis as secretary of war. The Army troops stationed in Leavenworth played umpire, usually managing to ride in a day or two after each raid. Perhaps Lieutenant Colonel Joseph Johnston of Abingdon, Virginia, saw to this; perhaps not. Neither he nor Captain H. H. Sibley nor Lieutenant J. E. B. Stuart ever made public utterances on the matter. But they were there, commanding the Federal troops. And somehow, Kansas adopted a proslavery constitution, with an amazing number of cemeteries voting.

James Buchanan inherited the intrigue-ridden Washington mess in 1857. John Floyd's son, John Buchanan, had been Governor of Virginia, too, and carried the state for Buchanan. The new President named John B. Floyd Secretary of War; Jefferson Davis rode back to Mississippi to be re-elected to the Senate.

John Buchanan Floyd (it was another Buchanan family, he claimed, not the President's) grew up in Abingdon, Virginia. Lieutenant Colonel Johnston was a boyhood friend. Floyd married a home-town girl, one of the daughters of Brigadier General Francis Preston. Other Preston daughters married James McDowell, Floyd's predecessor as governor, and Wade Hampton of South Carolina, said to be the South's wealthiest cotton and sugar operator. And two of General Preston's sons were cutting swathes. William C. had been president of the University of South Carolina, then moved on to the Senate; John S., a most capable orator for States' rights and Secession, served in the South Carolina Senate after 1848.

Despite these distinguished relatives, John Buchanan Floyd was in trouble. He had already grappled with Jefferson Davis on the appropriate carving of several political pasties. Gruff old Edmund Ruffin, the great Virginia scientist and Secessionist, growled that he wouldn't trust Floyd either as a politician or as a neighbor.

Now here he was, strategically placed at a strategic time. Perhaps he could recoup and prove his worth to The Cause. At least, the Knights of the Golden Circle trusted him. And Joe Johnston, cautiously herding those damned Abolitionists away from the Kansas polling places, trusted him.

The West—there was the crisis. Floyd glowered out of his office window at the pink mud spraying off the carriage wheels on Constitution Avenue. March, 1857; one week as Mr. Secretary. Time to take a first step? He fingered the stack of papers on his desk and frowned. With one hundred million dollars in gold sluicing off those California hills each year, there was greater need than ever to hold the West for the South. Aside from the Kansans and the confounded German Socialists in St. Louis, just one bee's nest offered a threat to creation of a South-West confederation when Secession came. The Mormons had buzzed with amazing industry on their salt-rimed desert. The beehive was their symbol; they were swarmers. Heathen polygamists, claiming to be Israelites rather than Gentiles—but efficient, determined swarmers. Thousands of new converts from England as well as from the Northeast had walked, pulling handcarts, those fifteen hundred miles from railhead to Salt Lake. Sugar-beet seed had been smuggled in from France. That devil Brigham Young declared coffee-drinking and the use of tobacco downright sins—probably in order to save community funds for the "self-sufficient empire" he boasted about. But, worst of all, the Mormons were gun-wise Free-Soilers. They must be crushed and scattered before any Western confederation sprang into being and California was seized.

Leavenworth. The scrawl on the envelope caught his eye. Leavenworth. By glory, that might be the answer. It was a report from Captain Brent, the Leavenworth quartermaster. Atop it was a one-year contract renewal just drawn up with the freighting combine of Russell, Majors & Waddell. Floyd's eyes darted down the page. Up to five million pounds, eh? Almost enough to—hmmm. Yes, almost enough freight for an emergency expedition to Utah. Worth looking into that. Now, who would have the latest news on Utah? Hadn't some official been killed there recently—from ambush? Yes, that's right—from ambush. Russell, Majors & Waddell. Up to five million pounds of cartage. If they could do that, they could do more.

3.
THE $5,000,000 TEMPLE NAILS

No signposts pointed to the Russell, Majors & Waddell headquarters at Leavenworth, Kansas. Strangers merely followed the smell from the river wharves out past the fort. Then, in the slab-board, pig-roamed town, bellows and shouting pinpointed the location of the gaunt new warehouses, the tannery and meat-packing shed, the corrals jam-packed with oxen and, beyond, seemingly to the horizon, row upon row of huge, canvas-topped wagons lined up as neatly as General Harney's cadre on an inspection day. This was the Far West's most elaborate effort to build a monopoly. The partners were as obvious about it as a Comanche war party on a prairie hilltop.

Trade with Santa Fe built slowly after Lieutenant Zebulon Pike's explorations of the Southwest in 1807–08 and his polite imprisonment at the Spanish capital beyond the Sangre de Cristo Mountains. By 1830, wagons loaded with calico, tinware, muskets, flour, rum and corn liquor were smuggled out of Missouri and over the buffalo grass and mesquite to Raton Pass, the Las Vegas pueblos, Glorieta Pass and Santa Fe.

Alexander Majors, born in Franklin County, Kentucky, brought his young family to western Missouri in 1835, farmed for a decade, then ventured on a trading expedition to Indian villages up the Kaw. The profits enabled him to buy six wagons and trade down the Santa Fe Trail from Independence, Missouri. The trip established a record—he was back in ninety-two days, with a five-thousand-dollar profit.

The feat was the more remarkable because of the work rules used by this soft-spoken giant. There is no record that Majors ever attended school. Yet he had learned to read and write fluently, and heredity had blessed him with eloquence plus the will to live in harmony with convictions. Methodist circuit-riders and Baptist lay preachers were organizing the massive frenzy of camp meetings in Missouri. A generation later, Alexander Majors might have turned to the "cloth" and become a revivalist. Instead, he used the Bible as his "highest court" for ethical decisions and business judgments, and developed eloquence by studying it.

So, in astonishing contrast to the frontier's harshness, Majors ran his freighting enterprise with Calvinist discipline. No work or travel was permitted on the Sabbath. Every employee must sign a pledge that read:

While I am in the employ of A. Majors, I agree not to use profane language, not to get drunk, not to gamble, not to treat the animals cruelly, and not to do anything incompatible with the conduct of a gentleman. I agree, if I violate any of the above conditions, to accept my discharge without any pay for my services.

The pledge signed, and carefully filed, Majors presented to each new hand a leather-bound Bible and later, as his business developed, a copy of his crisp, learned "Rules for Wagon Masters."

Supplementing these, "Ol' Gospel," as the bullwhackers nicknamed him, delivered a one- or two-hour lecture on morality and clean living at warehouse prayer meetings before each wagon train jingled west. And he started every day on the trail with a prayer service.

He backed up this piety with golden-rule convictions. On the trail, he worked as long and hard as anyone. He paid top wages, saw that employees' families were comfortable, provided for the widows and children of men who died on the plains, matched joke with joke and scuttlebutt with scuttlebutt around the campfires. Back home, he would get down on a puncheon floor, puff out his beard and play bucking horse or charging buffalo for any bullwhacker's toddler. By 1854, he had one hundred wagons, twelve hundred oxen and 120 men on the trails, owned slave plantations in central Missouri and held the United States Army's contract to supply provisions for Fort Union, the great new command post dominating the Santa Fe Trail between Raton Pass and Las Vegas.

The frontier freighter's life was as rugged as the mountain man's had been a generation before and, in some respects, more dangerous. Catastrophe in the shapes of blizzards, Indian attacks, starvation, and desert breakdowns forced him to perfect his techniques. Each wagon, outfitted with a toolbox and assorted pieces of hardwood for repairs on the trail, could carry a five-thousand-pound load. The twelve-ox teams trundled them at two or three miles an hour. But Indian warriors could shriek and kick their ponies up to bursts of twenty miles an hour. A freighter's rifle was as important as his oxen's health in those four- and six-month crawls through prairie, desert and bleak timber-line passes. But the profits could be huge, so the competition was keen.

William H. Russell minced up the walk to Majors' home in Westport—the future Kansas City—one winter afternoon in 1854. Born in Vermont, he came to Missouri with his stepfather, hired out as a store clerk, then married a Baptist minister's daughter and glibly built a fortune in land speculation, hemp-bagging, loans, and contract freighting. He also served competently as county treasurer for fifteen years and Lexington postmaster for four years. Now, he and fellow churchman William B. Waddell owned an investment-and-trading firm. Russell was the dreamer and glib "front man." Waddell, a dour grandson of Scotland born in Virginia and raised in Kentucky, was the detailer and book-balancer. They teamed well.

Russell's years as county treasurer and postmaster had trained him in politics, he believed. He had every confidence that he could maneuver in Washington as skillfully as he did in Lexington. It was possible, he explained to the frowning Waddell, to secure the contract for freighting all of the Army supplies west of the Missouri. But Alexander Majors was essential to the scheme. Not only because Majors held that Fort Union contract; it was the charm the calm giant cast over bullwhackers as well as savage Indians. It was common gossip, wasn't it, that the only time the Apaches did capture him, he lectured them so movingly from the torture stake that the tribal grandmothers orated in his defense and forced the war chief to let him ride off, scot-free, with all his equipment? Majors was essential to a monopoly contract.

Russell sold the plan to Majors, too. Considering the times, it was a logical one. The Abolitionists had reached Kansas and built Lawrence. Guns barked on both banks of the Missouri River. The term "border ruffian" had become an arrogant boast in the saloons and livery stables.

Lieutenant Colonel Joseph Johnston and Captain H. H. Sibley, both stationed at Fort Leavenworth, were personal friends of Secretary of War Davis. It would be sound strategy for the Army to have all its supplies handled by one firm, particularly if the firm was owned by devoted Missourians and slaveholders. And Majors could not swing such an operation alone. Wasn't it true that he had no taste for political matters and was happiest out on the trail with his trains?

In March, 1855, the War Department signed a two-year monopoly contract with Majors & Russell, who in turn subcontracted to Russell, Majors & Waddell and a swarm of holding companies dreamed up by Russell. That summer, the warehouses and pens went up at Leavenworth, two miles from the fort. The great prairie parking lot was readied for the trains to trek back from the red man's wilderness. Then, in September, William H. Russell formed a Washington partnership with Luther R. Smoot. They opened a bank under the name of Smoot, Russell & Co. This was it. Russell swam proudly in the mainstream of national politics. Really, it seemed no more turbulent than some of the county commissioners' meetings back in Lexington.

More than twenty-seven thousand settlers swarmed into Kansas during 1856–57. The Lawrences' New England Emigrant Aid Society hired excellent publicists—and suppliers. The looting and murder intensified. Missourians, clattering back from the sack of Lawrence, stored part of their booty in the Russell, Majors & Waddell warehouses. A few months later, Abolitionist raiders stormed into Leavenworth and, before troops could be summoned from the fort, plundered a warehouse, helped themselves to hams and jerked beef in the packing plant, and drove off a herd of oxen and mules. Nevertheless, the supply trains got through without mishap. The firm admitted to a profit of $150,000 for 1856.

Several trains were already on the road in June, 1857, when Captain Thomas L. Brent hurried to the offices. An army was being formed at once, he announced, to proceed against the Mormons. The veteran Indian fighter General W. S. Harney would lead it personally. As sole provisioners to the Army in the West, Russell, Majors & Waddell must round up another three million pounds of supplies and have them on the road by mid-July.

Russell's eyes popped. There were Washington rumors, but both he and Smoot discounted them. Mr. Floyd, the new secretary of war, had been most gracious during Russell's spring visit in Washington. They had chatted leisurely about the outlook in Kansas. Floyd even invited Russell to his home for dinner and a gala evening. Not so much as a hint of a Mormon expedition passed the secretary's lips. Good heavens! The order would bankrupt Russell, Majors & Waddell. Where was Majors? Off in the field somewhere. Probably checking on his confounded Bibles. Send a messenger for him. Even so— It can't be done.

Captain Brent was unctuously serene. The War Department would stand all losses; word of honor. No need, even, to waste time by drawing up a new contract.

Majors hurried into Leavenworth. Buyers rode down to Westport, up to St. Joseph. The news preceded them. Ox prices suddenly doubled. Stores demanded cash. The bankers, musing, decided loan rates must be higher. Bullwhackers reached the conclusion that Utah was a dinged far piece; them heathen Mormons were dead shots as well as madmen. Big risk—more money.

When, somehow, working round the clock, eyes ringed and shoulders sagging, Majors got the wagon trains moving, Russell, Majors & Waddell had five hundred thousand dollars' worth of new short-term notes and due bills. Majors and Waddell agreed privately that there should have been a contract; praise be that Russell had such good friends in Congress and that splendid relationship with Mr. Floyd.

The showy caravan, the gallant dragoons and spit-'n'-polish infantry, made a brave show as they rolled into Nebraska. The *Nebraska City News* gloried that "a thousand whips are cracking, 16,000 tails are gaily snapping the flies away, two thousand drivers shrieking, eight thousand wagon wheels squeaking, all anxious to join the anti-Mormon fray."

The paper hadn't heard about two grim-faced riders hurrying northwest across Iowa. Feramorz Little and Ephraim Hanks were members of the mail conductor troop the Mormons had organized to deliver mail between Independence, Missouri, and Salt Lake City. They hurried home now to report that the United States postmaster had shown them orders straight from Washington to halt all mail deliveries for Utah. Then, by word or gesture, the postmaster or someone else indicated that it might be quite an experience for them to ride past Fort Leavenworth on the way west. They did. They learned what was coming.

Hulking behind a desk twelve hundred miles west, staring glumly out on the raw foundation walls of the great Tabernacle, Brigham Young held firm, clear views about James Buchanan and his slinking, fox-faced Cabinet. Despite the street brawls in New York and Ohio, the pitched battles in Missouri and Illinois, the Mormons kept faith with the concepts of the United States Constitution. The five hundred men of the Mormon Battalion sent out to join Kearny's expedition against Santa Fe in 1846 achieved the longest military march in history before they were disbanded at San Bernardino, California. When the Mexican War ended, the church Council of Twelve organized the state of Deseret, swore in Young as governor and sent a formal petition off to Congress. Deseret, a *Book of Mormon* word, means honeybee; a beehive was in the coat of arms. The boundaries proposed, to be sure, made the state somewhat larger than Texas; but most of it was wasteland—canyons and mesa.

Congress refused to recognize Deseret, but approved much of it as the Territory of Utah, with Brigham Young as governor. However, other territorial officials must come from Washington.

They came—with lean faces, sticky hands, and large carpetbags. Several spoke in liquid drawls, strutted the village streets, and asked endless questions about routes west toward California.

Then W. W. Drummond arrived, with Washington credentials. Out of his wagon swished a hippy young brunette. Drummond introduced his Ada. Ada addressed one and all as "dahlin'." Salt Lake eyebrows hoisted right back to the hairline the day Ada waggled up to sit on the bench beside new Associate Justice Drummond of the Territorial Supreme Court.

That night, a mail conductor rode east with an urgent letter for Washington. The reply came in a few weeks. Justice Drummond's wife and family were still at home in the east, saddened by dear Papa's dangerous mission among the heathen and Indians. Ada filled the description of one Ada Caroll, a whore-about-town. Ada had vanished from the Twelfth Street red lights two or three months ago.

The Mormons believed in the right of plural marriage for their priests, and cited early Christian history in evidence. They were equally adamant that adultery should be punished by death. Reports and requests headed east. Judge Drummond was recalled, Ada still in bouncy tow. A safe two thousand miles from Temple Square, Drummond began to spin yarns. Some of them, considering his Methodist and Baptist audiences, were lulus.

Drummond's stories were still tavern favorites when news of A. W. Babbitt's murder reached Washington. Territorial Secretary Babbitt had started east; his mutilated body was discovered on the banks of the Sweetwater River. Some claimed he was murdered by Indians. The Church knew better. The Mormons, too, had juvenile delinquents. Porter Rockwell and the "Avenging Angels" handled this type of problem. Two young Mormons known to have itchy trigger fingers were trailed to Faust's Ranch. One refused to surrender and was killed on the spot. Rockwell rode back to Salt Lake with the word that the second one had died, too, "trying to escape."

Babbitt's death plus Drummond's stories gave Floyd and his confederates all the emotional ammunition needed to go to work on pious, timid James Buchanan. Brigham Young wasn't too surprised when Porter Rockwell galloped into the Mormon gathering at Cottonwood Canyon on July 24, with unshaven, dust-caked Feramorz Little and Ephraim Hanks trailing. It was a church holiday, but Young gave them audience.

Joseph Smith had established a church militia called the Nauvoo Legion. The Council of Twelve kept it in pert existence. General Daniel H. Wells, its commander, was called into the conference. Major Howard Egan arrived later. Egan had joined with the doughty Major George Chorpenning in pioneering mail deliveries between Salt Lake and California. After 1850, he drove numerous herds of cattle across the savage Nevada desert and the Sierras to sell for beef and leather in West Slope gold camps. Many of the Mormon Battalion's fighters were lingering in San Francisco, Sacramento, Marysville, to prosper in the trade boom. "Call them home, Major Egan. Call them home."

The scheming behind Washington's indignation clarified when mail conductors rode in with word that Colonel Albert Sidney Johnston was being ordered north to replace "Hem-and-haw" Harney as commander of Buchanan's Army of Utah. Johnston, like Floyd, had married a Preston—probably a Kentucky cousin of the Abingdon Prestons. She died; Johnston wandered into Texas. What with excellent soldiering, and a duel or two, he rose to secretary of war in the Republic of Texas. Then he switched to the United States Army as a colonel of cavalry. Secretary of War Davis agreed with the regiment's Lieutenant Colonel Robert E. Lee that it was a happy day for the Army when Johnston made the switch.

Now, with this "fair-haired boy" galloping up the High Plains, the plot thickened. Did it hark back to Joseph Smith's 1844 prophecy of civil war? The Abolitionists had really slammed down the gauntlet with their Kansas challenge. There was brutal, brash war there; no question about it. Were the proslavers retaliating with an army, piously financed by all of America's taxpayers, that would remove the only antislavery forces between Kansas and California? Would it then march back to Kansas and, on one pretext or another, mop up the Free-Staters? Hmmm. Time to call in the editors of the *Deseret News*.

On September 23, 1857, the *Deseret News* reached back to Saxon frankness for some of the phrases on its front page.

TROOPS FOR UTAH

From the dawn of our government until now there has never been anything so outrageous, unconstitutional, illegal, inhuman and in every way occasionless, unjustifiable and wanton a waste of the people's treasure to compass their oppressions and destruction, as is to be found in the sending of troops to Utah. What said our equal rights government when its citizens were successfully driven from Ohio, Missouri, and Illinois, SOLELY for daring to exercise freedom of conscience and worship? "YOUR CAUSE IS JUST, BUT WE CAN DO NOTHING FOR YOU." While state after state, in its sovereignity was hounding and harassing a numerous class of American citizens, a great and powerful Government not only looked tamely on, but actually hugged itself with joy, and abetted those fiendish persecutions, as was proven to all the world by the Government requisition of 500 men from citizens whom they disfranchised, and who were in Indian country with their wives and children in tents and wagons, and using all diligence to leave the borders of "Columbia, (Once) free and equal," but now priest, politician, speculator and editor ridden nigh unto destruction. . . .

It is most readily obvious to all that the administration of our government is becoming rotten even unto loathing, when anonymous liars and whoring, lying venomous late associate justice can incite the expenditure of millions of public treasure in an unjust outrageously wicked and illegal movement against a peaceful and known zealously loyal people inhabitating a region that had been reclaimed and which no others desired, or would now occupy were it laid waste for their entrance. Dear Uncle Sam, we were reared and taught under the broad folds of the Star-Spangled Banner, and notwithstanding you have deprived us of our Eastern mail, we are well aware of the designs of those who are eating your very vitals, and forewarn you that Utah alone cannot avert your speedy dissolution, unless you shake yourself of the vampires now preying upon you, cease your ungodly crusade against an innocent people, return to the old landmarks meting even-handed justice to all.

Weeks before, the Nauvoo Legion had moved in to Echo Canyon, erected ramparts along its rim, piled up rocks to roll down on the Army of Utah, and prepared to flood the canyon so that the wagons could not move. So began our most unique war, in which not a man was killed.

In October, Lot Smith and forty young Mormon commandos, guided by the ever-active Porter Rockwell, rode out on the Wyoming plains to harass the Army.

The gay, brave march reported by the *Nebraska City News* hadn't frolicked well. General Harney had reason to be cautious about the Far West; he'd been there. He wrote letters of protest against starting the march in midsummer. Mr. Floyd read them and beamed. Things were working out; now he had an alibi to transfer the command to Albert Sidney Johnston; Senator Davis would be pleased, too.

But the Continental Divide maintained ugly, snow-plumed indifference. The trail through South Pass remained as awesome and treacherous as it had been for Mormon handcarts and Oregon wagons. September frosted alder groves aflame against the taffy-colored cliffs and iced the gloomy gorge paths.

On October 4, two of the Russell, Majors & Waddell wagon trains lumbered through to Simpson's Hollow on the Green River. Another—Train No. 26—was fifteen or twenty miles behind. Colonel Alexander and the advance guard of the Army of Utah were across the river. Everyone was fagged. Not even the card players stayed up after nine o'clock.

Major Lot Smith and his forty Nauvoo commandos formed a ghostly circle around the wagon trains about midnight, then fired off a few shots to waken the dragoons and bullwhackers. "Don't want to see anybody get hurt," Major Smith announced. "Go get your clothes and such. Then start walkin' —fast."

The wagons made a lovely glow above the hills. Before the breakfast detail at Train No. 26 could awaken Wagonmaster Simpson to ponder it, Smith and the forty rode in. The ceremony was monotonously identical. Smith and the boys had a rough time chousing the three trains' bullocks over Green River, but a week later they trailed seven hundred of them into Salt Lake. The seventy-five wagons that they eventually burned held three hundred thousand pounds of ham, bacon, sugar, and flour; enough to last the Army of Utah for three months.

Colonel Alexander hurriedly assembled the remaining trains into a nine-mile column, and ordered an advance on Salt Lake. Now a dragoon rode alongside each wagon. But General Wells and the Nauvoo Legion preceded them, carefully burning all the grass along the trail; there wasn't enough grazing left for a goat. Then, sixty miles out, a messenger from Johnston spurred in. The column must turn back and try another route. Alexander stuffed the order in his pocket and held the column stock-still for a week. A second Johnston dispatch shifted the route again. This time Alexander moved. But the pace was funereal; the oxen were gaunt and sullen.

Russell, Majors & Waddell's foresight had added a large herd of reserve oxen to the Army columns. About nine hundred of these, plus some mules, finally reached Green River. They could be rushed in to replace Alexander's starving beasts.

But Porter Rockwell and a troop of seventy-five rode up on

November 1, tut-tutted the guards against hurting anybody—and trailed all nine hundred off to the West. They would come in real handy when the Council handed down that order to abandon Salt Lake and march for the southwest deserts.

Colonel Johnston showed up with the rest of the Army two days later, pondered, then ordered a march to abandoned Fort Bridger, fifty miles west of Green River but 150 miles east of Salt Lake. There the United States troops could make out for the winter and, if the worst came to the worst, eat the oxen. The remaining wagons formed an eighteen-mile column.

The march began on November 6; the weather promptly enlisted with the Nauvoo Legion. Seven inches of snow fell before dusk. Wagons were parked and teams turned loose. Porter Rockwell and his cowboys waited patiently behind a ridge. While the Army slumbered, they frolicked off with another five hundred oxen.

Two nights later, the temperature tumbled below zero. More than half of the remaining oxen froze to death.

Finally, eleven of the trains reached Bridger. But it took them weeks. The surviving oxen stumbled them in, a few wagons at a time, under heavy guard, then rested overnight and went back for more. The Nauvoo Legion, without loss of a man, had repeated the tactics used by the Russians in 1812 to destroy Napoleon's armies.

When spring, 1858, finally came, the Mormons graciously allowed Alfred Cumming, the new territorial governor sent out by Buchanan, to enter Salt Lake. But as he passed through Echo Canyon during the night, General Wells marched his fighting men around campfires in plain view of the governor, scurried them on the double to march around the next fires. Governor Cumming was convinced he beheld a vast army.

Promptly, too, Brigham Young ordered all of Salt Lake's women and children moved into desert camps, then stationed men on Temple Square to fire the town if Johnston's army entered. "After this season," he told his people, "when this ignorant army has passed off, I shall never again say to a man, 'Stay your rifle ball,' when our enemies assail us, but shall say, 'Slay them where you find them.' But the army that is now upon our borders are in ignorance and know not what they are doing nor the spirit that prompts them, or they would ere now have been visited with swift destruction."

Mediators came in; councils were held. Brigham Young agreed to step down as governor, and to allow the Army to pass through Salt Lake City on condition that it did not stop until it was across the Jordan River. Thus, after staying a while near the mouth of Bingham Canyon, the Army moved on to Cedar Valley, fifty miles west, and established Camp Floyd. Brigham Young, as spiritual leader of his people, continued to direct the important affairs of the territory much the same as he had while serving as governor.

All told, the Army of Utah cost the Federal government more than five million dollars, and brought Russell, Majors & Waddell to the brink of bankruptcy. The Mormons, buoyed by the dashing tactics of their Nauvoo Legion, achieved greater power and prestige, and became more belligerent against slavery and the South. The New Englanders and New Yorkers, as suspicious as Brigham Young of the true motives for the expedition, began to use Johnston's march as evidence that, "by goldurn, if an army can fumble through to Salt Lake in the winter, then a mail service really could use that Central Route to California the year around."

Was Floyd's scheme utterly worthless? Would no monuments rise to honor his army of Utah?

Yes. There was one. And it still gleams gloriously above Salt Lake City in 1960. Alexander Majors learned about it thirty-six years later in a Chicago hotel room. This is how he reported it:

One afternoon in Chicago, Mr. J. F. Wells of Salt Lake City called on me. "Do you remember the 75 wagons you lost in the vicinity of Green River back in '57?" he asked.

"I reckon I do," I answered. "They were captured by Lot Smith, who was serving under General Wells."

"Yes," my visitor said. "My father. I want to tell you a little incident connected with that raid. Nails were worth 60¢ a lb in Salt Lake then. When the news was received of the capture and burning of those wagons, a lot of us boys were sent out with axes, hammers and chisels to break up the wagons in still smaller fragments, and extract every nail we could find. But that isn't all. The nails we extracted from your wagons were afterwards used in the roof of the Tabernacle which was then under construction."

4.
PIKE'S PEAK AND BUSTED

James Rupe and Charles Morehead, Jr., rode with the Army of Utah as Russell, Majors & Waddell's "field bosses." They checked in the wagons when the gaunt, half-frozen oxen staggered them up to the Fort Bridger enclosure and, by Christmas Eve, 1857, had a comprehensive picture of the catastrophe. On December 27, they wrapped their reports and bills of lading in waterproof canvas and began the twelve-hundred-mile journey to Leavenworth.

Bucking snow-clogged passes, northers, wolves and Indians, they averaged forty miles a day across the trackless wilderness and rode into Leavenworth on January 26, 1858. While accountants totted up the losses, Majors and Waddell telegraphed Russell in Washington, sent the new office boy, William Cody, off with messages to the Rupe and Morehead homes, then settled into an afternoon's cross-examination beside a roaring Franklin stove. Army couriers had brought rumors. Both partners were convinced that their losses would be staggering. Now Russell must really prove his mettle. There was not so much as a scrap of paper to show any War Department responsibility for the burned wagon trains, the frozen teams or the fifteen hundred mules and oxen the Nauvoo Legion drove off to Salt Lake.

Yet, despite this threat of bankruptcy, Majors was fascinated by the miracle of the Rupe and Morehead journey. Ever since the Mexican War and the stampede to the California gold fields, plainsmen had pretty much accepted the edict of Jefferson Davis and other government officials that the Southern Route through Santa Fe and El Paso del Norte was the only year-round trail across the continent. Even William Gilpin, the West Point graduate who strove so ardently to develop the city of Centropolis at the Missouri-Mississippi junction, fell in line with this concept by arguing that the first transcontinental railroad should be built beside the Santa Fe Trail. And in September, 1857, after Congress finally passed the bill authorizing a six-hundred-thousand-dollar subsidy for semiweekly mail service to California, Postmaster General Aaron Brown awarded the contract to

The Butterfield Co., with a specific proviso that the route run through Arkansas, Texas-New Mexico to San Diego and San Francisco.

But now an army of infantrymen and lumbering wagons had proved that the grim peaks and ten-thousand-foot passes of the Rockies could be crossed as late as November and, more amazing still, two lone riders had recrossed this "uninhabitable wilderness" in midwinter. If horse-and-rider communication was possible between Missouri and Salt Lake in December and January, why couldn't the same route be used all the way to California? It was hundreds—yes, perhaps a thousand—miles shorter than the weary, roundabout jog across the Southwest. Word had already filtered back about the veterans of the Mormon Battalion who skedaddled out of San Francisco and the mother lode towns to vanish up the passes toward Lake Tahoe. And a year or two back, the brave Major Chorpenning finally did make it through with mail deliveries between Sacramento and Salt Lake. If he could do it, and the Mormon Battalion veterans could do it, wasn't the entire route feasible the year round? How much of this "safe Southern Route" was truth, and how much was politics?

Billy Cody rode in from the telegraph office the morning after Rupe's and Morehead's arrival with a message from Russell; the two riders were to bring their reports to Washington as soon as they felt able to coach across Missouri to the Jefferson City railhead. The accountants had worked most of the night, too. Even they broke the traditional composure of the mathematician to express sympathy and reassure Majors—in polite asides—of their confidence that he could "straighten out this tragic affair." The Nauvoo Legion and Utah's winter, in partnership, had so far cost the firm $493,553.01. Russell must move quickly. The gossip would seep from the accounting room out to Westport, St. Joseph and Lexington banks and merchants within a few days.

Russell and his new banking partner, Smoot, were meanwhile working effectively as Capitol Hill lobbyists. They engineered another two-year monopoly contract for all military supplies west of the Missouri, then, by showing facts and figures on the hijacking rates the Missourians charged for Army of Utah supplies and loans, boosted the firm's cartage rates.

Some time in February, with Rupe and Morehead in attendance, Russell secured an appointment with Secretary of War Floyd. The politician was abject. The Army of Utah costs mounted daily; another three thousand troops were being assembled at Fort Leavenworth to march to Johnston's relief; the budget was exhausted. Really—he sighed—he held himself responsible for all this. Confidentially, Methodist to Baptist, his Christian motives had surpassed his military judgment in approving the expedition's start so late in the summer. As everyone knew, that Central Route wilderness was a death trap; it could never be regularly traveled. But, at least Johnston was on the scene. His guns would put an end to Mormon polygamy and godlessness.

Russell nodded agreement—five hundred thousand dollars' worth. Mr. Secretary, then, did concede the indebtedness to Russell, Majors & Waddell?

Why, yes. Of course. But, no budget. Floyd's hands fluttered in silent imprecation against the Capitol Hill misers.

Would it be possible—Russell's eyes almost popped their sockets at the thought—would it be possible to draw drafts or notes of some kind on the War Department against 1858 earnings? After all, the new contracts called for two or three times as much outlay. Also, they stipulated that the village of Nebraska City, 150 miles up the Missouri, was to be developed as a new supply base. Mr. Majors was taking steps to sell his Westport property and move up there. If the Secretary could see fit . . .

Floyd *hmmed* and finger-tapped the desk. Not a bad idea at all, at all. The Department would not be in any danger. And—he smiled inwardly—this would put the firm utterly in his power and lessen the likelihood of this adventurous little fellow's sniffing out Abolitionist support, or becoming too nosy about operations in Kansas and Utah. Why, yes, he said aloud, he thought something along that line might be feasible. He would let Mr. Russell know within a day or two.

During March, Floyd wrote letters to New York and Washington bankers, asking them to honor War Department acceptances issued to Russell, Majors & Waddell. August Belmont took one hundred thousand dollars' worth. In all, four hundred thousand dollars was raised. Russell also secured loans, at high rates, in Philadelphia. Waddell and the accountants juggled books and stalled creditors. The firm struggled on.

Majors, meanwhile, boated his household goods and retinue of slaves upriver to Nebraska City. His beloved wife, Catherine, had passed away in January, 1856. Desperately lonely, and with heavy social obligations, he had married Susan Wetzel in the spring of 1857. But Catherine still haunted Westport; memories of her were everywhere. Perhaps, in a new home, the loneliness and ache would lessen.

Nebraska City, like every other village on the river, had

dreams of big-city glory. An upstate New Yorker named Julius Sterling Morton settled here in 1854 and founded a weekly newspaper, the *Nebraska City News*. He was probably the author of that doggerel description of the Army of Utah fly-swishing up the prairie in the summer of 1857. A Methodist preacher named John Chivington rode in, too. Chivington, the son of a Kentucky War of 1812 veteran, was burly and black-bearded. Strangely, the cloth had claimed him; Methodists around Quincy, Illinois, praised his eloquence at camp meetings. He and a brother had already split, violently, on the subject of slavery. Reverend Chivington worked with Morton in the Abolitionist cause, as well as on the plans to make Nebraska City a great "port for the West." The Army of Utah march strengthened both their convictions of the Central Route's potential as the great east-west throughway across the continent.

Then, during the spring and summer of 1858, Cherokees and Georgians justified these convictions by lighting the fuse on a migration that would not only lead to the Pony Express but doom the Floyd-Johnston "Secesh" dreams for a Western confederation.

For centuries there had been rumors of gold in the Rocky Mountains. Spanish explorers came looking for hidden treasure. Indians brought gold, in dust and nuggets, to trading posts along the North and South Platte rivers and the Arkansas. If the Spaniards found the treasure, they did not tell about it. Neither the Indians nor the mountain men had tried or wanted to develop the mines. They knew that the lure of gold would surely bring thousands to their hunting grounds, men who would destroy the game and ruin their trapping-and-trading business.

A party of California-bound Cherokees from Georgia, who took a short cut along the foot of the Rockies, in 1850 panned "colors" in a stream they named Ralston Creek, near present-day Denver. But since the amount of gold that they found was small, they trekked on. In the summer of 1857, soldiers reported meeting on the South Platte a small party of Missourians who claimed they had prospected in the Pike's Peak area for a number of months, and displayed gold in bottles and little buckskin bags. Frightened by Indian hostilities, they were going back to "the States" for reinforcements. Fall Leaf, Delaware Indian guide to Major Sedgwick's military expedition in the summer of 1857, displayed gold nuggets in Lawrence, Kansas, that autumn, and told he had found them near the Rocky Mountains. He promised to lead a party to the gold fields in the spring.

First to reach Cherry Creek in 1858 was a party led by William Green Russell of Georgia. He had been with the Cherokees in 1850 when they found gold on Ralston Creek. The original Russell party numbered eighteen; but, by the time they reached the mouth of Cherry Creek, another seventy-five to one hundred stragglers had joined them. They prospected in numerous places and found some color. But, by July, most of the men were discouraged. In response to Russell's call for volunteers to stay with him, twelve men declared their willingness to remain in the mountains. This group prospected various streams until, on the Little Dry Creek branch of the South Platte, they found gold in "paying quantity."

Fall Leaf failed to keep his promise. The Lawrence party started west without him in late May and, on June 5, numbered forty-six men, two women and a child. One of the women, Julia Archibald Holmes, was the wife of James Holmes, a recent follower of John Brown. She was a women's rights advocate, the object of some ridicule; she wore "the bloomers," and asked to take her turn at standing guard along the trail. Late that summer, she became the first white woman ever to climb Pike's Peak.

Only two or three of the Lawrence party were experienced miners. They camped for a time on the Fontaine qui Bouille, near the Garden of the Gods, and sent two parties toward South Park. When they learned of the success of Russell's party on Little Dry Creek, some headed up the South Platte. There, more experienced in handling real estate than in mining, they laid out Montana City, six miles from the confluence of Cherry Creek and the Platte. But after erecting a few log houses, they decided it would be more advantageous to have a townsite near the mouth of Cherry Creek, where the so-called Trappers' Trail from Taos, New Mexico, and from the Arkansas River to Fort Laramie, crossed the South Platte.

Accordingly, on September 24, they laid claim to the land on the east bank of Cherry Creek, and formally organized the St. Charles Town Company. John Smith and William McGaa, (known as Jack Jones), two Indian traders who, with their Indian wives, had previously set up tepees near the mouth of Cherry Creek, were taken into this realty venture. On October 2, the Kansans started back to Lawrence for the winter, intending to perfect plans there for their town.

In the meantime, news of gold discoveries had reached the towns along the Missouri River. On August 27, 1858, the Kansas City *Journal of Commerce* reported: "There is perfect furore in Kansas City on the subject of the Pike's Peak mines. We have no hesitation in saying in a fortnight the road from Kansas City to Council Grove, and then west to the mines, will be lined with gold-seekers for the new Eldorado." And: "Great excitement is now rife in this city, and on every corner can be heard the usual conversation incident to the gold fever mania. How far is it there? How long will it take to make the trip?" Parties were organized at Plattsmouth, Omaha, Florence and Bellevue, Nebraska, at Council Bluffs, Iowa, and in many Missouri towns. Little thought was given to the dangers of winter on the prairies.

With wagons daily arriving at the mouth of Cherry Creek, a mass meeting was called on October 30 to discuss plans for founding a town in the V formed by Cherry Creek and the South Platte. The new community, the meeting voted, would be named Auraria (from the Latin word for "gold"), in honor of Auraria, Georgia, five miles from Dahlonega, the home of William Green Russell.

Back in Leavenworth, General William Larimer, a former banker and railway president of Pittsburgh, Pennsylvania, who had lost heavily in the panic of 1857, proposed getting up a party to start for Pike's Peak. Eighty or more men volunteered to accompany him. But when the start was made in October, the party totaled only six. On the way five others joined them, including officers appointed by Governor James W. Denver, the most recent in Buchanan's long list of governors for Kansas Territory, to perfect the organization of "Arapahoe County, Kansas Territory," the western boundary of which was the Rocky Mountains. Before leaving, General Larimer and his son called on William H. Russell and discussed townsites, stage lines and similar undertakings. Russell, the Larimers reported, gave them much helpful advice about Western travel. "But," according to young Larimer, "we could find no one who had ever been to Cherry Creek."

The Larimer party reached the mouth of Cherry Creek on November 16 after forty-seven days on the road. When the general found that a settlement named Auraria already had been organized, he immediately crossed to the east side of the creek and laid claim to the site of the projected but undeveloped St. Charles townsite. He and his son quickly erected a cabin, then organized the Denver City Town Company, giving the new townsite the name of Governor Denver.

By mid-November, Auraria was reported to have from fifty to seventy-five houses "put up." Denver City also was building winter quarters. It is estimated that by December there were six hundred men scattered along the South Platte and its branches within fifteen miles of Auraria and Denver. Because of the snow in the mountains, most of them stayed close to the settlements.

Of major concern to the Cherry Creek settlers was the lack of mail service. The nearest mail office was Fort Laramie on the Oregon Trail, some two hundred miles to the north. There, an "express" left letters and papers on the average of once a month. Arrangements were made with Jim Sanders, known also as Saunders, an Indian trader, to drive over to Fort Laramie each month. On November 23, General Larimer wrote his wife to direct letters in care of Sanders & Co. Express. "It will cost twenty-five cents for each letter and fifteen cents for newspapers," he reported. "Let all your letters be good large ones and send no papers except important ones; but do write me often."

Soon afterward Sanders and his squaw headed north in an open wagon for Fort Laramie. They were back on January 8, with more than one hundred letters and a number of papers. Men stood in line as the mail was given out.

On the very day that Sanders returned, a friend of his, George A. Jackson, who had prospected along every stream from Fort Laramie to Cherry Creek, made one of the most important discoveries in the Rocky Mountains. Jackson was wintering near "Arrapahoe Bar," twelve miles west of Denver. On an elk hunt up Clear Creek, he made camp to rest his dog, Drum, who had been lamed in a "hell of a fight with a carcajou." Jackson built a big fire to thaw the gravel along the stream. There, from rim rock, he dug eight "treaty cups of dirt filled with fine colors." There also was a nugget of coarse gold. "I've got the diggin's at last," Jackson jotted in his journal that night.

About the same time in January, other prospectors discovered the yellow metal in a branch of Boulder Creek, and named the place Gold Run. About the end of January, Deadwood Diggings sprang up on South Boulder, in a gulch filled with fallen timber. Soon afterward, a gold-bearing quartz vein was found in what was named Gold Hill. New arrivals kept coming to the Pike's Peak country during the winter from all parts of the country. Store agents distributed thousands of copies of brochures, guidebooks and other materials boosting various border towns as outfitting points. Said a Kansas City correspondent of the *Missouri Republican* on March 21:

Here they come by every steamboat hundreds of them, hundreds after hundreds from every place—Hoosiers, Suckers, Corn Crackers, Buckeyes, Redhorses, Arabs and Egyptians—some with ox wagons, some with mules, but the greatest number on foot, with their knap-sacks and old-fashioned rifles and shotguns; some with their long-tailed blues, others in jeans and bob-tailed jockeys; in their roundabouts, slouched hats, caps and sacks. There are a few hand-carts in the crowd. They form themselves into companies of ten, twenty, and as high as forty-five men have marched out, two-and-two, with a captain and a clerk, eight men to a hand-cart, divided into four reliefs, two at a time pulling the cart. . . . Onward they move, in solemn order, day after day, old and young, tall and slender, short and fat, handsome and ugly, the strong and the weak.

It was estimated that at least seventy-five thousand persons would be in the Pike's Peak area by autumn. Word of a mild, pleasant winter at the mines and of the finding of many prospects sent canvas-topped wagons swaying across the prairies with PIKE'S PEAK OR BUST painted in large letters on their sides. By mid-April the roads leading west from "the River" were white with wagon tops. Many large parties camped along the creeks waiting for better grass to green farther west.

But when it was learned that gold was not yet arrivng at the border towns from the diggings in sufficient quantities to justify the belief that the mines were paying, an undercurrent of discontent set in. Many who were going back had not even been able to turn a shovelful of dirt because of the snow and frozen ground. Some had suffered hardships or had seen fellow travelers sicken and die by the wayside. Hysteria seized many. In the ebb of the gold tide, some twenty-five hundred wagons headed away from Pike's Peak, back to the States.

Through it all, not even Billy Cody was half as starry-eyed about Pike's Peak gold as William H. Russell. General Larimer sold him a share in the Denver City Town Company, and thus a thirty-acre plot in what would be the heart of Colorado's capital was set aside in Russell's name. Congress was in a lusty pre-election uproar over the "Mormon War fiasco." Investigating committees demanded copies of all contracts, orders, correspondence concerning it. In the hearings that followed, Russell, Majors & Waddell came in for verbal spankings as "war profiteers."

Secretary Floyd bustled to provide logical alibis for these arrogant Republicans and Northern Democrats. Also, he saw opportunity looming to oust Thomas S. Jessup as quartermaster general of the Army and put his boyhood friend, Lieutenant Colonel Joseph Johnston, in the job. He did take time to shake his head at Russell over a pitcher of shrub one summer evening, and warn him that congressional inquisitiveness might make it advisable to shift the Army's cartage contract to another firm in 1860.

This may have spurted the little man off into the very path that Floyd was marking with a large No Trespass sign. Or perhaps the ego was flexing again and Russell saw, gleaming atop Pike's Peak, a millionaire fairyland even prettier than the one the Nauvoo Legion had shattered. Early in 1859, Russell and John S. Jones, another Missouri supply contractor, organized the Leavenworth & Pike's Peak Express Company to run stagecoaches and a mail delivery between Missouri and Denver City.

Waddell flew into a rage when he heard the news. The bitter letters between Washington and Leavenworth almost wrecked the partnership then and there. Majors also was brought into the squabble. He, too, refused to take any stock in the new firm and went back to Nebraska City. His own affairs were broadening; his farmer instinct warned him against trusting all his "eggs" to Russell's ambitious jugglings. He owned a store in Westport Landing and operated at least five hundred wagons in his separate account that year.

The express company invested lavishly in Concord coaches, prairie schooners, horses and mules, and built dozens of way stations across Kansas and Nebraska to the banks of the South Platte. Then, only a week before the line opened, Russell bustled down to St. Louis and pledged another $144,000 to J. M. Hockaday & Co. for their new United States Mail contract between the Mississippi and Salt Lake. The L. & P. P. was in business all across the Rockies and Wyoming desert to Temple Square, only 750 miles from the Pacific. When the first coach left Leavenworth, with a band and parade, Jones & Russell expenses had zoomed to one thousand dollars per day.

Horace Greeley, bombastic editor of the *New York Tribune*, rode "deadhead" on one of the first stages. He wrote long stories about the firm's array of wagons outside Leavenworth, the glories of the prairie, the building boom in Denver City. Russell went into ecstasies over them and sent clippings to all his acquaintances. Waddell and Majors gravely watched the books, and saw the L. & P. P. sink more deeply into the red.

Scarcely had the dust settled from those first stagecoach wheels than word came down from the gulches that John H.

Gregory, who had been prospecting for several weeks, had struck a rich gold lode. George A. Jackson, in the meantime, had interested some Chicago men in developing his find on a branch of Clear Creek; almost coincident with the announcement of Gregory's strike, the story of Jackson's diggings on Chicago Creek (present-day Idaho Springs) was published. Denver City was almost depopulated overnight. Buildings that were being constructed were left unroofed. Everyone who could possibly get away headed for the hills.

Constantly, Denver's press advocated regular United States Mail service for the Cherry Creek area and nearby mines. On March 28, Washington announced that a post office had been established at Coraville, in the Pike's Peak region; Mathias Snyder, formerly of Virginia, was postmaster. This office was to be sustained from its net proceeds, not to exceed five hundred dollars per annum. There was no contract for transportation of the mails. The Washington reporter was careful to point out that if the Post Route Bill had passed, and a contract had been made under it, this service would have cost the government from thirty to forty thousand dollars a year. "The contractors," he concluded, "will be mainly compensated for their outlay in the carrying of passengers." He failed to point out that a mail line through a vast, uninhabited stretch of country, servicing a small population, could not possibly make money on passengers; a large government subsidy was essential.

From the scanty evidence available, it is apparent that the Coraville post office was part of the Leavenworth & Pike's Peak Express office of Jones & Russell in Denver City. Since the people in the area were asking for regular United States mail, Russell may have thought that the charge of twenty-five cents a letter made by the Express Company could be collected more readily if the patrons thought they were paying through an official post office. The office of Coraville was discontinued June 25, 1859. A few covers are still extant bearing the Coraville postmark, but they are exceedingly rare. Only a few ever were stamped, and those were done through a misunderstanding.

During August and September, discoveries were made of both placer and quartz—yielding gold on the Upper Blue and its tributaries. Men were prospecting from the head of Del Norte to the head of the Big Laramie, ranging west as far as the mouth of the White River. It was estimated that the miners at work made "from three to five dollars a day to the hand." Mining districts were formed. Miners' courts conducted the affairs of the areas. Although the Pike's Peak coun-

55

try lay mostly in Arapahoe County, Kansas Territory, it was too far away from a seat of government. In December, 1859, the "people of Western Kansas" formed their own provisional government of Jefferson Territory. They hoped for statehood soon.

The Leavenworth & Pike's Peak Express had, since its inception, given exceptional service. But, as the experienced and conservative Alex Majors had anticipated when he refused to back the line, it was not paying expenses. The cards were down by late fall. The L. & P. P. had run up debts of five hundred thousand dollars, and failed to meet the payments on its short-term notes, meanwhile borrowing willy-nilly from Russell, Majors & Waddell funds and raiding their warehouses and corrals for supplies. In brief, when it failed—as it inevitably would—the freighting monopoly would vanish with it.

The partners went into conference. The decision was made to reorganize the stage line, and have it taken over by Russell, Majors & Waddell. Then more ominous news came in from Washington. The military contract to Utah would not be renewed for 1860. Instead, Floyd and his new quartermaster general, Brigadier General Joseph Johnston, offered Russell, Majors & Waddell the 1860–61 contract for military-supply cartage to New Mexico posts.

Alex Majors took a long walk alone, out the snowy road to the Leavenworth landing and back. Mr. Floyd had always bothered him. There was something unclean about the man. And now, despite this Republican and Northern Democrat fury against the Mormon War, there was no valid reason to boot Russell, Majors & Waddell off the Utah route and transfer them to the Santa Fe Trail. It would be far more logical to cut them off altogether. No co-operation could be expected from Butterfield's drivers and guards in warding off Indian attacks or helping mired and ditched wagons. Instead, there would be rivalry—perhaps open fights—because everyone would know that Leavenworth & Pike's Peak stages were actually pioneering that shorter Central Route to California.

What was behind it all? What was there in the fact that Louis McLane, general manager of the California division of Wells Fargo, was General Johnston's brother-in-law? Wells Fargo was, of course, a "power behind the throne" of John Butterfield's stage line. Postmaster General Brown was a Tennesseean and a fiery Old South patriot. McLane had migrated to the Pacific coast from Baltimore, where his father had been president of the Baltimore & Ohio Railroad.

Joe Johnston married his sister. Johnston and Floyd were old friends, and ardent Virginians. Now Russell, Majors & Waddell wagon trains were being deprived of Central Route deliveries just six months after Russell recklessly had pioneered Denver and Salt Lake passenger and mail service.

What did it add up to? Majors had never really studied the Slavery-Abolitionist issue. He was a businessman. Brought up in Missouri, he took slavery for granted. But talks with Chivington and Morton at Nebraska City had already caused him to look thoughtfully at the slaves working in his kitchens and barns. Now, if proslavers in Buchanan's retinue were using the government's power not only to further their cause but to enrich relatives and associates, the time had come for soul-searching. He didn't want it. Yet truth was truth. Moreover, Russell, Majors & Waddell was actually in bankruptcy right now.

The bearded giant was still pondering when Russell popped up with the idea of a spectacular *coup de grâce* that might save the firm. Why not, he proposed, organize a fast-mail express that would deliver letters to California by the Central Route? Butterfield's stages were taking a lumbering thirty—yes, even thirty-five—days to deliver mail between St. Louis and San Francisco. Now the railroad had reached St. Joseph. Pony riders should be able to make it to San Francisco, via the Central Route, in fifteen—twelve—perhaps even ten days. This, if successful, might very well force Congress to award Russell, Majors & Waddell the United States Mail contract in 1861. With that subsidy of seven hundred thousand dollars or more, they could squeak through.

Majors took another long night walk. This would really put the fat in the fire. But why not? They might as well go bankrupt with a vengeance! And the other matter—that larger, biting matter of conscience and truth? There was something bigger in all of this than a bank account. He was still pondering it the afternoon he met Russell's train in St. Joseph and again that night, as he read his Bible in the Patee House bedroom.

5.
ORPHANS PREFERRED

WANTED

YOUNG SKINNY WIRY FELLOWS not over eighteen. Must be expert riders willing to risk death daily. Orphans preferred. WAGES $25 per week. Apply, *Central Overland Express*, Alta Bldg., Montgomery Street.

The two-inch, single-column advertisement, scheduled for issues of the *Alta California* during late February and early March, 1860, exploded into a front-page story before the compositor picked the first "cap W" off his font.

A few hours after press time, an express messenger galloped away from the Wells Fargo building a few doors down Montgomery Street, having been promised a bonus if the letters he carried for Mr. John Butterfield, the postmaster general, and certain Washington lobbyists caught up with the stage lumbering down the Ox-bow toward Los Angeles.

Collis P. Huntington stared out the windows of Huntington & Hopkins toward the black masts of Golden Gate shipping, read the story again, shook his head and growled, "Constructive murder." But he jotted himself a reminder note to inquire about rates and the possibility of obtaining New York, Boston and Washington newspapers as well as letters via Pony Express.

Two stagecoach drivers had tied reins on dashboards, and were leaning back and chawing cigar-clipping cuds reflectively when, in a Sierra pass, the northbound run for Virginia City shrilled the news to the southbound. Even the Wells Fargo messenger on the down stage, after worried glances at the big green box loaded with raw silver, lowered his rifle and engaged in ten or twelve syllables of conversation. The decision rendered, after fifty words and fourteen tobacco squirts in eleven minutes, was, "Three to one th' boys don't make it."

Yet those odds, echoed from Jones' Canvas Hotel to Montgomery Street, were a gambler's prayer that the Pony would get through. It began to look as though the three

Fates had held another knitting party and a long talk, if you believed in those old Greek superstitions. Anyway, things seemed to shape up that way. So, some kind of prayer was in order—especially among Northerners and those with fixed minds about Abolition and Union.

California hadn't fared too well in Washington these thirteen years. John Charles Frémont, "The Pathfinder," had come down the Pacific Slope via the Central Route in the 1840's; Kit Carson was his guide. The insurrection Frémont talked up against Mexican rule timetabled neatly with the United States' declaration of war against Mexico in 1846. The Bear Flag Republic, established by the Americans, folded when Commodore John Sloat arrived off Monterey with orders to seize the capitol buildings and claim California as United States territory. Then Commodore Robert F. Stockton, a New Jersey neighbor to Zebulon Pike's descendants, assumed command of United States Navy forces in the Pacific; he appointed Frémont governor of California. General Kearny's army, largely Missourians plus the famed Mormon Battalion, crossed the deserts from Santa Fe that winter. Kearny outranked Stockton.

The Californians, having won freedom from Mexico with ease, now faced the messy traditions of Washington power plays. Los Angeles rebelled against highhandedness by Kearny's local administrator. Frémont and Stockton both stormed back to the Potomac, bellowed imprecations and resigned their commissions.

California Territory slipped into military rule until the discovery of gold, in a millrace at John Sutter's bucolic New Helvetia, turned San Francisco and Sacramento into bawdy, filthy boom towns, impoverished Sutter and brought on a regime of Vigilante committees and "necktie parties." The citizen government that emerged was dominated by Free-Staters.

Northerners had taken steamers out of Boston, New York and Philadelphia, transferred to muleback for the jounce across Panama and Nicaragua, then reshipped north up the Pacific to the Golden Gate. Others used the Central Route's Mormon-Oregon Trail into Utah, plunged blindly across the Nevada deserts and Sierra passes to the mother lode country behind Sacramento and Sutter's ruined farming idyl. Either way, they beat the Southerners, jogging out via their weary Ox-bow Route.

After the Yankees, by alacrity and cunning, captured California's government, they built San Francisco up its golden hills in a street pattern that made Philadelphians homesick, and applied for statehood as a free, nonslave domain. The ruckus this created in United States Senate chambers brought Henry Clay tottering out of retirement and caused Daniel Webster to lose most of the Abolitionist vote. The Compromise of 1850, sired by Douglas of Illinois with Clay and Webster holding the halter of mare Columbia, not only sustained the Northerners in California but aided the "squatter sovereignty" techniques of the New England Emigrant Aid Society in Kansas as well as the ballyhoo to Scandinavians and Germans about the "loveliness" of the Wisconsin, Minnesota and Nebraska frontiers.

However, as the Mexicans, Frémont, Stockton, and finally the Army had learned, capturing California was one thing; holding it was quite another matter.

Zachary Taylor's death in July, 1850, seemed to have ended the succession of United States presidents who were stanchly and aggressively pro-Union. Millard Fillmore, although a New Yorker, became a creature of proslavery forces in Congress. Franklin Pierce, another son of a state governor, fell into the same trap partly because of frustrations about the Democratic party, partly because of personal unfitness for the job. James Buchanan, the frightened Democrats' choice in 1856, was emotionally ready for carpet slippers, sherry flip, and a cushioned settle beside a Pennsylvania fireplace.

Southerners filled the critical Cabinet positions of secretaries of navy, war and treasury through most of these three terms. Vice Presidents King of Alabama and Breckenridge of Kentucky presided over the Senate between 1853 and 1861. Aaron V. Brown of Tennessee and Joseph Holt of Kentucky successively ruled the dreary, graft-ridden office of postmaster general. Working desperately for The Cause, the Southerners overcame the natural suspicions of Georgian toward Virginian and piedmonter for highlander. For thirteen nervously groping years, while Vermonters still stiffened necks toward York Staters and Pennsylvanians looked askance at Down East, this Southern bloc ran the United States. The Ox-bow Route to California was blessed; the Central Route was cursed. The Navy frolicked off to Africa to buy dromedaries for Secretary of War Davis' camel corps. The post office awarded mail subsidies with the stipulation that the Ox-bow Route be used. The Army managed to arrive a day or two late to prevent raids against Kansas Abolitionists, but was more prompt about frustrating Kansas raids into Missouri.

Through it all, the Knights of the Golden Circle built a

careful case for a slave empire that would extend from Cuba and Mexico across all the West. There is evidence that more than one hundred thousand rifles were stored in Arizona, southern California and Nevada by 1860, waiting for the signal to reconquer California and swing it back into the proslave columns, either as a "friendly power" or as part of a new confederacy.

There is, also, voluminous evidence that the Mormon War was either deliberately generated or made possible by this ambition. If Albert Sidney Johnston was not aware of such a "hidden agenda," he was at least a Southerner of proved allegiance to the proslavery and States'-rights cause; thus the transfer of command of the Army of Utah to him. General Harney's valid protests against the late start of the 1857 march provided the hoped-for alibi.

As it developed, 1858 would have been the logical year for Southern secession, followed by quick conquest of Mexico and the trans-Mississippi West. George E. Pickett, the rowdy Virginia careerist who would later launch Pickett's Charge at Gettysburg, commanded United States Army forces in Washington Territory that year. William Walker, the Nashville, Tennessee, "freebooter" and proslaver, had been ousted from control of Nicaragua in May, 1857, only because of outraged screams by New York and California shipping interests and President Pierce's fears of Great Britain.

But, with Buchanan vacillating between crying spells and shrill prayer, and the South in Secesh, Walker could have retaken Nicaragua in a week, then calmly closed the Panama Isthmus to all Unionist traffic until the West's rebellion was assured. Neatly arranged in the same package were Butterfield's stage line's using the all-Southern route for the only transcontinental mail and passenger service, plus Jefferson Davis' camel corps freshly arrived in Texas.

But, as the Virginia City stage-drivers opined, "Them Fates must have held another meetin'." The Nauvoo Legion, judiciously combining weather and horsemanship, bobbled Johnston's campaign and handed him an ignominious defeat that not even Ulysses S. Grant could later excel. By the summer of 1858, the Mormons were stronger than ever. So the Central Route's "center" remained secure, manned by a "beehive" that was belligerently antislavery.

That summer, too, the "Pike's Peak or Bust" wagons plowed dusty ruts across Nebraska, Iowa, and Kansas to the very foot of the Continental Divide. So the eastern frontier of the Central Route advanced five hundred miles beyond the Missouri.

Meanwhile, Ethan and Hosea Grosh advanced the western frontier of the Central Route 150 perilous miles across the Sierra Nevada. Sons of a Pennsylvania preacher, the Grosh brothers panned fruitlessly for gold through the mother lode country, then, following a hunch, headed for the Sierras' eastern slopes behind Lake Tahoe. They found gold outcroppings on a savagely bleak peak that would one day be named Mount Davidson. But their claim, like the name of the man who murdered them, was never registered. A sheepherder named Harry Tompkins Paige Comstock took over their cabin, registered the claim and began to pan nuggets. He soon tired of the job. The veins petered out or disappeared into masses of blue quartz. When, after two months, a group of sourdoughs offered him eleven thousand dollars cash, Comstock sold out. By spring, 1859, Sacramento and San Francisco had the whisper, from an assay office, that that "damned blue quartz" Comstock had tossed aside was smeltering out at $1,595 in gold and $4,791 in silver per ton. Comstock's Lode repeated the Sutter's Fort frenzy of 1849; Virginia City (named by a homesick Southerner) was built up around it. So the western frontier of the Central Route moved 150 Sierra miles toward Salt Lake.

There she stood. The Fates had met, finished their knitting, and voted a straight Abolitionist ticket. Virginia City —Salt Lake—Denver. All that remained was to find the combination of desperate businessmen and foolhardy youngsters who would literally "thread the needle" by establishing regular communication between Denver, Salt Lake, and Virginia City. And, struggling fervently to win a place in his Southland's hall of fame, John Buchanan Floyd had unwittingly made that tenuous thread of the Central Route inevitable, because the day he forced the Army of Utah provisions contract on Russell, Majors & Waddell, he enabled all the American West to "hold for the Union."

Some foreboding of destiny must have welled up in Alexander Majors when he stalked across the prairie those nights after the October, 1859, conferences splashed BANKRUPTCY in bold type across the future for Russell, Majors & Waddell. It must have shone, too, for pint-sized William H. Russell since, pompous as he was, he now realized that the currents in Washington's politics were strong and deep—with quicksand underfoot. Certainly something larger than a desperate gamble against bankruptcy drove the three partners into the gargantuan task of building, during three midwinter months, 163 relay stations and corrals across nineteen hundred miles of wilderness; hiring eighty to one hundred youngsters who were willing to "risk death daily" at twenty-five dollars per week; manning the way stations with hostlers as deft with rifles and Bowie knives as they were with currycombs and blacksmith tongs; buying four hundred to six hundred ponies that could outrun any Indian cayuse or mustang; briskly announcing a timetable so precise that Mormon housewives and Nebraska schoolteachers alike would learn to set clocks by "the minute the Pony Express rider rode past."

It seems impossible that even an army of Alexander Majors, Ben Ficklins, Bolivar Roberts, Howard Egans and W. W. Finneys could have achieved this between January, 1860, and April 3, 1860. Yet there it is in the record. These five achieved the miracle, while Russell bustled to Chicago, New York, Philadelphia and Washington to open Pony Express offices, and made his suave supersalesman "pitch" to bankers, politicians, editors, gamblers and traders willing to pay five dollars for a half-ounce of "news" delivered between the Atlantic and Pacific seaboards in twelve or thirteen days.

Raymond W. and Mary Lund Settle—who, among the hundreds of writer-historians sparked by the drama of the Pony Express, seem to have done the most thorough job of research—report in their *Empire on Wheels* that Russell telegraphed his son at Leavenworth on January 27, 1860, saying: "Have determined to establish a Pony Express to Sacramento, California, commencing 3rd of April. Time ten days." This was just sixty-seven days before the first runs set off from St. Joseph and San Francisco.

The plans must have been put on paper several months before, with the telegram as a sort of "official news release" that the son could hand out to journalists, as he promptly did. The Settles conclude that the decision to embark on the venture was reached during the October, 1859, conferences when Russell, Majors & Waddell took over the "busted" Leavenworth & Pike's Peak Express Company, and renamed it Central Overland California & Pike's Peak Express Company (while bankruptcy loomed so clearly that Mrs. Waddell took brisk steps to have one hundred thousand dollars or more of the family fortune transferred to her personal account). Thereafter, the secret was held in Russell, Majors & Waddell's "front office" until Russell, back in Washington, gave the signal.

It was so well kept, as the Settles' punctilious details bear out, that not even the Leavenworth & Pike's Peak division managers knew about it before January. Ben Ficklin, the gruff, trail-wise superintendent for L. & P. P., rode across the frozen plains in late January to let contracts for home and

63

swing stations, then battled on to Salt Lake to buy two hundred of the best, wiriest ponies, hire Howard Egan and start construction of adobe stations across the Nevada deserts. In midwinter, too, Egan or other Mormons must have slipped across the Sierras to set off the chain reaction that developed the Alta Telegraph Building in Sacramento as western terminal for the Pony Express and hired the competent W. W. Finney as Pacific Slope manager.

The route, as laid out, swung north by west across the Kansas plains from St. Joseph to Fort Kearny, followed the Oregon and Mormon trails through Julesburg to Fort Laramie, kept on along the North Platte past Red Bluffs and Independence Rock, crossed the Continental Divide at desolate South Pass and through the agony of mountaintop desert and gloomy gorge, dropped to that ancient sea bed still centered by its "last puddle"—Salt Lake.

Since 1830, wagon trains, handcarts, and Army columns had searched out the easiest grades, then lumbered on, leaving only rock scratches, campfire ashes, and headstones to mark their passing. Nature, curbed by the cruelest weather patterns on the continent, still reigned. Even the half-wild mountain men had shrugged and moved out when a clerk in London's Bond Street innocently ended the pelts market for the ponderous beaver hat by inventing the lighter, cheaper silk hat. (The clerk's employers promptly fired him. Then the London police arrested him for wearing the "topper" on the street and so "disturbing the peace.")

But now, for the first time, fortress homes were to be built all along the Central Route; messengers were to pound across the nineteen hundred miles each week of the year with a precision that still wins commendation from jet pilots. A decade later, the world would gasp at the "miracle" of the transcontinental railroad built along the same trail in a matter of six years. Yet Alexander Majors, Ben Ficklin, Howard Egan, Bolivar Roberts, and W. W. Finney achieved the same "miracle" during sixty frantic days and nights in February and March, 1860.

Their construction program, while obvious, pioneered techniques that would be copied by the transcontinental telegraph in 1861–62, and by the Central and Union Pacific railroads after the Civil War. Finney, Egan, Ficklin, the deadly J. A. "Jack" Slade and Alexander Majors himself divided the route into sections, rounded up construction crews and riflemen, co-ordinated their operations with the routings of Russell, Majors & Waddell wagon trains, then "set to."

Majors personally supervised the improvement of L. & P. P. way stations and the construction of new swing and home stations across Kansas to the Denver-Oregon Trail junction at Julesburg.

Ficklin stalked with cougar persistence back and forth across the Continental Divide, urging along the lean-tos, dugouts and sod huts that would serve as stations through Wyoming and eastern Utah.

Howard Egan pushed wagon trains out into the "Paiute Hell" west of Salt Lake to build huts and corrals on the mail route he had pioneered with Major Chorpenning in 1854–55.

William Finney, with lavish help from Ben Holladay, bought 250 mules and ponies, hired twenty-one lean youngsters as riders and station agents, then organized them into a wagon train and set out through the Sierras, building stations and laying out supplies while they moved east.

Some of the stations—doubtlessly east of the Rockies—were lavishly outfitted with supplies. The Settles' research uncovered Denver records claiming that materials sent out to stations between Laramie and central Kansas included brooms, candles, buckets, rope, window glass, doors, tinware, putty, stovepipes, hardware, turpentine, castor oil, horse liniments, and medicines. The food supplies included macaroni, dried fruits, hams, bacon, pickled tripe, coffee, tea, spices, corned beef, sugar, sorghum, and corn meal. (The lists were included in legal briefs of lawsuits filed against Russell, Majors & Waddell during and after the war. Thus the question remains as to whether the Pony Express riders, or the stationmasters, ever really lavished in these creature comforts.)

Quick as crocuses sprouting on a sunny south slope, the job was done. Some of the swing stations, where the Express riders changed horses, weren't much larger than a modern station wagon. The relay stations where riders lived between runs, were large enough to hold fifteen to twenty men and a *remuda* of horses during Indian attacks. Slimy mountain dugout, cedar-ribbed mesa cabin, gaunt adobe monolith on the Nevada desert—within sixty days the Central Route was open, and manned, from the Missouri to the Pacific.

Would it stay open? Could the youngsters who came clamoring for death-risked-daily-at-twenty-five-dollars-per-week be able to run the thread of national destiny between these crude shelters, tie East and West into a coherent, co-operative Union and, in the doing, "fate" an 1865 Appomattox?

In they strolled—at San Francisco and Sacramento—at Salt Lake and Nebraska City and St. Joseph. Haslam—Harrington—Ranahan. Westcott—King—Kelley—Keetley. Avis—Fred—Brink—Beatley. Mormons and Baptists—Catholics and Quakers—Irish and German youngsters who had clumped down New York gangplanks from the Old World only months before—desert kids who had never seen a steamboat or a steam engine, and never would.

Many of them would have been tagged "juvenile delinquents" in 1960. A few would become statesmen and world-famous figures. All were destined to become immortals—even though their names have been lost forever. One by one, they took the Alex Majors oath and received a leather-bound Bible, a gun, a Bowie knife, a scarlet flannel shirt and a pair of denim Levi's.

That was it. The gate was opening on the Central Route. On April 3, 1860, the Pony Express was ready to run.

6.
MOCHILA'S GLORY

Clem Huniker knew that his eyes were bulging a bit. Starched collars always did that. For this day of days, Mrs. Huniker had dipped his shirt collar, cuffs and bib, too, in the slimy stuff. Every time he breathed, he crackled like a prairie fire. His neck and chest would be sore for a week. But worth it! April 3, 1860 A.D. They'd be printing that one in red on future calendars. It was going to work, by glory! It was-s-s-s going to-o-o wor-r-rk. He could feel that a lot deeper than the collar.

The telegraph ended its chatter. He whirled so rapidly that he almost slid off the stool. "Hear that," he shrilled. "Sixty-five miles an hour between Palmyra and Shelbina! Ol' Addison ain't rollin'. He's flyin' between the rail joints."

"A wife and six lovely children. And him out getting himself killed for the sake of a few letters." Mrs. Huniker patted a crease out of her skirt and sniffed. "I'll give Addison Clark a piece of my mind for dinner—if he's alive."

Clem started to grin, thought better of it and gulped. You couldn't have kept Mama away from the station today with anything less than a troop of Leavenworth cavalry, sabers at the charge. Sunday-go-to-meetin' petticoat; the black silk dress with the bustle. Even those hand-painted china beads that Uncle Zeke brought from Hankow, and th' silly lace poke bonnet he'd ordered from Chicago last Christmas. By glory, she hadn't looked prettier at her son's wedding. Talk sharp to his best friend for breakin' the H. &. St. J. speed record, would she? Hah. More likely, she'd throw the ironstone soup tureen at him if he didn't make up th' time those durn Chicago an' Detroit connections had lost.

"Yes'm," he said aloud. "Don't you worry about Add." He walked across the office, put an arm across her shoulders, and squeezed that ticklish place on her right side until she giggled. "Hoist up now," he laughed. "Mister Majors and all of them are out there on the platform talkin'. Here's your chance to meet 'em."

He turned his back politely. Mrs. Huniker stood up, grasped the bulges at each side of her hips and, with the dexterity of a Kiowa dancer, began to wriggle the whalebone stays back down into walking position. Suddenly, the opportunity proved too tempting. Clem plunged a thumb and forefinger inside the starched collar, pulled hard and held it free through two wonderful full breaths. Then the silk dress stopped rustling. Mama coughed. Clem eased the collar back into the welt across his gullet and slipped into his frock coat. "Now, mind," he said, while he tugged the lapels straight. "Don't breathe one word about that two-hundred-thousand-dollar bet of Mr. Russell's. All I know is the chatter come over the line from Hannibal."

"Baptist deacon, indeed." Mrs. Huniker sniffed.

"Baptist deacon in Missouri's one thing," he said as he took her arm. "Playin' Mr. Big in Washington is something else again. After all, some senator or New York banker wagers two hundred thousand dollars that Pony Express won't make it from Sacramento to St. Joseph in ten days. Then somebody's got to stand up for our side. One of those fellows out there is from a New York newspaper, so mum's the word. There's two more come on special from Chicago and St. Louis. By jiminy, I hope Addison keeps that thing on the track. Gotta hurry, Mama. Lots to do."

The one-car special that Addison Clark and his locomotive, The Missouri, were jack-rabbiting across the hills from Hannibal wouldn't *boo—hoo* around that Patee House curve for at least another hour. But the platform was crowded already, with another crowd almost as big gaping around the Pike's Peak Stable doors. A whole steamboat load of folks had come upriver from Westport Landing and Leavenworth; another one had swept down from Nebraska City about noon, with a five-piece German band playing "Skip-a to My Lou" and "What Was Your Name in the States?" The side porches of the Patee House seemed solid blue and silver with uniforms of the officers who had ridden over from Fort Leavenworth. Even some Indian bucks were squatted, quiet as copper-tinted statues, along the station's south wall.

"One of them Kiowa," Clem confided as they threaded toward Alexander Majors' towering figure, "said this mornin' that there's real bad prairie fires all across Kansas. Been burnin' for a week, he said. Could hold the boys up for days, y'know."

"Baptist justice."

"Now, Mama. Ease your throttle." Clem tightened his grip on her elbow, and sighed.

Majors, Russell, and Jeff Thompson, with an attentive gallery of bankers, merchants, and bullwhackers, clustered around a young man drowning in a mustard-yellow tweed suit three sizes too large for his skinny shoulders. A pearl-gray top hat rested perilously on his bulging forehead. He punctuated his conversation with headshakes, twitches of his shaggy pink eyebrows, and right-arm gestures reminiscent of Hon. Stephen A. Douglas hollering toward crescendo on the Senate floor. "It's that reporter f'om N' York," Clem whispered, and arm-braked Mama to a "red-ball" stop.

Jeff Thompson got his licks in now, and matched the youngster flourish for flourish. "I repeat, Mr. Ferris!" Jeff really had his dander up. "The day must come when the mail services of the United States of America and the state of Missouri equal the efficiency and dispatch of the railroads and the telegraph. The shabby treatment accorded the correspondence of the citizenry of this country is a disgrace, sir, to all civilized mankind."

Ferris had a fold of newsprint paper in one hand and a pencil stub in the other. The pink eyebrows shot up again; the hat teetered. "You want to be quoted on that?" He leered.

"It's your pencil, son. You're going to write what you please anyway. And danged if I'd come all the way to New York—even to horsewhip you. I said it. And you can add this to it. The day's going to come when trains on this railroad will have names like Pacific Express and Overland Limited. Us, or our children, will submit an addressed missive for friends in San Francisco to the postmaster on the way to the depot. Our train will reach the Pacific five—perhaps even four —days later. Our friends will be at the station to meet us, because that letter, traveling without pause for refreshment, toiletries and the—uh—other travails of the human body, will have preceded us by a day or two."

Clem gulped a gasp of admiration in past the collar. But Ferris stuffed the paper and pencil back in his pocket and shook his head. "Hope you're right," he said, "but my editors would never pass it. It's too visionary. The postal service can never be that good."

"Sorry to hear you say that, young man." Russell edged around Thompson and poked a finger in Ferris' midriff. "Is your editor acquainted with Mr. Anthony Trollope of the British Postal Service?"

"Trollope! Of course. I interviewed him twice last year. He's worse than his dear mother. Those English mince over here, get a speck of mud on their gaiters in Washington, have dinner with Horace Greeley, attend two tea parties and a concert in Boston, then go home and write books about the 'abominable Americans.' Hogwash. They know what they're going to say before they leave Liverpool. It's all a trick to earn easy money with a bad travel book."

"Literature is your field, Mr. Ferris." Russell's voice was as rustly silky as Mama's petticoat. "Transportation is our specialty. I had the pleasure of two evenings in Mr. Trollope's company at Washington last year. I found him most stimulating. He expressed honest horror in the discovery that the Washington post office has only one window where residents may inquire for letters and—yes—their home-town newspapers."

"All of 'em two or three months old and practically ripped to pieces." Ferris nodded violently. "You don't have to be a British fop to realize that."

"Precisely." Russell purred. "That is what fascinated me when Mr. Trollope described the advantages of the government postal system in Great Britain. Containers for the deposit of mail on street corners. Regular delivery of correspondence to homes and businesses. Train schedules are so organized, as I understood him, that a train for Scotland, let us say, will not depart until the mail pouches for Scotland have been transferred from the Dover coach and Southampton train. Finally, it seems, they have outfitted some kind of railway carriage that enables letters to be sorted en route."

"Yup." Ferris frowned, reached into his pocket, then shook his head. "No. We're a Tammany paper. There'd be forty thousand Irishmen with shillelaghs storming the office if we ever ran a piece praising anything English. Anyway, Congress will never give the Postmaster General that much of a budget."

Majors cleared his throat, glanced thoughtfully at Russell and Thompson. "Somehow," he said, "Congress has managed to scrape up funds to subsidize the longest, slowest land route to California—and for six years, too."

"Well—eh—that is—" Ferris glanced at Jeff Thompson, then stared away across the river. "Yes. Yes. Of course. We're a Democratic paper, you see. We—uh—supported President Buchanan. It's—well—it's too touchy. Say, what's the latest news on our gallant locomotive race?"

Majors' beard quivered in silent laughter. He glanced toward the station and saw Clem. "Why, Mr. Huniker, sir." He strode through the crowd, clapped Clem on the shoulder.

"Good to see you, too, Mr. Majors." Clem grasped the big hand and pumped it. "Addison Clark's been bustin' speed records all across Missouri. But, first away, Mrs. Huniker, I'm honored to introduce Mr. Majors to you. This splendid creature, Mr. Majors, is mother of four of the finest youngsters in St. Joseph. Would you believe it?"

"Impossible! Impossible!" Majors boomed, then swept off his rakish black drover's hat and bowed so low his beard brushed his ankles. "Ma'am, I am honored."

Mrs. Huniker wriggled, blushed, and curtsied wordlessly. She held out her hand. Then her eyes widened. Her lips opened in a piercing scream. She hurtled for the safety of Clem's breast.

"You know, your good husband—" Majors was saying. A shadow whirled across the platform in the instant of Mrs. Huniker's scream. Something hit the platform beside him with a crash. A wet, coal-black muzzle eased along his shoulder—and whinnied.

Clem began patting Mama's cheek, alternately cooing, "There, there, now, Maw," and growling, "Blamed fool kid."

Majors turned, eyed Billy Cody and the mustang slowly up and down and up again, then patted the pony's nose. "Well-l-l-l?" he finally asked.

Billy's grin faded. His eyes studied the saddle, the mustang's mane, the station roof, the Kansas sky, then slowly sidled back to meet the giant wagonmaster's. "G-g-g-gosh," he stuttered, "I didn't mean nothin'. Honest."

Russell stormed in past the mustang's hurricane deck, glowered up at Billy's spang-new Levi's and red flannel shirt, then stood there, waving his hands—so mad that no words would come out.

Majors didn't even look at him. His eyes held Billy's. He patted the pony's neck with slow, soft deliberation. Billy's backsides began to twitch. His pop used to act the selfsame way before he said, "Best fetch me a shingle butt about three inches wide, young feller. Git it back here on the double. 'N' then unfurl your britches."

"You aren't a show-off fool, boy," he heard Majors saying. "What's afoot?"

"Alexander-r-r." Russell finally found voice. "I've warned you a dozen times about that hellion. Now—"

Majors waggled a hand. "In a moment, William. Be right with you." His eyes held steady on Billy's.

Billy broke. He had to grit his teeth to talk without blubbering. "Yes, sir." He stared straight back. "I got it comin'. Goldurn it, sir. I was jus' tryin' to show you I'm good enough. Bill Richardson wants you should come down to the stables right away. They keep snitchin' hairs out of his cayuse's tail and mane—for makin' souvenirs. Bill can't stop 'em. There's even a captain and a lieutenant colonel down there doin' it. Bill says that cayuse ain't fit to ride today. He wants you."

"Alexander, I'm—"

Majors' right hand waggled again. "What do you think you're good enough for, Billy?"

The question wasn't necessary. The answer was brighter than the Kansas bank of the river. Somehow the youngster had got hold of a Pony Express uniform. It fit perfectly. And his eyes were as forlorn as a lovesick beagle's. But, the boy did it. He'd have to tell it—out loud.

Billy's eyes darted away from Majors' again. Some lady was staring up at him, grinning. Willikers, if it wasn't the one that screamed and fell into Mr. Huniker's arms. She was still leanin' heavy. But her eyes weren't mad. They were blue and twinkly, like Mom's, an' matched her gray hair. Looked kinda as if she was gonna smile.

Billy's head straightened. "Mr. Majors, sir. Mr. Ficklin and all the others say I'm too young to be an Express. Gotta be sixteen, they say, and shorter'n what I am. I been practicin' this pony for a month, teachin' him to run and jump. When —when Bill sent me up here for you, seemed like it was my only chancet to show we're good enough for the run. We been jumpin' these tracks every night fer two weeks. Nellie 'n' me, sir, can clear 'em at a dead run and never put a hoof beyond that third board. See. Right down there. Them's my chalk marks. I—I guess I got real crazy, sir. I'm sorry. I—I'll be waitin' down at the stables for—for anythin' you say."

Billy turned his head and blinked. His right heel thumped Nellie lightly atop her third rib. The mustang whirled, sprinted a few yards down the platform's edge, sprang like a frightened jack rabbit catercorner over the H. & St. J. track, and settled into a canter down the road. Billy sat ramrod straight, eyes riveted broodily on the emerald sweep of transriver prairie and the bluffs that seemed to lift like beckoning hands toward the blue horizon.

"By God, Alexander— Madam, I humbly beg your pardon—" Russell flushed, flourished his top hat at Mrs. Huniker, bowed and put the hat on backwards. "Alexander, that—that—b— You've got to get rid of that young hoodlum. He'll kill somebody. And—and we'll have to pay for it."

Majors stared after the red-and-blue figure. Would those brave colors really ride down San Francisco's Market Street —with cheers and band music? Would the Pony surge like a small comet in steady orbit across the West's eternity of snow and precipice and searing desert? Only reckless youngsters like Billy could do it. Had they hired the right ones? "Yes, William," he decided. "Billy's going—west."

"Go anywhere. Makes no difference. West? How d'you know he's going west? Eh? My G—mhhhh. Alexander, you aren't going to give that fool a run, are you? Eh?"

Majors stared down at him.

"Well, Alex. Your business, of course. You—you run the Pony, eh. That's our agreement. Just—keep him off this platform. Important guests." He beamed, bowed, and hurried back toward the New York reporter.

Majors turned to Mrs. Huniker. "Ma'am, I'm terribly sorry about that boy. I trust you sustained no injury?"

Mama squeezed Clem's arm ever so slightly. "Both our boys are married and moved away," she said, and sighed. "Is that the Billy Cody Clem told me about?"

"The same." Majors nodded. "He's really an earnest worker and truthful."

"And very handsome." Mama sighed again.

"I'll be honored, ma'am, if you and Clem could join me for dinner at the Patee House after the ceremonies this evening." Majors' eyes met Mama's; they both smiled. "You see, Clem prevented me and Billy from engaging in some perilous daydreaming right along in here two months ago. Now the boy's frightened you. It seems fated, ma'am, that we become better acquainted."

"I've been thinking that way, too." Mama's face dimpled. She gave the little giggle that always made Clem want to get down on a rug and roll and bark. "Mr. Clark will be with us for dinner and overnight—if he doesn't break his foolish old neck getting here. I—I think Billy might like to hear him tell about the trip. Could you and Billy come to our house to dinner?"

Clem gawped—first at Mama, then at Majors. Both of them had their hands in the air, laughing their heads off like they had a secret joke. Far away he heard the sudden chatter of the telegraph against the tin can. "You—you two talk a bit," he muttered. "There's another report comin' in." He strode off. Damn—durn if he ever would understand women.

"Cam to Joe—Cam to Joe—Cam to Joe." The staccato was jubilant. Through Cameron and still on the track? Zowie! Must be a world's speed record. Clem flipped the switch, tapped his call, listened. "S-o-m-e-t-h-i-n-g—y-e-l-l-o-w—f-l-y-i-n-g—l-o-w—j-u-s-t—s-h-o-t—t-h-r-o-u-g-h—t-o-w-n—I-f—i-t—w-a-s—o-l-d—m-a-n—C-l-a-r-k—h-e—d-u-s-t-e-d—C-a-m-e-r-o-n—a-t—4-4-9." Clem acknowledged, flexed his wrist to give a rundown on the station crowd. The Hamilton operator butted in. "W-o-o-d-u-p—h-e-r-e—t-o-o-k—1-5—s-e-c-o-n-d-s—w-i-t-h—a-l-l—h-a-n-d-s—h-e-a-v-i-n-g—A-d-d—s-a-y-s—e-n-o-u-g-h—d-e-a-d—p-i-g-s—n—c-o-w-s—b-e-t-w-e-e-n—h-e-r-e—a-n-d—H-a-n-n-i-b-a-l—t-o—b-a-r-b-e-c-u-e—a-l-l—M-i-s-s-o-u-r-i—H-a-w."

Clem snorted, gave the boys a run-down on the crowd scene, then settled back in his chair. Things were coming clearer now. They usually did if you kept the wax out of your ears. He'd figured that probably little Russell was paying a whopping big fee for a special train to race those Pony letters clear across Missouri. But it wasn't that way at all. What was it Quincy had relayed? The fellow had told him there were only forty-six letters in the pouch. Five by six is thirty; carry three. Just $260 for Russell, Majors & Waddell out of that first run of the Pony Express. Eighty riders at twenty-five dollars a week; twenty, add two zeros; two thousand dollars a week right there. Majors said no rider must carry more than twenty pounds of mail. Well, suppose he did; right up to the last half-ounce. That would be 640 letters. Multiply it by five dollars. The best any Pony Express trip could ever hope to earn would be $3,200. It wouldn't even buy the boys' beans and bacon.

So that's what Jeff Thompson and Colonel Haywood were up to! Out fishing for a government mail contract right along with Russell, Majors & Waddell. Strange, the way changes get to happen. Nobody ever really thought much about government mail. It wandered in by steamboat now and then. Once in a while, you'd drop by the United States Post Office on the off chance you might have something. If there was a letter, it was nice to know how things were with the writer two—or three—or maybe six weeks back. You hoped he was still alive.

Letters that really mattered came privately, via an express company like Wells Fargo or a stagecoach driver or maybe a sales drummer who made a sideline of delivering letters and small bundles, at two bits apiece, when he went from town to town.

Vanderbilt's steamship lines, they said, had the California mail and parcel business so well organized that it took six or seven years to get the money for Butterfield through Congress—even with all those lobbyists he had working for him, and the Ox-bow Trail to boot.

It was really smart of Jeff Thompson to give Russell a free train to whisk his Pony letters across Missouri. Then Ferris and all the others would get to write about it. Pretty soon, United States Mail would be coming by railroad. Then it would be worth your time to stop by the post office almost every day.

There would have to be more than one window in Washington, too. Even that's one more than Buchanan must have in the White House. He didn't see a thing, they said.

Majors and Mama promenaded down the platform, going on like they were old sweethearts. There'd be no living with her for a month. He sighed, pulled the collar away from his gullet for two more free breaths, then was frocked and waiting at the door when they sauntered up.

"Addison went through Cameron fifteen minutes ago," he said. "If he don't decide t' jump th' track an' rent that outfit for contract plowin', he's bound to be here just after six o'clock."

"Wonderful. I'll get right down to the stables." Majors pulled out his watch. "Suppose we can get Bill started by six thirty?"

"I'll tell th' mayor. He could start his speech before Add pulls in. Sixty miles an hour all across the state of Missouri! It's never been done before by mortal man. We're breakin' records just so the Pony Express can break some more. No sense for Jeff to ruin it all with a big speech."

Majors saluted them and strode off. Mama beamed after him, then rustled into Clem's cubicle to readjust her stays. Clem hurried up the platform and had said, "Be in about six o'clock" at least twenty times before he reached Russell and Thompson.

It was five forty-four before Thompson finished studying his notes, held up his hands for silence and began talking. He said pretty much what he'd said to Ferris earlier; just didn't lay it on quite so thick about the United States Post Office. (After all, you award contracts to people who say nice things about you—even when you're a government!)

He was going full tilt—and so well that even the Army lieutenants stopped promenading past the family carriages—when the long, shrill wail of an angry baby, magnified one hundred times, echoed down the hills. The women gasped, then began to laugh and squeal. The men, neat as a chorus line, shucked their watches out of vest pockets, stared at them, and held them there. Jeff left his speech in midsentence, raised his arms, and led in three cheers and a tiger.

Smoke boiled up across a hillside in a narrow, straight cloud. A flash of gleaming yellow, a distant clatter; the long, eerie *booooo—hooooo* echoed again. The Missouri came around the Patee House curve so fast that it seemed her funnel was acting as a pivot to whip-snap the coach across lots to the station. The whole train rocked and creaked like a runaway perambulator when Addison and the brakemen finally did skid her to a stop.

The back door of the coach creaked open. Colonel Haywood, the H. & St. J. superintendent, and George Davis, the roadmaster, clumped out with the Pony Express messenger between them. Their clothes were crumpled and torn, their faces black with wood smoke and soot. The messenger's left eye had swollen shut from a bash against a seat arm, "about a hundred dead cows back." Colonel Haywood bellowed to Clem for a towel for his face and hands, then grunted to the mayor, "It's a question which is broken the most—us or the record."

Jeff resumed his speech, with interlardings of praise for "the Missouri and her gallant crew," then signed off after another ten minutes. Russell made a speech, too, and would have said a lot more if Alex Majors hadn't stood with watch in hand, staring. He hadn't even finished the part about "immortal glory" when Majors took a valise from the messenger, handed it to Russell, and signaled Bill Richardson to ride in closer.

Russell took the tiny packets of letters from the valise, slid them into the *mochila* boxes, locked the boxes, and handed the key to Majors. Jeff Thompson moved up alongside Bill, spoke briefly about glory, greatness and destiny, then slapped the pony on the rump. Bill lifted his hat, bowed, and galloped down the narrow lane of cheering people. Five minutes later, the steamboat *Denver* hooted three times as she pulled away from the pier. The cheers echoed back. Majors, Russell, Thompson, Haywood, and Davis clustered at the end of the platform.

The *Denver* appeared in midstream, sparks gushing from her stack as she nosed straight across the current. Bill didn't wait for the tie-up on the Kansas shore. With a deck-long run, the pony cleared the last three feet of water, hit the bank in a spurt of dust, and sprinted away toward the bluffs. The red shirt dimmed to leaf size, to a weaving "devil's paintbrush," to a sunset speck—and vanished.

Russell pulled out his watch to break the brooding silence. "Well, that's that. I hope Finney's on schedule in San Francisco. I told him to hire a band and three fire companies."

George Davis stared down at him, sniffed, then limped away. He pulled out the bandanna to wipe his face again. Judging by the way his eyes smarted, there was enough charcoal stuck under the lids to filter a barrel of moonshine. Patches of black and white hair dangled from the Missouri's cowcatcher. He shuddered. Clark still sat in the window beside his throttle, jaws working with the rhythm of his locomotive's pistons. Since Mrs. Huniker had rustled home to start dinner, Clem had climbed up beside him. They stared out across the prairie, where Bill's shirt still flashed for an instant, like a distant cardinal's wing.

The roadmaster spraddled his legs, clamped his fists against his aching hips, and glowered at them. Add's chomp seemed to slow a bit. He and Clem stared dreamily away toward Kansas.

"My hero," Davis purred.

Add's jaws stopped. He nudged Clem. "You hear somethin'?"

"Didn't hear a thing." Clem's eyes widened. "Too early in the year for a cyclone."

Davis' fists jammed deeper. His breath rasped. "You big Presbyterian ape," he snarled. "You deliberately tried to kill us."

Add stared down at him, *tchked* a brown jet against the edge of the platform at Davis' feet and turned back toward Clem. "Must be a minstrel show in town," he drawled. "There's one of the end men down there. Wot say, after dinner tonight, I treat you and Mama?" He stuck his head out of the window, and beamed. "Where's your troupe playin', bub? You got any tickets on you?"

"I can fire you. And blackball you on every railroad from here to Timbuktu."

Clem's head poked out beside Add's. "Y'know," he mused, "I bet the ol' skinflint would, too."

Davis sneered back at them. "An' the night before I do, you know what I'll do? I'll hog-tie you into one of them damn seats back there—alone. Then I'll open the Missouri's throttle wide, jump off and walk over to th' sheriff's office to file charges against you for stealing a train."

Add's head sank against his chest. He belched. "I'll sure as hell hate to go. It's so nice up here—and clean. Gawd, suppose it happened. I'd have to go off somewhere, hire out as a roadmaster, an' come crawlin' home nights covered with soot and . . ." He pointed down at Davis, shook his head, and howled. Clem howled with him. They beat one another on the back and collapsed against the cab window.

Davis gloomed up at them like a frustrated Satan, foot tapping. "Try to run a decent railroad," he announced to the world. "What they do? Hire a lot of imbeciles an' tell you to go an' make glory with 'em. When you girls have put your dolls to bed, I'll buy you a drink."

Clem poked Add in the chest. His eyes were saucer big. "Add, 'ja hear that? Sounded like our beloved roadmaster— Why, hello there, Mr. Davis. Good to see you, sir. Just got in town, didja? You're lookin' fine. Be right down, Mr. Davis, sir."

"Come to think about it"—Davis leered—"I withdraw the offer. That hairy fool'll probably get a raise out of this. You're buyin', Mr. Clark! Hurry up. I'm thirsty." He stalked off toward the Patee House.

Mama took one look at Add and Clem rollicking up the walk a half-hour later, then met them at the kitchen door with wintergreen-oil gargles and ordered each to chew two cloves for a full five minutes before they washed up.

Majors and Billy Cody strode in at about seven. Billy had his hat on the side of his head again, and couldn't wait to get it off before burbling the news. He'd go back west with Mr. Ficklin next week to try out for a run on the Julesburg division—up the Platte toward Wyoming. Addison took to the youngster as quickly as Mama had. He was all for going over to the stables after dinner, to get a pony and try team-jumping across the track with Billy. Mama got so mad she stamped her foot.

Next morning was like one of those breathless days in August when everybody stares out across Kansas to look for whirling, greasy green cloud funnels. Your head just jerked over there. Then you realized nothing could possibly happen for another week and a half. Or maybe never.

Bill Richardson rode in that afternoon. Those prairie fires were bad. But he had met his relay on schedule. He rubbed down his horse, hung the red shirt and blue jeans on a hook, and went back to work.

Leavenworth tapped a brief report on the third day that an inbound L. & P. P. stage had passed the Pony going full tilt one hundred miles out of Julesburg. There were some telegrams of congratulations and such for Russell, Majors & Waddell including a long-winded, mush-mouthed thing from the White House. Clem was just putting it in an envelope to take down to the Patee House when Hannibal clamored again. That one was for Russell, too—and from Washington. It said: "Waterbury, New York, threatening. Three hundred thousand urgent. Smoot."

Clem shook his head. Real pleasant at times to be a plain telegraph operator. They set up a Pony Express that can't possibly earn its keep. Right away, somebody yells for three hundred thousand dollars. You could probably get to feel downright sorry for that little Russell fellow.

Ben Ficklin crackled up the Patee's steps on the tenth of April. The westbound Pony had got to Laramie three hours late; no incident otherwise. The editor of the *St. Joseph Times* had heard about it, sent a reporter over, then telegraphed a fifty-word jumble on to New York. Back that afternoon came another jumble. So next day the *Times* rolled with a front-page story about Russell's two-hundred-thousand-dollar bet with a New York banker. Ferris must have confirmed it, on some sort of a share-coverage agreement with the *Times*. Clem didn't even pursue the subject when Mama led up to it during dinner that night. Too confusing. A yell for three hundred thousand dollars from Washington; a casual bet for two hundred thousand dollars in New York—and a Pony Express that couldn't possibly ever earn so much as its feed bills. Just too confusing to talk about.

Anyway, the Patee House was full again the night of April 12. There were people up in the tower all evening with field glasses, staring out toward the Kansas bluffs. They were back up there at dawn on the thirteenth. The ten days of the alleged bet would be up at noon, the story said. People began to walk down to the riverbank, some of them with lunch boxes and fish poles. Clem saw no sense in it. There'd be shouting and a helluva *boom* from that toy cannon on the Patee House lawn if and when the eastbound did show. If it didn't—well, he didn't like funerals.

It was after eleven when the door squeaked and Russell's raspy little voice said, "G'day, Mr. Huniker. Like to get this off right away, if you please." He shoved a piece of paper under the wicket. There were beads of sweat under his nose.

His eyes kept rolling this side and that, but never at Clem. "It can go at once, Mr. Huniker?"

"Yes, sir." Clem nodded. "Line's clear. I'll bat 'er right out. Washington, eh. Lessee. That'll be two dollars and fifty-five cents."

Russell's eyes rolled again. He licked his lips and shoved two ten-dollar bills through to Clem. "We—uh—won't mention this, Mr. Huniker, will we? Eh? And—uh—you'll keep the change? Eh?"

"I'm the most forgetful man in Missouri, Mr. Russell." He almost bit his tongue on that one. "So—I don't need no tips or bribes. Thank you."

"Oh. No offense. Really. No offense." The eyes rolled again. "You'll get it off immediately, won't you?" Russell turned and darted out the station door.

Clem read the telegram. It was to John Buchanan Floyd, United States secretary of war. "Imperative New Mexico contract be activated. Financial situation desperate. Beg privilege conference your earliest convenience week of April 20. Bill Russell."

He tapped out the message, signed off, put on his coat, then finally looked back at the wicket. The two bills were still there. He picked them up, dropped one in the cash drawer, stared at it a moment, then fished it back out. He counted two dollars and fifty-five cents from his own purse, clanked it in and put the tens in an envelope.

Bill Richardson, Ben Ficklin, Billy Cody and a dozen hangers-on stood in the Pike's Peak Stable door, staring away toward the river. Young Cody had the Levi's and red shirt on again; a canvas bag bulged beside him. Clem tapped him on the shoulder.

"Gee whillikers." Billy's eyes were saucer big. "Suppose Mr. Fry will make it? Won't—won't it be terrible?"

"He does or he don't." Clem grunted. "You goin' out with Mr. Ficklin today?"

"Yes, sir. We're leavin' in about an hour."

"You seen your ma this week?"

"Yes, sir. Rode over night before last."

"Gonna send her money regular?"

"You bet. I made a deal with Mr. Majors. He's taking it out of my pay and passin' it right over to her."

"You be a good boy, son. Mama's took a shine to you. She's murder when somebody lets her down."

"Yes, sir."

Clem thrust out the envelope. "Tuck this in your kit. You'll have to buy extra duds for them Rockies."

Billy peered at the bills. "My—my gosh, sir. That's almost a week's salary. You—you can't afford that."

Clem leered. "Oh, you know. Us railroaders—" He got that far. The cannon banged from the Patee lawn. Up from the bank the cheers began to roll. Bill Richardson snapped his watch shut and leaned against the door. "Glory," he groaned. "We done it—with five minutes to spare."

7.
AWAKE THE WINDS!
by Agnes Wright Spring

There never sets the sun on rolling plains,
Nor evening shadows soothe the desert heat,
But ghostly riders flit on ghostly mounts
And skim the twilit ways with silent feet—
The men who brought the eager-waited mails,
Forgotten men who ride forgotten trails.

They come again to gallop sleeping roads,
These wraiths that race along the windy way;
They mark again the starlight in the sand
Until they see the streaks of coming day—
Then vanish like the dust of desert gales,
Forgotten men who ride forgotten trails.

CHARLES JOSEF CAREY, "Pony Express Courier"

Historians of the Pony Express would find many factors which determined the success or failure of this noble experiment. They would examine the long miles of sand and granite, of peaks and plains, where there were no towns, no signs of human habitation. Here, it would seem, are blank pages. Blinded by the idealism of this great effort, they would become naïve about it and look for sentimental reasons. Russell, Majors & Waddell, however, were neither sentimental nor naïve. They had four million dollars invested in their freighting operations, and were willing to risk five hundred thousand dollars on the new mail route. They knew perfectly well the telegraph would follow them and the railroads would soon complete the east-west circuit.

Yet the historians are inclined to be very sad for these

hardheaded businessmen and weep about their losses. Why were Russell, Majors & Waddell willing to make that gamble? There was only one reason: they wanted the mail contract; they wanted and expected to be subsidized by the government for the risk they were taking. Russell, in Washington, was sure of it; he had been encouraged by Senator Gwin and others. They had every right and expectation. Once they had the mail rights, the ownership of the railroad would follow.

Why didn't they get these rights, this subsidization? Because a Southern politician, Secretary of War John B. Floyd, was against them. Not singlehandedly, for all the Southerners wanted the Southern Route. But Floyd encouraged Russell, helped to finance him, and finally ruined him, thus bringing down the whole R-M-W empire into ruins. The tragedy of the Pony Express can be laid finally and completely at the door of the Virginian, Floyd. It is in the record. Most historians of these fraught years alleged that Floyd did not plan it. Let us see.

The 1860 newspapers give hints of the drama. Scraps of the record are to be found in the *Sacramento Union*, which tells how W. W. Finney, the agent in charge, had detailed "his men and secured his stock along the route." He had 129 mules and horses of California stock adapted for riding and packing purposes. It was difficult to establish stations. The first explorers in 1827 tried three times to cross the Sierras. One party of two, with seven horses and a mule, struck across the desert. Twenty days later they staggered into an Indian camp at Great Lake, barely conscious, with one horse left.

It was across these deserts of alkali and sage that the Pony Express must forge, yet in spite of all obstacles the riders persisted. On April 3, the *Alta Californian* in San Francisco announced: "The mail to be carried Horse Express will be made up at the Alta Telegraph office at Sacramento. The stations are 300 miles from Sacramento toward Salt Lake. Another division, headed by Major Egan, extends from Salt Lake eastward to Saint Joseph. "The newspapers predicted the mail would take about thirteen days.

Bill Richardson, the ex-sailor, was far out on the starlit Kansas grass-sea when James Randall tossed a *mochila* over the back of a beautiful palomino pony on San Francisco's Montgomery Street. There were only 85 letters in this first eastbound run of Pony Express; a pitiful $425 in income for Russell, Majors & Waddell.

Like the brass band, both Randall and the palomino were showpieces. Horse and rider clattered only as far as the docks,

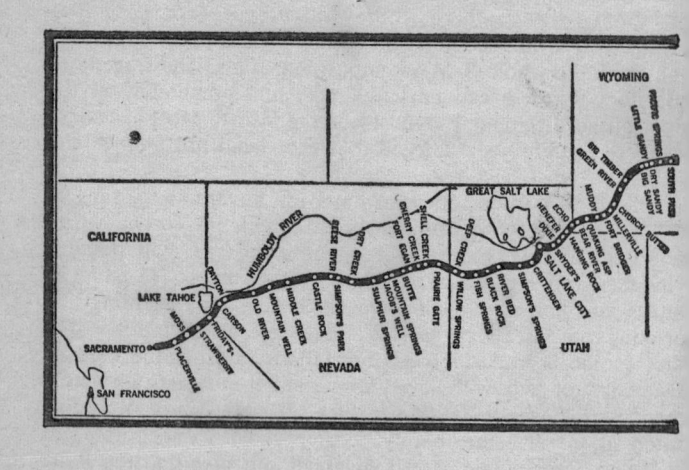

The route of the Pony Express.

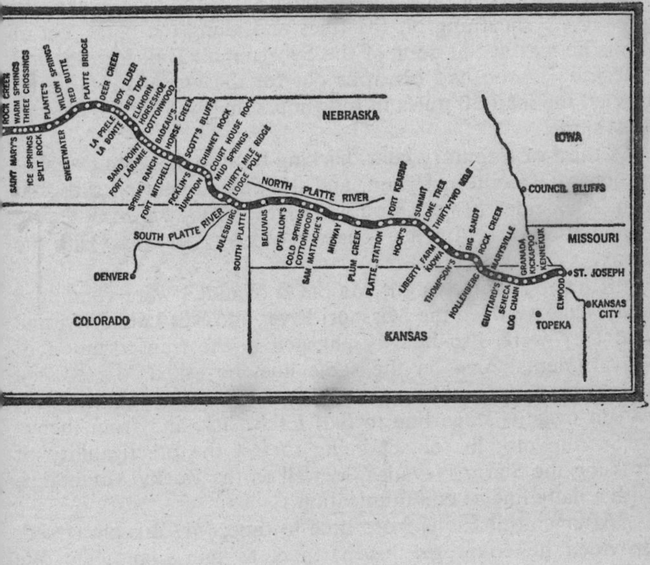

ROCK CREEK
WARM SPRINGS
THREE CROSSINGS
PLANTE'S
WILLOW SPRINGS
RED BUTTE
PLATTE BRIDGE
DEER CREEK
BOX ELDER
BED TICK
ELKHORN
HORSESHOE
COTTONWOOD
BADEAU'S
HORSE CREEK
SCOTT'S BLUFFS
CHIMNEY ROCK
COURT HOUSE ROCK
MUD SPRINGS
THIRTY MILE RIDGE
LODGE POLE
SAINT MARY'S
ICE SPRINGS
SPLIT ROCK
SWEETWATER
LA PRELE
LA BONTE
SAND POINT
FORT LARAMIE
SPRING RANCH
FORT MITCHELL
FICKLIN'S
JUNCTION
NEBRASKA
IOWA
COUNCIL BLUFFS
NORTH PLATTE RIVER
FORT KEARNY
SUMMIT
LONE TREE
THIRTY-TWO MILE
BIG SANDY
ROCK CREEK
MARYSVILLE
GRANADA
KICKAPOO
KENNEKUK
MISSOURI
ST. JOSEPH
ELWOOD
KANSAS CITY
TOPEKA
KANSAS
LOG CHAIN
SENECA
GUITTARD'S
HOLLENBERG
THOMPSON'S
KIOWA
LIBERTY FARM
HOCK'S
PLATTE STATION
PLUM CREEK
MIDWAY
SAM MATTACHE'S
COTTONWOOD
COLD SPRINGS
O'FALLON'S
BEAUVAIS
SOUTH PLATTE
JULESBURG
SOUTH PLATTE RIVER
DENVER
COLORADO

where the steamboat *Antelope* waited for the trip up the Bay to Sacramento. The real test began in the pitch-black small hours of April 4th when the *Antelope* chuffed into the Sacramento wharf. Finney, perhaps Bolivar Roberts, and Sam Hamilton were waiting. Mountain-bred Sam Hamilton was as restless as his white mustang. His friend Warren "Boston" Upson was waiting at the Sportsman's Hall relay station, 60 miles up in the Sierras. Fog and rain threatened. And fog and rain at sea level meant a slashing blizzard in the Sierra passes.

So a growl, silent prayers, and the hiss of spurs along the mustang's flank were the only send-off the first Pony run received in Sacramento. Hamilton ran eight re-mounts ragged in the race that night. The rain became sleet; the sleet slicked to ghostly ice sheathing on the trees and along the path. Yet at dawn he was at the door of the Sportsman's Hall lean-to, and "Boston" Upson had his arms out for the *mochila*. Hamilton carried the mail 60 miles in four hours, halfway up the Sierras' west slope.

A third of a century later, harking back to the grim determination of Hamilton, Upson, and the other riders on that first run, Alexander Majors would offer the following meandering explanation of California Senator Gwin's relationship with the Pony.

"Knowing that Russell, Majors & Waddell were running a daily stage between the Missouri River and Salt Lake City, and that they were also heavily engaged in the transportation of Government stores on the same line, he asked Mr. Russell if his company could not be induced to start a pony express, to run over its stage line to Salt Lake City, and from thence to Sacramento; his object being to test the practicability of crossing the Sierra Nevadas, as well as the Rocky Mountains, with a daily line of communication.

"After consultations from time to time, Mr. Russell agreed, provided he could get his partners to join him. . . . We both decided that it could not be made possible to pay expenses. He urged us to reconsider. As soon as we demonstrated the feasibility of such a scheme he [Senator Gwin] would use all his influence with Congress to get a subsidy to help pay the expenses of such a line . . . that the public mind had already accepted the idea that such a route open at all seasons was an impossibility; that as soon as we proved the contrary, he would come to our aid with a subsidy.

"After listening to all Mr. Russell had to say upon the subject, we concluded to sustain him. . . . Within sixty days . . . we were ready to start ponies. . . . To do the work the Pony Express required about one hundred and ninety stations, two hundred men for station-keepers, and eighty riders; riders made an average ride of thirty-three and one-third miles. In doing this each man rode three ponies on his part of the route; some of the riders, however, rode much greater distances in times of emergency.

"The Pony Express carried messages written on tissue paper, weighing one-half ounce, a charge of five dollars being made for each dispatch carried.

"As anticipated, the amount of business transacted over this line was not sufficient to pay one-tenth of the expenses, to say nothing about the amount of the capital invested. In this, however, we were not disappointed, for we knew, as stated at the outset, that it could not be made a paying institution, and was undertaken solely to prove that the route over which it ran could be made a permanent thoroughfare for travel at all seasons of the year, proving, as far as the paramount object was concerned, a complete success.

"Two important events transpired during the term of the Pony's existence; one was the carrying of President Buchanan's last message to Congress, in December, 1860, from the Missouri River to Sacramento, a distance of two thousand miles, in eight days and some hours. The other was the carrying of President Lincoln's inaugural address of March 4, 1861, over the same route in seven days and, I think, seventeen hours, being the quickest time, taking the distance into consideration, on record in this or any other country, as far as I know.

"One of the most remarkable feats ever accomplished was made by F. X. Aubery, who traveled the distance of eight hundred miles, between Santa Fe, New Mexico, and Independence, Missouri, in five days and thirteen hours. This ride, in my opinion, in one respect was the most remarkable one ever made by any man. The entire distance was ridden without stopping to rest, and having a change of horses only once in every one hundred or two hundred miles. He kept a lead horse by his side most of the time, so that when the one he was riding gave out entirely, he changed the saddle to the extra horse, left the horse he had been riding and went on again at full speed.

"At the time he made this ride, in much of the territory he passed through he was liable to meet hostile Indians, so that his adventure was daring in more ways than one. In the first place, the man who attempted to ride eight hundred miles in the time he did took his life in his hands. There is perhaps not one man in a million who could have lived to finish such a journey.

"Mr. Aubery was a Canadian Frenchman, of low stature, short limbs, built, to use a homely simile, like a jack-screw, and was in the very zenith of his manhood, full of pluck and daring.

"It was said he made this ride upon a bet of one thousand dollars that he could not cover this distance in eight days. . . .

"In the Spring of 1860 Bolivar Roberts, superintendent of the Western Division of the Pony Express, came to Carson City, Nevada, which was then in St. Mary's County, Utah, to engage riders and station men for a pony express route about to be established across the great plains by Russell, Majors & Waddell. In a few days fifty or sixty men were engaged, and started off across the Great American Desert to establish stations, etc.

"Among that number the writer can recall to memory the following: Bob Haslam ("Pony Bob"), Jay G. Kelley, Sam Gilson, Jim McNaughton, Jose Zowgaltz, Mike Kelley, Jimmy Buckton, and 'Irish Tom'."

The first Pony Express, say the records, left St. Joseph at 6:30 P.M. on April 3, 1860, and arrived in Salt Lake at 6:25 P.M. on April 9. That meant a seven-day mail delivery from Chicago and eight or nine days from Washington and New York City. The route, using the facilities of the Central Overland California & Pike's Peak Company, followed the ruts of the Oregon Trail and the forty-niners' wagons to Marysville, Kansas, then arrowed north by west up Nebraska valleys to Fort Kearny on the south shore of the Platte River.

Jim Beatley, "Doc" Brink, and Mel Baughn are the riders listed as the relays who carried that first *mochila* west from Bill Richardson's junction station at Seneca, Kansas. Meanwhile, eastward across the continent, Sam Hamilton and "Boston" Upson rode, walked, and slid, with the audacity of charmed lives, up the flooded gorge of the American River and on across snow-blocked Sierra passes with the eighty-five letters—$425 worth—that Californians were entrusting to this epochal gamble. Upson, twenty-year-old son of a prosperous California publisher, gritted through fifty-five miles of drifts in the Sierra passes, yet averaged almost seven miles an hour in delivering the *mochila* to "Pony Bob" Haslam at Friday's Station near Lake Tahoe.

Haslam raced eastward down the Sierra slopes into blinding Nevada desert in the very hours that Baughn was darting westward toward the grim, weedy mounds of abandoned furniture, bleached bones, and rusty tools that, since the forty-niners, had ringed Fort Kearny like the stinking litter of a battlefield. West from Kearny, the trail was idyllic wilderness beside the gurgling waters of the Platte into bloody Julesburg. Not much is on record concerning Pony Express activities along the route from Julesburg, in the northeastern corner of Colorado, through the southwestern tip of Nebraska, and west across what is now Wyoming. Lucius Beebe tells us that historian Hamilton Basso once remarked of Wyoming: "Nowhere on earth has mankind in passing left fewer traces of his going."

Maps of this section of the route, with names of home and relay stations, vary. There was no town on this route, nor was there a newspaper. There were two forts, Laramie and Bridger, and a conglomeration of dugouts, huts, stations and stores. Because of the strenuous nature of the work, the riders did not remain many months on the job. Some background has been obtained from firsthand observation of the country through which the ponies ran, from reminiscences of old-timers and from the book *The City of the Saints*, in which Sir Richard F. Burton, an English traveler who left St. Joseph by stage in August, 1860, detailed his observations along the route. Our basic list of Pony Express stations is taken from the government contract with the Butterfield Company, authorizing the Overland Mail Company to maintain the Central Route, beginning July 1, 1861.

Distances between the stations have been authenticated by L. C. Bishop, an experienced engineer from Wyoming. At first, Pony Express stations were about twenty-five miles apart, but as semiweekly service replaced the original weekly schedule, the distances were shortened by setting up new stations, whose locations were determined largely by the terrain. If the prairie was smooth and the road good, the Pony rider would cover more miles without a relay.

At the relay station, the rider turned over the *mochila* of mail to the next rider, and rested until time for his return trip. The swing stations often were of extremely crude construction, with few if any comforts, and sufficient only to shelter a stationkeeper and from two to four stock-tenders, who cared for the animals. Most of these original, primitive stations had dirt floors, and their windows, if there were any, and door openings were covered with hides. The stable, for convenience, was close to the station.

Julesburg, at the Upper Ford or California Crossing of the South Platte, was the first station in what is now Colorado. One of the larger and best-known stations, it comprised a station house, stable, outbuildings, and a blacksmith shop, made chiefly of cedar logs. Though it was later called Overland City, the first name, Julesburg, clung. It had been named for a French-Canadian Indian trader, Jules Reni, who originally had a ranch on the site. When the Pike's Peak stageline was first launched, Reni was hired as station agent by Superintendent B. D. Williams. It soon became common knowledge that "Old Jules" was involved in the theft of horses and other nefarious doings. Later, when Benjamin F. Ficklin became superintendent, he hired J. A. "Jack" Slade as division agent and told him to clean up the line from Julesburg to Horseshoe Station. He at once dismissed Jules Reni.

Much has been written connecting Slade with thieves and murderers. Some writers made unsubstantiated claims that he pillaged emigrants, stole horses and mules, and committed other crimes. Luke Voorhees, an old stageman who knew him and worked with men who knew him, said that Slade, when not drinking, was an excellent stage-line superintendent. He looked after a line that had to be conducted through Indian country. For a long time he negotiated business satisfactorily, with vigilance night and day. Mark Twain described him as a "matchless marksman with a Navy revolver."

Slade's most noted fight was with Jules Reni. The men often met and quarreled. In one of their disputes, Jules got the drop on Slade, and with a double-barreled shotgun put fifteen buckshot into Slade's body. Jules thought he had killed Slade, and coolly said to a bystander, "When he is dead, put him in one of these old dry-goods boxes and bury him."

Slade, according to Voorhees, was alive enough to hear Jules. He swore he would live long enough to wear one of Jules's ears on his watch chain. When the stage arrived, Slade ordered the men to seize Jules. They proceeded to hang him until he was black in the face, then, upon his promise to leave the country and never return, they lowered him. Slade was sent to St. Louis to have the buckshot removed, but some pieces could not be extracted, and he carried them as reminders of eternal vengeance. On his return to the stage line, Slade learned that Reni had not left the area. He sent word that he would kill Jules on sight, then sent four men to Badeau's Ranch on the Platte River, near Fort Laramie, where he heard Jules was stopping. Not finding him there, they went to Chausau's ranch, where they captured him, bound his hands and feet, and placed him in a corral. Slade rode in, went to the corral, shot Jules in the mouth, then sent a second shot through his brain.

Voorhees claimed that Slade cut off Jules's ears and put

them in his pocket. He carried them for a long time, showing them when he would get on one of his sprees. When the stage line was moved, in 1862, to the Southern Route across the Laramie Plains, in present northern Colorado, Slade built the Virginia Dale Station, which he named for his wife; it is still standing. Drinking and resulting brawls finally brought on his dismissal. He went with a wagon train of supplies to Montana, and, as the result of another spree, he was hanged.

Sir Richard Burton visited the Julesburg Station in the autumn of 1860, when a German-English keeper and his wife served "coffee boiled down to tannin, . . . meat subjected to half sod, half stew, and, lastly, bread raised with sour milk corrected with soda. . . ."

One of the riders who often dashed in or out of Julesburg on a foam-flecked mount was Theodore Rand, called "Little Yank" because of his small size. Most of the time his run was between Julesburg and Box Elder, a distance of 110 miles. Because of the favorable terrain, Rand often made the run in nine hours. His horses, purchased in Illinois or Iowa, were well built and good sized.

David R. Jay, who took the Express-rider oath when very young, usually rode out of Marysville, Kansas, but sometimes covered the trip from Fort Kearny to Julesburg.

Jim Moore, later a ranchman in the South Platte Valley and Wyoming, finished the westbound run from Midway to Julesburg one day in June, 1860, just as a rider pulled in with the eastbound mail. The boy who was supposed to relay east had been killed the day before. Stopping only to eat, Moore took the mail and raced back to Midway. He covered the round trip of 280 miles in fourteen hours and forty-six minutes. No regular-branch Pony Express system was established from Julesburg to Denver by the Central Overland California & Pike's Peak or Overland Mail Company. Occasionally, William N. Byers, editor of the *Rocky Mountain News*, in Denver, hired men on horseback to carry relayed Pony Express dispatches from Julesburg, but, according to Byers, that was a very expensive process. The usual procedure was to transport telegraphic messages by stagecoach to Denver from the end of the telegraph line. Many of these messages had been carried by Pony Express to the dispatching telegraph station. The *News* carried a regular telegraphic service, which was referred to as having come by Pony.

At Julesburg, the road forked. The stage-and-freight road to the Denver-Pike's Peak area followed the south bank of the Platte. The Pony Express rider, however, after obtaining a new mount, forded the river, which was wide, shallow, and full of treacherous quicksand, and headed north. The road wound over the divide between the North and South forks of the Platte, following the bank of Lodge Pole Creek, which headed in the Laramie Mountains, seventy-five miles to the northwest. The stations, in westward order, were: Nine Mile Station or Lodge Pole, Pole Creek Number 2 or Thirty Mile Ridge, Pole Creek Number 3 or Midway.

The last named was a dugout in the hillside, facing the creek. According to Burton, "the ceiling was a fine festoonwork of soot, and the floor was much like the ground outside, only not nearly so clean. In a corner stood the usual 'bunk,' a mass of mingled rags and buffalo robes; the center of the room was occupied by a rickety table, and boxes, turned up on their long sides, acted as chairs. The unescapable stove was there, filling the interior with the aroma of meat. As usual, the materials for ablution, a 'dipper' or cup, a dingy tin skillet of scanty size, a bit of coarse gritty soap, and a public towel . . . were deposited upon a rickety settle outside." Many of the small relay stations were of this character.

From Midway, at an altitude of about thirty-five hundred feet, the Pony rider crossed a divide and, following an abrupt descent, clattered down into the head of a broad arroyo, where he pulled up in front of a sod house, called Mud Springs Station. This "soddy" was roofed with juniper. Meals were served in an open shed, where birds hopped about picking up stray crumbs from the table. Sleeping quarters were a doorless dormitory at the side of the shed.

It was ninety miles from Mud Springs to Fort Laramie. Jack Keetley, of Marysville, Kansas, known as the Joyous Jockey, sometimes covered the run. Henry Avis, who earlier had accompanied Major Dripps to Fort Laramie with supplies, completed the ninety miles, then continued on to Horseshoe. He, too, carried Lincoln's inaugural address. At another time, when one of the riders refused to go on his run because of an Indian scare, Avis doubled back and is said to have won a three-hundred-dollar bonus from Russell, Majors & Waddell. He lived to the age of eighty-six years.

Bill Cates also carried Lincoln's message over the windswept, snow-covered hills for seventy-five miles on the Wyoming route. According to Cates, the closer he came to the mountains, the tougher it got. "We had the best horses," he said, "but several of them were killed on this run—and considering what we had to fight, the record was the most wonderful ever made by the Pony Express."

Beyond Mud Springs there were a number of well-known landmarks, familiar to emigrants for years, from which Pony Express stations took their names, including Court House Rock, Chimney Rock, and Scott's Bluffs. Between Court House Rock and Chimney Rock was Junction Station, and Ficklin's Station followed Chimney Rock.

This was an area of *mauvaises terres* or badlands, a tract about sixty miles wide and 150 miles long. Although the valley was green in season, the road along the river was rough and broken. Warm winds often raised sand and dust in clouds, sometimes almost blinding the riders.

Near Scott's Bluffs, rider Charles H. Cliff was once attacked by Indians. He received three balls in his body and many more in his clothing, but lived to be eighty years old.

Horse Creek Station was kept by a French Creole, son of an old soldier. From there the route ran twelve miles over sandy, heavy river bottom to Cold Springs or Spring Ranch, then on thirteen miles to Badeau's Ranch, called Laramie City and later known as Verdling's Ranch. Badeau sold liquor, Indian goods, and supplies; horses were changed there.

Now the road ran between high earth banks where Indian attacks had occurred, then over a short cut, away from a bend of the Platte, to a hilltop. From there Laramie Peak, highest mountain in the region, seemed very close though it was sixty miles away. To the right, the broad valley was dotted with thickets of red willow and cottonwoods, in many of which the white tips of Oglala Sioux lodges could be glimpsed.

Westward the road wound up steep hills, then switched abruptly down sandy draws toward the Fort Laramie crossing of Laramie's Fork, a stream of fine, clear water about 660 feet wide. The rider splashed through and pulled to a stop in front of the sutler's store which served as headquarters for mail delivery.

Fort Laramie, called Fort John and Fort William in the days of the American Fur Company in the 1830's, was now a cantonment with barracks, storehouses, officers' quarters, a guardhouse and stores skirting a parade ground. It had been purchased by the United States Government in 1849, upon the recommendation of John Charles Frémont.

Edward Bush and Louis Dean rode in this area. Dean's widow, in later years, recalled how he had dashed up to one of the stations one afternoon to find "scalped heads of three occupants of the little cabin stuck on poles around the smoldering embers of the station, corral and hay supply."

The ninety-one-mile stretch of country between Fort Laramie and Deer Creek was said to be one of the worst sections on the entire route, although, in season, it was a mass of color from the brilliant wild flowers that carpeted the hillsides.

Beyond the fort were two roads. One, the longer, led to the right, hugging the Platte River. The other, usually used, went up the Platte valley to Seth Ward's ranch, called Sand Point or Nine-Mile House, where Ward, for many years sutler at the fort, operated a small store. The rider dashed on twelve miles to the station at the crossing of Cottonwood Creek. Although the stream was often dry, it might, after a rain or flash flood, run ten feet deep. It was not to be taken without inspection on a night run.

About thirty-six miles west of Fort Laramie was Horseshoe Station, a trading post with substantial buildings, and residence of the agent, Jack Slade. One of the men hired by Slade as a Pony Express rider was Michael "Mike" Whalen, a large, genial Irishman from New York City.

On the back of the general waybill which reached St. Joseph by Pony Express on October 15, 1860, was the following message:

FORT LARAMIE, October 12, 12:20 A.M.

The rider from the Horse Shoe Station, together with others, report that the Sioux Indians have killed two white persons and one half-breed, and drove off considerable stock. It was supposed to be a war party of Sioux, returning from the Ute country.

Mr. Bromley, agent of the Express, adds all his ponies have been run off by the Indians on Bear River, which has delayed the Express twenty-four hours.

From Horseshoe, a cutoff led ten miles over undulating ridges, crooked and dented with dry creek beds and arroyos, to Elkhorn, a swing station. Onward fifteen miles was La Bonte, on La Bonte River, built in the autumn of 1860, with a strong corral suitable for a stockade against Indians. The stagemen lived in a brush wickiup.

From Bed Tick, ten miles beyond La Bonte, an extremely rough road wound through broken red hills for eight miles until it reached the valley of the Platte again, to cross La Prele (Lapierelle) or Rush River, a stream about sixteen feet wide, on whose bank was La Prele Station.

Next, after a run of ten miles, came Box Elder Station, a ranch with a competent stationmaster, who provided good food. Continuing, the Pony forded a creek and crossed rugged hills, cut by watercourses that often ran bank full after a rain. Up the smooth stretch of valley ahead raced the rider, to come, in ten miles, to Deer Creek, near the Upper Platte Indian Agency. There were a post office and blacksmith shop here, and a grog shop and store, run by M. Bissonette.

A waste of wild sage stretched ten miles from Deer Creek to Muddy Station or Bridger. Made of rock slabs placed one on the other without mortar, it had scant furnishings.

Fifteen miles beyond, at the upper crossing of the North Platte, was Platte Bridge Station, near the thousand-foot-span bridge built by Louis Guinard in 1859 at a cost of forty to sixty thousand dollars. Layovers here afforded plenty of opportunity to hunt grizzly bears, mountain goats, antelope, deer, rabbits, and sage hens in the pine-covered mountains nearby.

Across the river, on the north side, the land was rough, barren, and sandy for about ten miles to the next station, Red Butte, an old trading post. It was from this station that young Billy Cody, then only fifteen years old, made his famous nonstop ride of 322 miles. His regular run was to Three Crossings on the Sweetwater, about seventy-seven miles away. One day, when he reached Three Crossings, he found that the rider scheduled to relay west had been killed. Young Cody mounted a fresh horse and covered the next run, eighty-five miles farther west. Tossing the *mochila* to the waiting rider, he picked up the eastbound mail and galloped off on the return trip. When he pulled up at Red Butte Station, he had completed a ride of approximately 322 miles without rest. This nonstop record for endurance was unequaled by any other Pony Express rider. His average speed was fifteen miles an hour.

From the Butte, the route struck twelve miles over a high, rolling and barren prairie to Willow Springs Station, which provided a shed and a bunk for the keeper, but little else. Then, across a desolate waste, the route passed the Devil's Backbone, a jagged, broken landmark of huge sandstone boulders, and completed fourteen miles to Horse Creek Station.

Next came a sea of rabbit brush and sage over which sudden rain and hail often buffeted the rider in summer and blinding blizzards enveloped him in the winter. On the twelve-mile run through sand and alkali past Saleratus Lake, mirages often loomed. Beyond the lake was Sweetwater Station, near Independence Rock. This so-called "Register of the Desert," on which were inscribed thousands of travelers' names, rose domelike about one hundred feet in the air.

After crossing the swift, knee-deep Sweetwater River, the rider entered a valley luxuriant with flowering grasses, willows, cottonwoods, and white pine. About thirteen miles from Sweetwater Station, beyond Devil's Gate, a four-hundred-foot gorge through which the Sweetwater foamed, was a station kept by M. Plante, a Canadian.

Twelve miles on was Split Rock Station, then, out in open country, at the end of a fourteen-mile run, was Three Crossings Station. This was like a port in a storm. Travelers and riders, as well as stage-drivers, enjoyed stopping there because Mr. and Mrs. Moore served good, clean cooking, and kept the place "tidy." But mosquitoes in this valley were exceedingly annoying; and there were rattlesnakes.

The road then forded the river twice within fifty yards between rocky ridges, crossed a third ford, then wound through a waterless and grassless waste to Ice Springs, twelve miles farther, and Warm Springs, a similar distance.

Vast areas of greasewood and rabbit brush stretched almost as far as the eye could see, while the road gradually ascended the twelve miles to Saint Mary's Station, or Rocky Ridge, at an altitude of six thousand feet. Here the day might be hot and sultry, and the night frigid. Hailstorms of great intensity often struck in July and August. Sharp winds cut through a rider's clothing like a knife, unless he wore the skin clothing of the mountain men. The station was quite inadequate. Coyotes and wolves shadowed the livestock, and were a menace to any horseman who might have an accident on the trail. There was great danger of horses stepping into badger holes, and perhaps breaking a leg.

It was twelve miles from here to Rock Creek Station, then, westward, the rider pushed on across numerous small streams which flowed into the Sweetwater, including Strawberry Creek. Over steeper, rougher ground he traveled twelve miles, to Upper Sweetwater or South Pass, a level-topped bluff some twenty miles wide. The Pass, about 320 miles from Fort Laramie, lay atop the Continental Divide. Often without being aware of it, the rider had gained an altitude of 7,550 feet. In summer this was a sunshiny, grassy gateway; in winter it was called "that abominable country." An Ohio cavalryman who soldiered in the area in the 1860's wrote home that the tourists need not go to the Alps or Greenland to see snow. "Let them come to South Pass and patronize home industry," he said. "There are places here where the snow is ten feet deep for miles."

Thomas J. Ranahan, called "Irish Tommy," who later was one of the survivors of the Battle of Beecher Island with

Lieutenant Forsyth's men, used to drive stage over South Pass. Ranahan once told writer Arthur Chapman that "It was a hard run in winter, on account of the storms. Many a time 'Pony' riders would come in totally exhausted. In that case there was nothing to do but go on with the mail for him, and turn the ribbons over to someone else till I could pick up the stage at the next station."

The next station was Pacific Springs, twelve miles below the Pass. The crude station cabin commanded a view of the snow-capped Wind River Mountains. The prevailing west wind brought frequent showers. In warm weather it was necessary to build smudges in order to get relief from mosquitoes. Nights were always cold, even in August. At Pacific Springs, the Oregon, California, and Mormon trails united. Deeply worn ruts are still visible today, having survived a century of wind and weather.

A twelve-mile run over a gradually sloping red waste dotted with sage, greasewood, and thistles brought the rider to Dry Sandy Station, and fifteen miles more took him to Little Sandy. Between Dry Sandy and Little Sandy was Sublette's Cut-Off or Dry Drive, where the Oregon traffic turned northwestward to Fort Hall. The Pony Express route headed southwestward toward Fort Bridger.

Big Sandy Station, thirteen miles after Little Sandy, was on a clear, swift stream. The crossing was good, but in warm weather, riders and horses were pestered with green-headed horseflies that drew blood. Along a dusty, waterless, and grassless waste the road cut away from Big Sandy and traversed Simpson's Hollow. There, two large semicircles of black charred the ground, mute evidence of the burning of Russell, Majors & Waddell's wagon trains in 1857. Coyotes were often seen in this vicinity.

It was fifteen miles from Big Sandy to Big Timber, where horses were changed. Ten miles beyond was Green River, a home station for Pony Express riders, as well as for stagemen. It had the "indescribable scent of a Hindoo village," due no doubt to the burning of buffalo chips and the presence of sheep, horses, and cattle. There were willows, wild geraniums, asters, and quaking aspen. The store sold Valley Tan whisky. In low water, riders forded Green River diagonally. But when floods widened the stream to eight hundred feet, a ferry was used. In this area was the grave of a man named Farrel, said to have been one of Jack Slade's victims.

Four miles on up the valley was the store and grocery of Michael Martin. The road left the river and crossed badlands to Black's Fork, then went on to a station on Ham's

Fork, twenty miles from Green River. The shanty there was made of stones piled up against a dwarf cliff that acted as back wall. The door and windows were open holes, and parts of wagons had been fashioned into furniture. The proprietor was a Mormon who had married two Irish sisters. Indians frequented the place for a "bit" and a "sup."

An Express rider named Thomas Owen King once made the run eastward from Salt Lake City to Ham's Fork, 145 miles, in thirteen hours. He said that he often went to sleep in the saddle. One night, he discovered later, both he and a westbound rider were asleep in the saddle when they passed. The ponies kept running and stayed on the trail from habit.

Leaving Ham's Fork, the road forded Black's Fork three times, then veered across a long, pebbly flat past a curious, isolated mass of clay called Church Buttes. In this area riders found Mormons on the road with teams and handcarts.

At Millersville Station, twenty miles from Ham's Fork, a Mormon named Holmes and his English wife served good meals. Their home was built from wagon parts; ox-yoke bows were used as chair backs.

Up Black's Fork twelve miles was Fort Bridger, a cantonment with a post office, store, and other conveniences. Horses were changed here, but it was not a regular Pony Express station, since this was government property.

According to Arthur Chapman, Thomas Owen King, whose home station was Echo Canyon, sometimes rode to Fort Bridger. "On the first trip of the 'Pony' in April, 1860, King . . . rode twenty miles in fairly good weather. Then he changed horses, but five miles farther on he encountered a heavy storm. The trail was very narrow and the footing was bad. King's horse stumbled and the rider and *mochila* were thrown off. Before King could grasp it, the mail had been blown over a cliff. He quickly recovered it, and, by the time King reached the next station, he was on schedule."

From Fort Bridger, Pony rider Jeremiah M. Murphy often clattered over the rough pole bridges that spanned the small streams. In this valley it was hot in the daytime and cool at night. Down a very steep hill the pony zigzagged to a wooded bottom, to complete a twelve-mile run to Little Muddy Creek. On its banks stood Muddy Station, kept by Jean-Baptiste, a Canadian, and his English wife. Murphy, after riding the Express, was a prospector and government contractor. He lived to be ninety-seven years old.

Another Pony rider in and out of Fort Bridger was James T. Thompson. Later, as a frontier cavalryman, Thompson took part in Indian wars. He died at the age of eighty-seven.

Westward from Muddy the rider entered an area of broken spurs and hollows, sometimes perfectly bare, at other times covered with heavy vegetation. Hills of odd shapes and bluffs of red earth, capped with white clay, bore a thick growth of tall firs and pines. A long ascent wound along a crest of rising ground to the summit of Quaking Asp Hill, with its Quaking Asp Station, eleven miles from Muddy. Sharp curves and turns marked the descent of the devious route, which was bordered by stunted oak, box elder and heavy shrubbery. Riders here kept always on the alert for Indian signs.

Across a land broken by rock masses, canyons, ravines and water gaps, the next twelve-mile run led into a valley and across a divide to the plain through which meandered Bear River, one of the most important tributaries of the Great Salt Lake. Red cliffs and rocks rimmed the half-mile-wide valley where the Bear River Station was kept by Mr. Myers, a member of the Mormon Church. This was the last westward station within what later became the state of Wyoming. Thence the route led to Great Salt Lake.

8.
THROUGH PAIUTE HELL
by Frank C. Robertson

The Pony Express route through Utah and Nevada, supervised by Major Howard Egan and Bolivar Roberts, twisted across the desert battlegrounds of the Paiute War. Some of Roberts' boys had a respite at the western end of the trail. But Egan's riders, after they passed Lookout Pass, that jumping-off place into hell, never knew at what moment they might get their hair lifted.

Egan, the man who had discovered the trail five years earlier, was a devout Mormon. So were nearly all of his men. It had been Brigham Young's policy that it was cheaper to feed the Indians than to fight them. This friendship, combined with the threat of the Army in barracks at Camp Floyd, saved many lives and made it possible to operate the Pony Express across the Sierras.

Legend has it that the Indians along the way were the downtrodden and degraded Diggers. It is possible that at the time all Indians were lumped under that contemptuous term. However, the Indians who fought the Paiute War, then raging, were first-class fighting men from many tribes. They included not only Paiutes, Gosiutes, and small bands like the Parowans, but the warlike Bannocks and other Shoshonis. They were led by such able and implacable haters of the white man as Chiefs Tintic and Pocatello. Finally, peace-loving Chief Winnemucca was forced into the war by the course of events. All fought to preserve their ancestral homes.

Not all Indians were warlike. I often explored the past with Louis LeMaire, veteran merchant of Battle Mountain, Nevada. Mr. LeMaire's father was a pioneer. Even during those troublous times, the elder LeMaire employed Indians to cut hay that was sold to the soldiers and emigrants. According to Mr. LeMaire, his family never had the slightest difficulty with the Indians; the simple recipe was to treat them fairly.

That the Indian was inherently bad is a falsehood. During my own boyhood, my best friend was the son of a Paiute woman who had been taken prisoner by the Utes. Bishop Anson Call, of Bountiful, Utah, purchased her and her brother from Chief Yellow Metal of the Utes, to keep them from being roasted alive. The price was two sacks of flour. This woman, known affectionately as Aunt Ruth, was midwife to the community in which I was raised, and was one of the best-loved women I have ever known.

There were many adventurous young braves, however, who had a nose for trouble, and were in it wherever it could be smelled. One such I knew as a boy was a Shoshoni named Shinite. When the Modoc War broke out, he saddled his war pony and struck out for the scene of battle hundreds of miles away, arriving in time to get shot in the ankle; he was a cripple for life. His favorite expression when he got irked with anyone was, "One more sleep—me shoot-um." Young Indians of this type caused the Pony Express the most trouble. In warriors like Tintic and Pocatello they found leaders they were glad to follow.

The Indians had much provocation. One Express rider, who later became a driver for the Overland Mail, tells that a passenger deliberately shot and killed a harmless old Indian who was trying to shoot ground squirrels with a bow and arrow to feed his family. The Easterner wanted to write back to his people that he had killed an Indian. Such incidents were all too common. The Indians had no monopoly on viciousness.

The two important stations between Salt Lake and Lookout Pass were Camp Floyd and Faust's Ranch, sometimes called Rush Valley. The Army, three thousand strong, was at Camp Floyd, and there was little danger from Indians there. Both Secretary of War Floyd and the soldiers were unloved by the neighboring Mormons. The soldiers were paid eight dollars a month and had little to do. Here were the saloons and whorehouses which the saintly Mormons loathed, yet were able to abide because of the much-needed trade and gold they brought into the territory. And when the Army finally left, its supplies were sold at a fraction of their worth, bringing an added windfall, which was the basis of several large Utah fortunes.

Over a Wasatch pass from Camp Floyd, the colorful J. H. "Doc" Faust operated a horse ranch in Rush Valley that supplied many horses to the Pony Express. Some of his broncobusters became riders for the Express. Faust himself sometimes carried the mail, as well as providing one of the most comfortable stations along the route. In later years, he studied medicine and became a physician in Salt Lake City.

Beyond Lookout Pass—and it was assuredly well named—were such important stations as Simpson's Spring, Willow Creek, Deep Creek, Shell Creek, Ruby Valley, Fort Churchill, and others. The trail made a long elbow turn around one of the worst stretches of desert, still known locally as the Big Mud.

From Lookout Pass you look out over forbidding deserts of mountains and flats. Even today, you had best not venture to cross them without an ample supply of water. It is hot as the hinges of hell in summer, cold as the polar regions in winter. In winter, blizzards block the roads; in summer, cloudbursts wash them out.

That was the kind of country the Pony Express riders had to buck. And, always, there was danger from lurking Indians, who killed them whenever possible, or burned their stations and ran off with the horses. It took men of skill and daring to ride those hazardous trails. Even if a man reached his way station, he never knew but what he would find the attendant dead and the cabin burned. It happened again and again. There was nothing for him to do but press on with his tired horse, and hope to find the next station intact. One wonders why they did it. Yet there is no record of a Pony Express rider ever turning back.

Three decades later, Jay G. Kelley gave a forthright account to Alexander Majors of those Nevada desert rides. Here it is, as Majors printed it in his autobiography, *Seventy Years on the Frontier*. By that time a successful mining engineer in Denver, Kelley reminisced:

I . . . went out with Bol Roberts [in 1860] and I tell you it was no picnic. No amount of money could tempt me to repeat my experience of those days. To begin with, we had to build willow roads (corduroy fashion) across many places along the Carson River, carrying bundles of willows two and three hundred yards in our arms, while the mosquitoes were so thick it was difficult to discern whether the man was white or black, so thickly were they piled on his neck, face, and hands.

Arriving at the Sink of the Carson River, we began the erection of a fort to protect us from the Indians. As there were no rocks or logs in that vicinity, the fort was built of adobes . . . (dried brick), we tramped around all day in it in our bare feet. This we did for a week or more, and the mud being strongly impregnated with alkali (carbonate of soda), you can imagine the condition of our feet. They were much swollen, and resembled hams. Before that time I wore No. 6 boots, but ever since then No. 9s fit me snugly. . . .

We next built a fort of stone at Sand Springs, twenty-five miles from Carson Lake, and another at Cold Springs, thirty-seven miles east of Sand Springs.

At the latter station I was assigned to duty as assistant station-keeper, under Jim McNaughton. The war against the Piute Indians was then at its height, and we were in the middle of the Piute country, which made it necessary for us to keep a standing guard night and day. The Indians were often seen skulking around, but none of them ever came near enough for us to get a shot at them, till one dark night, when I was on guard, I noticed one of our horses prick up his ears and stare. I looked in the direction indicated and saw an Indian's head projecting above the wall.

My instructions were to shoot if I saw an Indian within shooting distance, as that would wake the boys quicker than anything else; so I fired and missed my man.

Later on we saw the Indian camp-fires on the mountain, and in the morning saw many tracks. They evidently intended to stampede our horses, and if necessary kill us. The next day one of our riders, a Mexican, rode into camp with a bullet hole through him from the left to the right side, having been shot by Indians while coming down Edwards Creek, in the Quakenasp bottom. This he told us as we assisted him off his horse. He was tenderly cared for, but died before surgical aid could reach him.

As I was the lightest man at the station, I was ordered to take the Mexican's place on the route. My weight was then 100 pounds. . . . Two days after taking the route . . . I had to ride through the forest of quakenasp trees where the Mexican had been shot. A trail had been cut through these little trees, just wide enough to allow horse and rider to pass. As the road was crooked and the branches came together from either side, just above my head when mounted, it was impossible to see ahead more than ten or fifteen yards, and it was two miles through the forest.

I expected to have trouble, and prepared for it by dropping my bridle reins on the neck of the horse, put my Sharp's rifle at full cock, kept both spurs into the flanks, and he went through that forest like a "streak of greased lightning."

At the top of the hill I dismounted to rest my horse, and looking back, saw the bushes moving in several places. As there were no cattle or game in that vicinity, I knew the movements must be caused by Indians, and was more positive of it when, after firing several shots at the spot where I saw the bushes moving, all agitation ceased. Several days after that, two United States soldiers, who were on their way to their command, were shot and killed from ambush of those bushes, and stripped of their clothing, by the red devils. . . .

One day I trotted into Sand Springs covered with dust and perspiration. Before reaching the station I saw a number of men running toward me, all carrying rifles, and as I supposed they took me for an Indian, I stopped and threw up my hands. It seemed they had a spy-glass in camp, and recognizing me had come to the conclusion I was being run in by Paiutes and were coming to my rescue. . . .

As I look back on those times I often wonder that we were not all killed. A short time before, Major Ormsby of Carson City, in command of seventy-five or eighty men, went to Pyramid Lake to give battle to the Piutes, who had been killing emigrants and prospectors by the wholesale. Nearly all the command were killed in a running fight of sixteen miles. In the fight Major Ormsby and the lamented Harry Meredith were killed. Another regiment of about seven hundred men, under the command of Col. Daniel E. Hungerford and Jack Hayes, the noted Texas ranger, was raised. Hungerford was the beau ideal of a soldier, the hero of three wars, and one of the best tacticians of his time. This command drove the Indians pell-mell for three miles to Mud Lake, killing and wounding them at every jump. Colonel Hungerford and Jack Hayes received, and were entitled to, great praise, for at the close of the war terms were made which have kept the Indians peaceable every since. . . . It is marvelous that the pony boys were not all killed. There were only four men at each station, and the Indians, who were then hostile, roamed all over the country in bands of 30 to 100.

What I consider my most narrow escape from death was being shot at one night by a lot of fool emigrants, who, when I took them to task about it on my return trip, excused themselves by saying, "We thought you was an Indian."

No rider left a more vivid account of those stirring days than Elijah N. "Nick" Wilson. His adventures have been recounted in the book *The White Indian Boy*, on which he collaborated with Howard R. Driggs. I had the privilege of knowing Mr. Wilson in the twilight of his life. He was known as a man of truth and veracity.

Nick Wilson ran away from his Mormon home in Grantsville, Utah, and lived for two years as a member of the family of the great Shoshoni chieftain Washakie. Even before that, he had played with Gosiute children and learned their language. This saved his life on several occasions while he rode for the Pony Express. He began his Pony Express career as a bronco rider for Doc Faust.

Once he found himself cut off in a narrow defile by four Indians. Turning back, he encountered three more. There was nothing left for him to do but to sit quietly and await his fate. His hopes went up a little when he recognized an Indian named Tabby whom he had known around his father's home in Grantsville. Then the one-eyed leader of the Indians took a ramrod out of his gun and marked a trail in the road. "We will burn the stations here and here," he said, "and we will kill the Pony men."

The Indians went aside to talk, then built a fire. Nick gave them all the tobacco he had, and Tabby came over for a talk. The other Indians, Tabby said, wanted to kill Nick. He would not agree; Nick's father was his friend. Nick must promise never to carry the mail there again. Nick insisted that the mail he carried must go through, then agreed not to ride that way again. He kept the promise, too, by transferring to another run.

Richard Erasmus Egan, another Pony rider, shed a sidelight view on this same Tabby, who had the qualities of a modern gangster. For years the Mormons kept losing cattle, which their friend Tabby always returned, and was given a suitable reward. Finally, the trusting Mormons learned that Tabby was in cahoots with the thieves.

One time Nick Wilson drove a bunch of horses to Antelope Station. When he arrived, the two hostlers were playing cards on the woodpile, and invited Nick to stay for dinner. While they were eating, they saw horses being driven away by two Indians. The boys started after them. The Indians raced into the cedars. As Nick entered the grove, one of the Indians shot him in the head with a flint-tipped arrow.

The hostlers tried to remove the arrow, but the shaft broke, leaving the flint in his head. Thinking he was dying, they rolled him under a tree, and lit out for the next station. Next morning, men came back to bury Wilson. He was still breathing, so they carried him to Cedar Wells, and sent a rider to Ruby Valley for a doctor. When the doctor came, he removed the arrowhead, then told the boys to keep a wet rag on Nick's head. Six days later, Major Howard Egan arrived and sent for the doctor again. This time the doctor decided that Nick might live and began to do something for him. Wilson lay unconscious for eighteen days, but was soon back on the job. For the rest of his life, because of the scar, he refused to take his hat off, even at mealtime.

Nick Wilson's first participation in an Indian battle had its amusing side. Riding from his home station at Shell Creek, he arrived at the Deep Creek Station. The relay was not there, so he rode on to Willow Creek. This station was kept by the redoubtable Pete Neece, who reported that Indians had killed the other rider.

Soon, seven Indians rode up and demanded food. Neece offered them twenty pounds of flour. They refused, demanding a sack of flour apiece. Neece threw the flour back in the cabin and ordered them to leave. Angered, they shot a lame cow in a nearby shed. Neece killed two of them; the others fled.

Knowing that there were about thirty Indians camped nearby, Neece and the boys prepared for a siege. There were four men at the station, including one who talked big but who began to cry when the chips were down. Just before dark, they saw the Indians coming. Neece moved his little force out in the brush a hundred yards from the cabin and told them to lie down a little way apart. "Soon as you fire," he whispered, "jump to one side." Nick Wilson says he had two pistols. He watched Neece. Whenever Neece jumped, he would jump. But he forgot to fire a shot. Finally, he landed in a little wash and stayed there.

When the firing ceased, he saw a number of little humps of sand which he believed to be Indians. He decided that his companions had been killed. After many hours, he crept toward the station to get a horse and try a dash back to Deep Creek. Then he heard his friends worrying about him. When he made himself known, Pete Neece asked him how far he had chased the Indians. Several Indians had been killed. Nick returned to Deep Creek a hero.

Nick volunteered as scout and interpreter for General Johnston. On trail with two other scouts, he encountered a boyhood friend named Yaiabi. Nick persuaded the Indian to go with him to the commander's camp. Yaiabi told the general that there were three hundred Indians camped nearby who were waiting for Chief Pocatello and fifty Bannock and Shoshoni braves. Because of this information, the soldiers were able to surprise the Indians in their camp and completely defeat them.

While the battle was on, Nick and his Indian friend watched from the top of a hill. It was a bloody encounter. They saw an Indian and a soldier in a hand-to-hand death struggle. As they fought, a squaw sank an ax into the soldier's back. An instant later, another soldier ran the squaw through with a bayonet.

On the way back to Camp Floyd, Nick was shot in the arm between the wrist and the elbow, and the same bullet killed a soldier. This ended Nick's career as a Pony Express rider.

The Mormon knowledge of and influence over the Indians was critical to the success of the Pony Express. Howard Egan, the superintendent of this most dangerous part of the route, appears to have had "the Indian sign" on the Indians. Once, having had six head of oxen stolen, he ordered an Indian to go out and return them. The Indian brought back not six but fifteen head of cattle.

In the western part of Nevada, where the Egan and Roberts divisions joined, things were just as hectic as they were farther east. Here the trouble seems to have been stirred up by two or three young white men who had captured two young squaws and held them prisoner in a cave. There were six thousand Paiutes in Carson Valley, and they had gone through a hard winter. The white men had killed or run off their game, and were destroying the pine trees upon which the Indians depended for their harvest of piñon nuts. There had been killings and retaliations.

A council was held between Numaga (known as Young Winnemucca, but no relative of old Chief Winnemucca), a half-breed Bannock named Mogoannoga, and a Shoshoni chief, probably the implacable Pocatello. Only Young Winnemucca was for peace.

The husband of one of the squaws tracked her to the cave, but was driven away. Mogoannoga gathered a war party, killed five white men, and drove off a herd of cattle. They headed for a larger encampment of Indians at Pyramid Lake, where a council was in progress.

Young Winnemucca argued for peace, warning his people that if war broke out they would be driven into the desert to perish. He threw himself on the ground and fasted for three days. But when he received word that the war had already begun, he rose to lead his people in what he knew would be a hopeless fight.

In the first battle, the militia, under Major Ormsby, was ambushed; more than forty were killed. Only Bartholomew

Riles and a few others survived. This disaster, on May 12, 1861, was comparable to Custer's defeat on the Little Big Horn. On June 3, the Pyramid Lake Indians were overtaken by a larger party of white men; twenty-five Indians were killed, fifty horses captured. The survivors fled north.

Meanwhile, death and destruction flamed along the Pony Express route. Bolivar Roberts and Howard Egan had to resort to every resource, chief of which was raw courage, to keep the mail going. They returned to Salt Lake to engage fresh recruits. A command under Lieutenant Weed dealt the Indians a final blow.

Examples of individual heroism are too numerous to be listed here, but it was at this time that Pony Bob Haslam made his famous ride, covering 380 miles in thirty-six hours.

This is the story as Pony Bob told it himself a half-century later when he was a gray-haired steward at Chicago's fashionable Hotel Auditorium.

Virginia City was only in its infancy and hourly expecting an Indian attack. A stone hotel on C Street was under construction and had reached an elevation of two stories. This was hastily transformed into a fort. The signal fires of Indians could be seen on every mountain peak.

When I reached Reed's Station on the Carson River with the eastbound mail, I found no change of horses. All had been seized by white men to take part in the impending battle. I fed my animal and started for the next station, Buckland's—afterwards known as Fort Churchill—15 miles down the river. It was my relay point, for I had already ridden 75 miles. But the rider waiting there refused to go on. The superintendent, W. C. Marley, was at the station. All of his persuasion could not prevail on the rider to take to the road. Turning to me, Marley said, "Bob, I will give you $50 if you will make this ride."

Within 10 minutes, when I had adjusted my Spencer rifle which was a seven shooter and my Colt's revolver, with two cylinders ready for use in case of an emergency, I started. It was 35 miles, without a change, to the Sink of the Carson. From there, I pushed on to Sand Springs, through an alkali bottom and sand hills, 30 miles, without a drop of water along the route. At Sand Springs I changed horses and continued to Cold Springs, 37 miles. Another change and a ride of 30 miles brought me to Smith's Creek, where I was relieved by J. G. Kelley. I had ridden 190 miles, stopping only to eat and change horses. [That run is on record as the fastest in the Pony's history.]

Nine hours later, I started back with the westbound mail. At Cold Springs, I found the station-keeper murdered and all the horses stolen. I watered my horse and started for Sand Springs. It was growing dark and my route lay through heavy sage brush, high enough in some places to conceal a horse. I closely watched every motion of my poor pony's ears, which is a signal for danger in an Indian country. The stillness of the night and the howling of the wolves and coyotes made cold chills run through me at times.

I reached Sand Springs, reported what had happened and advised the station-keeper to come with me to the Sink of the Carson. We rode on together; Sand Springs was attacked the following morning. At The Sink, station men reported having seen 50 warriors decked out in war-paint and reconnoitering. There were 15 men in the adobe here, well armed and ready for a fight. I rested for an hour and, after dark, started for Buckland's, where I arrived without mishap and only three and a half hours behind schedule. Mr. Marley was there. When I related my story to him, he raised my bonus from $50 to $100. All the excitement had braced me up. After another rest of one and a half hours, I crossed the Sierra Nevada again to Friday's Station at the foot of Lake Tahoe, and delivered the mail to the relay. I had traveled 380 miles within a few hours of schedule time.

Others were no less valiant. Major Egan, and William H. Streeper of Bountiful, Utah, once started for Salt Lake. At Deep Creek they found the scalped body of Rosier, the station-keeper. Three others were missing: the cook, and men named Applegate and Bolwinkle. They had been obliged to flee so hurriedly that "Bolly" had run off without his boots. When the cook could no longer keep up, he blew out his own brains. The other two made the next station in safety, but Bolly's lacerated feet kept him out of action for a considerable time.

William F. Fisher and George "Wash" Perkins set out eastward from Ruby Valley. They found Indians waiting for them in a defile, but put spurs to their horses and dashed through. A bullet struck Fisher's hat; an arrow stuck in Perkins' *mochila*. Perkins remained at Simpson's Spring, and Fisher took the mail on alone to Salt Lake, covering three hundred miles on six horses and two mules.

At Egan's Station Mike Holton and a rider named Wilson (not Nick) were surrounded by a party of eighty Indians, who ordered them to bake bread and then more bread. They expected a rider named Dennis. When he did not arrive, they concluded that he had been killed.

When all the flour was used up, the Indians tied Holton and Wilson to a wagon tongue, piled sagebrush at their feet and set it afire. Dennis, however, had seen the Indians, circled around them and met a company of dragoons under Lieutenant Weed. The dragoons arrived in time to save Holton and Wilson, kill eighteen Indians and capture sixty horses.

This appears to have broken the back of the Indian resistance, though sporadic attacks on isolated posts continued.

A pestilential thorn in the side of the Pony Express were white outlaws and horse thieves, who were constantly busy, though showing less courage than the Indian marauders. These gentry were not above killing Indians to incite them against the Pony Express, thus making their own thievery easier.

For eighteen months the boys of the Pony Express, Mormon and gentile, riding side by side, always in the very jaws of death, wrote a blazing page in history which for bravery and endurance has never been surpassed.

9.
BUT THE DEVIL'S IN WASHINGTON!

The world-wide effect of the Pony Express as a medium of favorable public relations for "those Americans" has never been adequately researched. There is no question, however, that it influenced public opinion in England, France, Germany, and power-hungry Russia. All of them knew the dire crisis confronting the United States on the slavery issue. Their diplomats and press were as aware of the "slave-and-cotton" South's advantages in dominating the West as Daniel Webster had been in 1850 when he thundered: "Peaceable secession! What would become of Missouri? Will she join the *arrondissement* of the slave States? Shall the man from the Yellow Stone and the Platte be connected, in the new republic, with the man who lives on the southern extremity of the Cape of Florida?"

Headlines in London, Paris, and Berlin about the Pony Express' success not only provided a dashing new hero figure for Europe's folklore about "golden America" but rallied confidence in the permanence of the Union throughout the ministries of Queen Victoria, Napoleon III, and Wilhelm I. Within weeks, garish color posters of "Le Poney-Post" galloping, with hussars-on-parade stance—and in a Turkish turban—away from hordes of leering Indians were hawked on the streets of Paris and London. Across Poland clattered the couriers of Czar Alexander II's diplomatic service, carrying newspaper reports and dispatches about the first runs. These would be referred to again in 1862–63 in considering Russia's hope to reclaim California as payment for formal recognition of the Confederate States of America.

The impact on New England and the North was even more meaningful. The national convention of the Republican party buzzed toward a May 25th call to order in Chicago. Political veterans were giving odds that this time a Republican candidate would win through to the White House. On April 30th, the brooding protagonists of secession walked out on the Democrats' national convention at Charleston, South Carolina; the convention adjourned without selecting candidates. A Democratic split, plus the thumping antislavery vote certain to be cast by the German and Scandinavian immigrants, could squeeze a Republican through the electoral college for the first time. California and Western-territory ballots would be critical, of course, to the outcome. There was desperate reason, then, for mail deliveries across the continent that would better the Ox-bow's time, and evade the risk of being deliberately "mislaid" for months at a junction point deep in slavery's realm.

So, alongside astute editorials forecasting the certainty of a first-ballot nomination for Senator William H. Seward of New York or an "every-reason-to-believe" second-ballot nomination for Governor Salmon P. Chase of Ohio, the New York, Boston, and Chicago dailies ran stories about the Pony's amazing relays, the torchlight parade, "led by the California Band, playing 'See, the Conquering Hero Comes,'" that cheered those first forty-six letters through downtown San Francisco; the ominous rumors of Paiute war bands sighted between Salt Lake and Virginia City.

Horace Greeley's *New York Tribune* pioneered a technique that journalists would rediscover in World War II when it ran off a weekly edition, on India paper, for Pony delivery to Denver, Salt Lake, and San Francisco subscribers.

Finally, and all-importantly, the success of the Pony Express activated the dawdling schemes for a transcontinental railroad and telegraph line. Edward Creighton, the bustling Irishman who pioneered telegraph lines across Missouri and Illinois, was finally rolling one up the Missouri River to Omaha. He and Alexander Majors were old friends. Doubtlessly, Majors played a role in Creighton's decision to ride to Salt Lake for a conference with Brigham Young as soon as the first call signal sputtered through to Omaha.

In Washington, too, the congratulations boomed at Russell in Capitol and War Department corridors seemed sincere, and the handshakes warm. Scores of notes (delivered "via runner" or oozed through the post office with "Official" franks) awaited him at the Smoot & Russell offices. A special railroad subcommittee of the House reported favorably on the plan to construct a transcontinental railroad from St. Joseph to the Platte River valley, thence west along the Pony Express route.

Even Secretary Floyd seemed jovial, but "desperately busy" and deeply disturbed by huge new expenses that were completely upsetting the departmental budget again. "Unfortunately, my dear Bill, I am not at—uh—liberty to disclose details regarding such—uh—matters of national security." No money was available—again—to pay for the five hundred thousand dollars' worth of livestock, supplies, and wagons destroyed by the Nauvoo Legion and its ally, Winter, eighteen months before. The atmosphere was more obviously frigid in the Quartermaster General's office. General Johnston was extremely busy. No decisions yet on the starting date for the New Mexico supply trains. "Certainly. Your message will be routed promptly to the General. Good day, sir."

The outlook brightened a bit at the Postmaster General's. Grim Aaron Brown was dead. His successor, Joseph Holt, though a Kentuckian, wasn't quite so snarling in defense of the Ox-bow Route. On May 11, Holt annulled Major Chorpenning's old contract for mail deliveries between Salt Lake and Sacramento, then awarded it to Central Overland California & Pike's Peak on the basis of "semimonthly" deliveries.

Fifteen years later, still trying to collect damages from Congress, Chorpenning would tell Isabella Bacon Bond and other house guests at his Washington apartment that he relayed transcontinental mail across the Central Route in 1859 by delivering Buchanan's second message to Congress from Washington to Sacramento in seventeen days, eight hours and thirty minutes. He lost the Sacramento–Salt Lake contract in 1860, he said, only because business rivals obtained a judgment on old due bills, attached his horses and mail coaches, then complained to Washington that mails were not being delivered. Chorpenning never specified his enemies. Perhaps he meant Russell and Ben Holladay. Perhaps Floyd, Joe Johnston's brother-in-law, and other Ox-bow champions were involved. In any case, Congress hemmed, hawed, denied.

Now, perhaps, fortune would finally smile on C. O. C. & P. P. and bankruptcy could be averted by a last-minute transcontinental mail contract. On May 12, Russell again wrote to Waddell that "I must have help. . . . Have $150,000 to pay this week and quite a large portion the middle of next week. Have about $60,000 at hand. . . . Really fighting so many hopes and fears I cannot be efficient at Washington."

Senator W. M. Gwin of California was Russell's best hope to obtain a substantial Federal subsidy for the Pony Express, or an annual million-dollar contract for joint coach and Pony Express deliveries via the Central Route. A hatchet-faced, wag-eared Tennessean who trimmed his hair in imitation of Calhoun's "beaver tail" and affected Henry Clay collars and stocks, Gwin talked openly of a Western confederation. He had recently assisted in the dispatch of California's antislavery junior senator, D. C. Broderick, via the gentlemanly Southern custom of a rigged duel. Currently he encouraged the legend that he gave Russell the idea for the Pony Express. Since Benjamin Franklin had designed a neat mail-courier-on-horseback stamp for the Colonies in the 1750's, and Great Britain routinely delivered mail to farms and estates via mounted courier, the senator's claim is as questionable as his loyalty to the Union. Furthermore, the great Californian Joaquin Miller would write, decades later, that "The Pony Express was a great feature in the gold mines of California long before anyone ever thought of putting it on the plains. Every creek, camp or 'city' had its Pony Express which ran to and from the nearest postoffice. At Yreka we had the Humbug Creek Express, the Deadwood Camp Express, etc. . . . The owner was always a bold, bright young fellow who owned the line, horses and all, and had his 'office' in some responsible store."

Again, testimony to debunk Gwin's claim and lend substance to the Chorpenning claim of a Pony Express in 1859 comes from the letters of Frederick Billings, the attorney and financier, for whom Billings, Montana, would be named. Writing his parents in Woodstock, Vermont, from Mexico City in 1859, young Billings reported. "We sent an express to Colima, something over 800 miles, and the man, the same man riding the whole distance, was back here in eight days, having ridden 1700 or 1800 miles. We expect the express to San Blas, close on to 2000 miles there and back, will be here in ten days after date of departure."

Senator Gwin, as well as Russell, must have known, too, the story of the Pony Express established by George Wilkins Kendall, the derring-do editor of *The New Orleans Picayune*. Kendall left New Orleans on muleback in 1846 to cover The Mexican War, and en route organized a system of pony-rider relays to rush his dispatches back to the city-room. When *The Baltimore Sun* learned of this, they signed on, too. Kendall's pony-messages, relayed from Vera Cruz and Mexico City to New Orleans and Baltimore, so mortified Federal officials in Washington that sharp orders went out again to speed up Washington–New Orleans mail deliveries from the twelve- to twenty-day average to an amazing eight to nine days.

Kendall scored his greatest triumph by leasing a ship to rush him home, in 1848, with details of the Guadalupe Hidalgo Peace Treaty. Full publication of the treaty in *The Baltimore Sun, The New York Herald* and *The Picayune*, days before the official White House announcement, added to Washington's choler against "the danged Pony-Press." Home again, Kendall dismissed his corps of riders and went back to dependence on the ambling, erratic United States mails.

However, Gwin was the senior senator from California, and Russell was either pompously naïve or had become so deeply enmeshed in the Secesh web that he could only nod assent to every "suggestion" made by Floyd and the proslavers. Obviously, reassignment of the transcontinental mail contract that spring would have been more logical than the cancellation of the Chorpenning contract. The Pony Express soon proved that the ten-day schedule of its initial run was not "luck" or happenstance. And mail couriers and coaches could go where the Pony went. Thus, Butterfield's Ox-bow Route was no longer the "quickest, most expedient" route for trans-West mail delivery. A dedicated legislator, even without a law degree, could have growled so loudly about this on the Senate floor that the change would have been pushed through Congress at once—especially in an election year.

But, again, evidence points to the conclusion that Russell had been marked—perhaps in 1858—as a "goat" for any mishaps that might occur in the slowdowns, supply transfers, funds appropriations, furtive "expeditions," and odd troop movements assigned to Floyd and his War Department minions by the master planners of Secession. Russell's reckless insistence on attempting to recoup the Russell, Majors & Waddell fortunes by launching the "sure-fire razzle-dazzle" of a Pony Express via the Central Route most certainly strengthened any "fall-guy" plan devised by Senator Jefferson Davis, Senator Robert Toombs, Floyd's brothers-in-law, and other plotters.

Now, quite in line with Floyd's eagerness to write more I.O.U. acceptances, Senator Gwin beamed on Russell, boomed praise of Pony Express across Capitol Hill—then held hands under the legislative table with the Ox-bow and slavery groups. Late in May, he showed up at committee meetings with a proposition to cancel the United States Mail contract with the Panama Isthmus steamers, and to create three official land routes. One road would be the Ox-bow, with a new connection out of New Orleans. The second route would provide semiweekly mails between St. Joseph and Placerville, California. The third would pierce the sacred lands of the Sioux and Blackfeet by operating between St. Paul, Minnesota, and Puget Sound (where Major Pickett still commanded United States troops). The proposition never got out of the committee room.

Russell was still hoodwinked. On June 13, he wrote Waddell about "being in treaty for tri-weekly mail at $600,000 which have hopes of closing today. . . . It will lay a foundation for a mail that will give us $1,200,000." The Postmaster General had, indeed, canceled the steamship-mail contracts. Funds were available, even with Buchanan's plunderbund Cabinet, to pay the $1,200,000 or more. But now the Democrats were in a purgatory of their own fashioning. The Republicans in that convention at Chicago Wigwam had proved as unpredictable as old John Brown. Seward would have been bad enough. Yet he was a suave New York politician, thoroughly familiar with Washington's tense games of deceit and double meaning. Seward would have been shrewd and placable about a peaceful Secession or another four years of Union and Southern bosses. But those damned New Englanders had ganged with their Illinois "cousins," sweetened up the St. Louis Germans and Wisconsin Swedes, then nominated that gangling, sway-backed bumpkin from Springfield —Abraham Lincoln. The man was as crazy as Mrs. Stowe. If the Democrats didn't win this time—well—anything could happen. Maybe it would have been better to push on with plans in 1858, after all! Well, done is done. By the clawhammered horns of Bull Durham, no California mail contract for that cussed Abolitionist Central Route before the election. Keep the pouches on the Ox-bow—and a sly eye on what's in 'em. After November, things'll be clearer.

Russell was sick with worry. He began to write daily letters to Waddell, some with the caution: "Don't let Majors know about this." Ben Ficklin slammed into Washington, testified at hearings on the mail contracts, and urged that the Pony Express be stepped up to a semiweekly service. Russell went into a rage, shrilled a "No," then wrote Waddell a series of letters accusing Ficklin of incompetence. Ficklin handed in his resignation. Waddell attempted a reconciliation, won only a screaming letter from Russell offering to sell all his interests in Russell, Majors & Waddell at once "for $500,000." Somewhere along the line, the little man stormed that Ficklin had made scathing remarks about "one of our stockholders (one too who had done more to save all than all the rest put together)." He never specified whether the stockholder might be Ben Holladay—or even John Buchanan Floyd! Ficklin's resignation was accepted as of July 1.

The grim determination of the Paiutes and their allies to rid Nevada of all the paleface invaders and to murder every Pony Express employee along the desert lifeline caused Egan and Roberts to hold up the trans-Sierra rides for a month. San Francisco bellowed, its newspapers charging that Senator Gwin was in on "the plot," that troops were deliberately being held in Camp Floyd while the Indians ran amuck. Eventually, for one reason or another, the Cavalry jogged West; the mail pile-up at Salt Lake and Sacramento rushed through by coach; Haslam, Bud Egan, Billy Fisher and the other youngsters put on the Levi's and red shirts again, rode out again to "risk death daily." And, somehow, by hook and crook, Majors dug up the twenty-five dollars every week, kept the supply trains on schedule while gaunt, saddle-sore Howard Egan and Bolivar Roberts roved the routes like guardian angels.

Russell paid little heed. From May on, he mentioned the Pony only once or twice in the stream of letters hurtled at Waddell. General Johnston kept stalling. Those "urgent matters" still prevented assignment of starting dates for the wagon trains to the New Mexico posts. The bullwhackers and wagonmasters had reported for duty in April, and had lolled around Leavenworth ever since—on full pay. The provisions were stacked in the warehouses; payments for them would fall due in a few weeks. The bullocks and horses grew fat and stupid in the corrals; the stockmen who provided them grumbled about overdue bills. "General Johnston is in conference, sir, and has ordered he is not to be disturbed. . . . Mr. Floyd left for Carolina this morning, Mr. Russell. He will be extremely sorry to have missed you."

The little man hung, drowning, to the straw of hope at the Postmaster General's. All the capital stock in Russell, Majors & Waddell, Central Overland Pacific & Pike's Peak, and other Great Plains enterprises launched by the three partners was mortgaged to St. Louis, New York, and Philadelphia banks. He and the firm's Eastern agents juggled accounts with frantic dexterity, borrowing here to make a part payment there. In late June, Russell waited nervously at the Postmaster General's until the chief clerk would take time to hear a plea for payment of $127,000 on the Salt Lake City mail contract. "Sorry, sir. That money isn't available just now."

Then, he wrote Waddell joyous news at the end of the month. Their rainbow was glowing. He had it on the highest authority that the matter of the transcontinental mail contract for the Central Route would be brought up at Buchanan's Cabinet meeting on July 10. There was "every assurance" that Russell, Majors & Waddell's good friends would see the matter through then and there.

He must have had reasons for the mirages of hope he saw during these months of doom. But, from the vantage of history, his naïveté seems amazing for a man already being referred to in Chicago, Salt Lake, and San Francisco papers as the "Napoleon of the West." Certainly he heard the cloakroom whispers of direful plight confronting the Democrats. As a "fall guy" for, hence a smirked-at intimate of Floyd, Johnston, Secretary of the Interior Thompson, and others, he knew details about the Democratic split that never reached the press. And the papers were a-scream with it.

In late June, the Democrats assembled again, but with the hauteur of in-laws marching into a divorce court. The meeting place had been carefully selected and, even to Russell, was indicative of the nation's crisis. Maryland was a border state between the proslave and protenement territories. And Maryland had grudgingly given up the swamp and pine-dune territory of the District of Columbia. Logically, both "regular Democrats" and the Southern walkouts selected Baltimore as the convention city. The regulars met first, on the twenty-third, to nominate Stephen A. Douglas of Illinois for President and Herschel V. Johnson of Georgia for Vice President, then adopt a weaselly compromise platform that plumped for the Union and held to Douglas' 1850 theory of squatter sovereignty for all territories, with the slavery question to be decided by popular vote.

The Southerners sat in the galleries, or buzzed in conferences, during the five days. John Buchanan Floyd came down from Washington. His brothers-in-law rolled in from South Carolina. John S. Preston had become famous throughout the South for gallant speeches to the South Carolina legislature. In these, he painted a starry future for the Republic of South Carolina, a confederacy of Americans who believed in the inherent rights of the states (and slavery), and the delights such brotherhood would provide across the South and West "uv ouh cont'nunt." Brother-in-law Wade Hampton shared most of these sentiments but was more disturbed for the moment by the tariff bill—sponsored by the dastardly

114

Yankee Morrill—that had just passed the House. It ordered another increase in import duties, as of March 2, 1861. Mr. Hampton gloomed over the retributions the British brokers might make against the cotton crop now in plump fold on his South Carolina, Alabama, and Mississippi properties.

Evenings the three attended the banquets and balls held at the town houses of Baltimore's shipowners and Eastern-shore planters. The orchestras played that haunting new tune, "Dixie."

The Southern Democrats assembled their convention on June 28. The full California delegation moved in with them. Coyly disregarding the instructions of state bosses in San Francisco, Senator Gwin had wheedled and cooed each delegate over to a States'-rights point of view. Latham, the junior senator hand-picked for the post of the murdered Broderick, openly avowed the "Gawd-given right of the white man to use his superior wisdom in guidin' th' destinies of them poor humans as has been cursed by color an' th' likes." There was smoky laughter, too, in the Gwin and Latham suites about the blessings that would be bestowed after the South walked to sun-drenched freedom, then, taking little brother California by the hand, aided it toward a confederacy of the West.

Efficiently, the South-West coalition nominated John C. Breckinridge of Kentucky for President and Joseph Lane of Oregon for Vice President, then plunked for restoration of the proslavery Lecompton Constitution in Kansas and the extension of slavery territory, plus "Billy be damned" to that Republican nonsense of free homesteads for settlers west of the Missouri.

With all of this just a week behind them, only a desperate man could have expected Buchanan's July 10 Cabinet meeting to approve a subsidy for California mails via the Central Route. That matter was well in hand. And what "Grandma" Buchanan didn't know was good for his blood pressure and crying spells. The subject, so far as records show, wasn't brought into the discussion.

So July 10, 1860, was doomsday for Russell, Majors & Waddell. But the Cabinet meeting wasn't the reason. Russell, according to the Settles and other researchers, was in New York, juggling Russell, Majors & Waddell's soaring bills with agents and, seemingly cocky as ever, frisking along Wall Street and Lower Broadway on interviews with bankers. Headed back to Washington that night or the next day, he chatted with Luke Lea, a Washington banker. Lea, reputedly, told him about a Godard Bailey, who used to deal in state bonds. Bailey's wife was a cousin to John Buchanan Floyd. He might prove helpful, not only in raising loans for Russell, Majors & Waddell but for ingenious "in the family" pursuit of payments on those War Department debts.

Bailey and Russell met a few days later. Bailey soon delivered $150,000 worth of Missouri and Tennessee state bonds to Russell, accepting Russell's I.O.U. note on Russell, Majors & Waddell in payment. Next day, Russell was back on Wall Street raising sixty- and ninety-day loans on Russell, Majors & Waddell notes, with the Tennessee and Missouri bonds as security. This money so soothed the more plaintive creditors that he journeyed to Leavenworth in late July for a meeting of C. O. C. & P. P.'s board of directors. "Very promising. Yes. Things look quite bright."

Back in New York, the bankers knew too much. The way matters were shaping up, Tennessee and Missouri bonds were risky. In all, Russell was able to raise only $97,000 on the $150,000 lot. Russell, Majors & Waddell creditors began to close in again. Russell went back to Bailey.

This time Bailey produced $387,000 worth of Missouri, South Carolina, and Florida bonds. (Oddly enough, he seemed to specialize in bonds from Southern states!) Russell handed over another I.O.U. Then, later testimony indicated, Bailey told Russell that all of the bonds must be returned before March 4, 1861. That would be Buchanan's last day in office. And Bailey's term expired the same day. Bailey was trust officer for the Department of the Interior. If Russell hadn't known it all along, he learned it then. Those bonds were "borrowed" from the Indian Trust Fund of the United States Government!

Whatever Russell's involvements were with Floyd and the Secesh plotters, he was in too deeply to quit now. The wagon trains at Leavenworth had finally received General Johnston's clearance orders to move out to New Mexico. Their hundreds of drivers and trainmasters had idled around town for five months—on full pay that Russell, Majors & Waddell could never bill back to the War Department. Missouri River merchants and brokers were clamoring for payment on Army supplies delivered to Russell, Majors & Waddell warehouses six and seven months ago.

The Missouri and South Carolina bonds of the second lot peddled readily in New York and Boston, but for only two-thirds their face value. Not a banker would touch the Floridas. Russell hustled the Floridas back to Bailey—and received a like amount in North Carolina bonds. These were acceptable on The Street. Yet the funds they yielded were far short of the million dollars needed to calm Russell's creditors. Markets were shaky. The oratorical booms for Secession resounded from Charleston to New Orleans.

In October, Russell got through to Floyd himself and secured another three hundred thousand dollars in War Department acceptances over the Secretary's signature. Even this wasn't enough. The creditors needed that cash at once to ride out the falling market. Russell finally admitted defeat to Waddell, and Waddell got the word to Majors in Nebraska City. The November week that the Germans, Scandinavians, and Free-Soilers teamed to give the White House lease to Abraham Lincoln, Majors and Waddell worked night and day to list their assets and debts, prepare deeds of trust, and generally straighten up personal affairs for bankruptcy proceedings.

Still, Russell gambled desperately on. He went back to Bailey again in late November, admitted the firm's perils, then proposed that he be given more bonds to sell on the declining market. Then, he told later, he planned to buy them all back "when the market hit bottom" and restore the entire lot to the Department of the Interior vaults.

Whatever the truth, Bailey did deliver another $330,000 in Indian Trust Fund securities. Again, they were Tennessee and Missouri state bonds. But this time, Bailey attached a hook. Russell could have the bonds on the condition that he give Bailey all of those I.O.U. acceptance notes that Mr. Floyd had signed. It was the week the world learned that South Carolina would, on December 20, call up a convention to determine secession from the United States.

In all the testimony that ground tediously through congressional hearings, injunctions, lawsuits, and even Supreme Court trials over the next decade, the picture of these Russell-Bailey-Floyd relationships would never focus. No congressman or attorney would ever probe the reasons behind that five-month delay in sending supplies to the New Mexico Army posts out of Leavenworth in 1860—not even when the discovery was made that Floyd had transferred 115,000 Army rifles, plus ammunition and other armaments, from "Northern posts" to Southern arsenals that year. Was this the real reason for the delay? Is that what the wagon trains finally carried around to the South's back door in September and October, after the strategy of secession had been decided? Did Russell know, or suspect, this? Would it be the most plausible reason for all Floyd's readiness with the acceptance notes—the neat business of leading a bumptious Lexington, Missouri, lamb to slaughter?

Was the Bailey theft of the Indian Trust bonds another

step in the same "fix," as some historians contend? Was this, too, part of a smooth plan to befog the Federal Government so thoroughly for the incoming Republicans that they could never "get their bearings" in time to fight Secesh?

These questions, and scores of others, have never been adequately answered. Nor has the time lag in Bailey's alleged "chicken out" ever been explained. He would testify that he finally wrote a letter of full confession to Jacob Thompson, Secretary of the Interior, on December 1. But then, he declared, he held it up for two weeks before giving it to a relative with instructions that it be delivered to Thompson on March 5. Bailey confessed a second time, he reported, directly to Senator Rice of Minnesota.

But the news didn't reach the White House until December 20. And that was the very day that the South Carolina convention, by a vote of 169–0, passed its Ordinance of Secession from the United States of America. Moreover, in New York on that selfsame day, Brigadier General Albert Sidney Johnston, hurriedly recalled from a vacation in Kentucky, walked up the gangplank of a Panama steamship to begin a record-breaking journey that would end, fifteen days later, in San Francisco, with his installation as new commanding general of United States forces on the Pacific Coast.

Buchanan and his cabinet fumed all evening, first about South Carolina, then about the bonds. A total of $870,000 worth of securities was missing. If the Republicans didn't know about it now, they would soon!

Floyd was implicated, and pleaded ignorance. But he sent a messenger to Russell in New York, ordering the little man to hurry back to Washington for "an emergency." Secret Service officers from the White House reached Russell, Majors & Waddell's office an hour after the messenger. They arrested Russell, took him back to Washington, and dumped him into the District of Columbia jail. A judge set Russell's bail at the astronomical sum of five hundred thousand dollars.

Floyd never flinched. There were still a few errands to do for The Cause. He began a five-day harangue with Buchanan, urging withdrawal of the pitiful handful of troops, under Major Anderson, manning the Charleston harbor forts. "There must," he cooed, "be no bloodshed." He failed to mention—after all, family is family—that brother-in-law John S. Preston was now aide-de-camp to General Pierre G. T. Beauregard, and desperately busy setting up gun batteries to blast Forts Moultrie and Sumter. Meanwhile, brother-in-law Wade Hampton galloped over the South Carolina hills, raising a regiment of "Hampton's Own" to march wherever Beauregard ordered.

The President cried and prayed, raged and prayed again. Then, finally, he held firm. "I would rather," he gritted at the unctuous Virginian, "be in the bottom of the Potomac tomorrow than that those forts in Charleston should fall into the hands of those who intend to take them. It will destroy me, sir. And, Mr. Floyd, if that thing occurs, it will cover your name with an infamy that all time cannot efface, for it is in vain that you will attempt to show that you have not some complicity in handing over those forts to those who take them."

With haughty calm, the President repeated the same convictions to the South Carolina Commissioners on December 29. Buchanan said he fired Floyd the same day. Southerners said that Floyd resigned. Either way, he had functioned splendidly for The Cause. The Federal arsenals in the North were all but empty. The United States Treasury was in about the same fix. Buchanan was scared silly. The only transcontinental United States Mail route was still the Ox-bow. A. S. Johnston was on his way to California. Joe Johnston would soon resign and come home to Virginia. The sole line of communication the Union had with the Far West was that hare-brained Pony Express. And its president was in the District of Columbia jail under five hundred thousand dollars bail. Welcome to Washington, Republicans!

10.
THE THREAD THAT HELD

The clouds presaging the cyclone of war roiled greasy black through the winter of 1860. Within a week of Floyd's flight from Washington, United States arsenals and forts in Georgia, Alabama, and Florida surrendered to state troops, well before the governments of these states voted on ordinances of secession. Many of the desperate steps taken by both Secession and Union forces during these last three months of Buchanan's Administration would become eternal puzzles to historians; all records pertaining to them would be lost or destroyed. This is still true of data that would solve one of the most puzzling and meaningful questions of all: *Why did the Pony Express keep running?*

The gamble to keep Russell, Majors & Waddell afloat had failed. The partners began bankruptcy proceedings in October. Russell's desperate persistence brought them the larger shame of the Bond Scandal in December. The superhuman achievements of Majors, Ficklin, Egan, Roberts, and Finney, the intent devotion of the twenty-five-dollar-a-week riders, stationkeepers, and supply-train bullwhackers had proved the expediency of the Central Route long before the first scarlet leaves announced September in the Wyoming gorges. Furthermore, the Pony was consistently losing fifteen to twenty thousand dollars a month in operational costs.

Why, then, through the bitter winter months of 1860–61, did a bankrupt firm keep the Pony in operation, meet its payrolls on precise schedule, faithfully supply relay and swing stations through blizzards and ice storms, and recruit scores of daredevil youngsters to replace those who "tuckered out" after four or five months on the deadly wilderness runs?

From all the evidence at hand comes one logical answer to the question. And it centers on the giant figure of Alexander Majors.

Russell returned to the St. Joseph frontier for only one brief visit between May, 1860, and April, 1861. Waddell kept frantically busy with bookkeeping, managing the warehouses, placating the local creditors and trying to save some of his fortune. Ben Ficklin rode upriver to visit Alex Majors at Nebraska City after his July 1 resignation. Ben Holladay, spinning his own web of loans around the C. O. C. & P. P., was busy in Utah and Nevada developing Ophir Mine and the other properties that would, for a few years, make him Russell's successor as the "Napoleon of the West."

Only the details of Majors' activities are missing for these critical months. It was typical of his humbleness and deep religious zeal that he never boasted of his achievements. Here and there, biographers report that all Pony Express riders were promptly ordered to take an oath of loyalty to the Union. They agree that Majors, native Kentuckian and Missouri slaveowner, administered that oath.

Known facts thus shape toward logic. Majors had become deeply disturbed by the issues of Secession and slavery and the future course of his beloved West. He was fighting toward personal decision in 1859 and early 1860. Russell and Waddell worried openly about his bluntness, innate honesty, and social logic. Hence they whispered business details to each other as furtively as proslave and pro-Abolition members of the Cabinet plotted behind "Grandma" Buchanan's back. Finally, when Russell's gambles and the Floyd plots combined to crash Russell, Majors & Waddell's dream empire in the weeks before the 1860 election, Waddell was chosen to deliver the grim news to Majors. Logically, then and there, the Pony Express would have folded as a business gamble.

But it had become something more. Had Majors' faithful roughnecks, the bullwhackers, told him what clanked and jangled in those cases rolling to New Mexico—and where else?—during September and October? Did Ben Ficklin unburden his soul to the big, quiet fellow during August fishing trips and prairie rides along the Pony run? Did Ficklin know details about the Floyd-Russell relationship that never got "on the record" of congressional hearings?

The Pony kept running. The money for payrolls and supplies kept showing up. The youngsters, sober as bishops, took that oath of allegiance to the Union and held to it with the same desperate seriousness with which they clung to the leather-bound Bibles.

Russell and Waddell didn't do it. Only Majors could have. And, because he did, the Pony Express veered California and Oregon, the huge gold and silver bonanzas of Nevada and Colorado, toward the Union cause during the most tenuous months of United States history. The gallant communication thread, made up of kids in Levi's and red shirts doubled over the frosty backs of half-wild mustangs, was held intact during that winter of 1860 by the will of a brooding pioneer who had sought peace of mind through prayer plus thought—and found the answer in his decision to give his all for human freedom. Majors and "the kids" maintained that "lifeline of the West" until Ben Ficklin teamed with Edward Creighton to weave the telegraph along the same route in 1861.

Long before Ben Holladay took over the C. O. C. & P. P. in April, 1861, drivers and stationmen had nicknamed the line "Clean Out of Cash and Poor Pay." Service deteriorated rapidly when Ben Ficklin's whiplash tongue and leprechaun energy vanished from the trail. The hostlers yanked harness off sweating teams, tossed down a bucket of oats and hurried back to their cribbage game. The wagon shops had orders to hold down costs, so they expanded them by ceasing to wash and lacquer the Concord coaches, oil the springs and snug up the shafts and wheels. The drivers, with pay overdue and no Ficklin to give them "blistered hell" for showing up ten minutes late, sauntered the creaky, shabby vehicles east and west as they pleased.

Yet, in those same crucial months, the Pony Express ran on punctilious schedule. There is no whisper, in all the thousands of pages of personal memoirs and journalese biography, of grumbles about the slow pay, the supply shortages, or the frantic economies that turned C. O. C. & P. P. from doughty pioneer to joke butt. The achievement record of the Pony that winter sings of the same trail skills and exquisite leadership that Majors, Ficklin, Egan, Roberts, and Finney displayed in fashioning and launching the Pony during that sixty-day miracle in February and March, 1860.

Bolivar Roberts and Howard Egan were still in the saddle—and that's no figure of speech—on the Utah and Nevada divisions. Jack Slade still roared along the Wyoming and Nebraska trail; he had recovered nicely from the double-barreled shotgun slugs Jules Reni had poured into him, and he now carried, for the edification of bartenders and greenhorns, one of Jules's ears in his pocket.

Was Majors still in command from Nebraska City? Was Ficklin working with him because he, too, realized the peril confronting the Union in the Far West if the Pony Express gave up?

In November, the Pony steeled for extraordinary effort to carry the presidential election news through to Sacramento. The Kansas and Nebraska relays raced the word that "Abe Lincoln's got it" from St. Joseph to Julesburg in less than two days and a half; the Julesburg-Denver relay reached Denver just sixty-nine hours after the dispatches left St. Joseph—an average speed of better than nine and a half miles an hour for the 665 miles. The same searing pace held across the Rockies and the Utah desert, then Pony Bob Haslam stepped it up to almost fifteen miles an hour by racing the 120 miles from Smith's Creek to Fort Churchill, Nevada, in eight hours and ten minutes.

Yet, in late December, the Pony bettered this record by delivering Buchanan's last message to Congress from the Missouri River to Sacramento in little more than eight days —an average of ten miles an hour for the two thousand miles, despite thirty-foot drifts in some of the Rockies' passes and the Paiute War bursting into a new spasm of murder and pitched battles across Nevada.

With these rides, the isolation of the Far West vanished forever. The time lags that had enabled Andrew Jackson to win immortality at the battle of New Orleans two weeks after a peace treaty between the United States and Great

Britain had been signed in Paris, that enabled Frémont and Stockton to set up a Bear Flag Republic and run headlong into the contrary orders carried by Kearny, were disappearing with the bison. One essential of teamwork is communication, and joint understanding of "what's going on." This is as paramount a law for a union of states and territories as it is for a business partnership or a marriage. The news provided by the Pony Express during the winter of 1860–61 finally enabled California, Nevada, Utah, and Colorado to become full-fledged co-operating members of the United States of America.

Side by side with the rip-snorting front-page stories about Russell and the Bond Scandal, about Floyd's traitorous deeds, newspapers from New York to San Francisco carried stories that were routinely headed "Via Pony Express." New York reported Johnston's arrival in San Francisco a week and a half after he stalked into the Presidio. The *Alta California* was hurling epithets at Jacob Thompson a week and a half after he resigned as Secretary of the Interior, fled into Virginia, then—assumedly following a delicious evening with Floyd and Quartermaster General Joseph Johnston at Abingdon—bustled home to Mississippi to start his campaign as state governor under the Confederate States of America.

The Secesh plotters had organized beautifully. States tumbled out of the Union with parade-ground precision. There were frightening demonstrations north of the Mason-Dixon line, too. Fernando Wood, Democratic mayor of New York City, met with his City Council on January 6, blandly urged that Manhattan, Brooklyn, Queens, the Bronx, and Staten Island secede from the United States to create the neutral Free Port of New York. The nation, he prophesied, would split into three factions—a Confederacy of the South, a Confederacy of the West, and the old United States of America, bounded by the Ohio and Mississippi rivers. A Free Port of New York, he pointed out, could gain much trade and wealth by dealing with all three. The Council turned him down. Yet Mayor Wood reflected the beliefs of millions in the North and West who sympathized with Secesh or became unconscious allies by favoring either neutrality or a confederacy of the West.

The day Wood made his bid, Florida's state troops seized the United States Arsenal at Apalachicola. Three days later, Mississippi seceded and, eight hundred miles east, General John Preston beamed while the new gun batteries around Sullivan and Moultrie churned shot across the bow of the unarmed merchant ship *Star of the West*. Obligingly, the *Star*'s captain veered about and hurried back to sea with the supplies Buchanan had sent down to besieged Major Anderson and his "regulars" in Fort Sumter. So, eleven days after Floyd left Washington and almost two months before Lincoln's inauguration, the South fired the first guns of the Civil War.

Florida on January 10 and Alabama the next day; Georgia on the 19th, Louisiana on the 26th—with noisy deftness, the Secession parade marched west. Gruff, tough old Sam Houston, Unionist to the end, fought the whole Texas convention. The cotton trust and politicos finally kicked him out and pushed through their ordinance, 166-7, on February 1, then rushed delegates off to Montgomery, Alabama, for the convention to form a provisional Confederacy government. "Mr. Floyd and Mr. Thompson cain't come back to testify before that ol' Congressional Hearin' on them Indian Trust Fund bonds, much as they'd like to. They've gone to Alabama—uh —visitin' kinfolk."

Arkansas "jined up" on February 8, when state troops seized the United States Arsenal at Little Rock. Next day, while Ex-Senator Robert Toombs of Georgia growled disgust and envy, Jefferson Davis was declared Provisional President of the Confederate States of America.

But there, leaving trembling anxiety, the westbound fuse of rebellion sputtered out. Far to the north, on Puget Sound, Major Pickett waited restlessly. At the Presidio, mysterious visitors to General Johnston entered and left by the side gate. Washington whinnied in dismay when word filtered back that Secesh troops had stopped mail coaches all along the Ox-bow, dumped the pouches beside the road, and appropriated coaches and horses for "the service of the Confederacy."

Still, out through the northers of the plains, up the glassy ice mounds of the Continental Divide, past the quaking-aspen ambushes and over "Paiute Hell," the Pony's red and blue held firm the thread of the West's destiny. Edward Creighton followed the route into Salt Lake City, held long conferences with Brigham Young, then rode on to California. By the time he returned to Nebraska, friends had incorporated the Pacific Telegraph Company. Skim down that list of the incorporators, and pause at the *F*'s for long deliberation. There it is: Benjamin F. Ficklin, ex-superintendent of the Central Overland Pacific & Pike's Peak and the Pony Express, Ficklin—Majors—Creighton—Brigham Young. Keep their names bright among the list of freedom's champions in the American West.

Construction of a transcontinental telegraph line along the Central Route began that same winter. Again, details have been lost, or patently neglected, by biographers. But, by the time Holladay and Wells Fargo moved onto the scene in the late spring of 1861, the Pony, in addition to the St. Joseph-Julesburg relays, was operating lickety-split as messenger service between the mobile terminals of the telegraph line—Fort Kearny, Nebraska, on the east and Fort Churchill, Nevada, on the West. Who did it if Alexander Majors, Ben Ficklin, and the Mormons didn't?

Back in Washington, William H. Russell slowly struggled from the maze Floyd, Thompson, Bailey, and masterminds of The Cause had spun. Friends raised money to pay his bail. Congressional committees yanked him in for questioning, pussyfooted, called him back again. His testimony had more holes than a barn door after pistol practice. It is best to say the truth is still unknown. Nevertheless, he remained president of Russell, Majors & Waddell and C. O. C. & P. P. He clung, with chameleon tenacity, to the dream of squaring off the 1858-59 account with the War Department, winning a transcontinental mail contract, and putting his empire back on its feet.

Buchanan finally dredged deep, found a little courage, and fought desperately to hold the remnants of the Union together until March 4. Now the postal bill swished through Congress like a frightened debutante—but the transcontinental contract was awarded to the Butterfield-Wells Fargo combine. Then there were summary orders that all operations be transferred to the Central Route. Mystery, again! Suddenly, in March, Russell signed a contract with both Wells Fargo and the new Kansas-Salt Lake competitor, Western Express. Under it, C. O. C. & P. P. would operate the mail service *and* Pony Express as far as Salt Lake; Wells Fargo would operate both the coach mails and the Pony from Salt Lake to the Pacific.

Thus, for the first time, the Pony Express was officially recognized by the Federal Government. In all, it had cost Russell, Majors & Waddell a minimum of five hundred thousand dollars to set up and operate. And, in that desperate winter of 1860, it had, mysteriously and magically, snuffed out the fuse of Secession intended for the Far West.

Some history books allege that Albert Sidney Johnston was faithful to the Union, held the proslavery and Western confederation plotters of California from open rebellion through that winter, and did not resign his command of the Department of the Pacific until "he learned of Texas' Secession." Texas seceded on February 1. The Pony Express hurried the news across the continent. The California newspapers gave it headlines—"Via Pony Express"—before February 15. General Johnston sat tight at the Presidio through February, through March, almost through April. Ditto for Major Pickett on Puget Sound.

There is more reason to believe the allegation of other historians that Gwin, Latham and their real "bosses" had more than one hundred thousand guns stashed away on ranches and in warehouses between Los Angeles and Seattle. Again, the indications are that Johnston was to take command when a signal was given—by either the Confederate States of America or the organizers of a confederacy of the West.

The scheme might have worked, with mails clanking willy-nilly via the Ox-bow or over the Panama Isthmus. But it couldn't work with the Pony Express jack-rabbiting newspapers and confidential dispatches across the continent on a ten- to seventeen-day schedule. The North was finally awake. The California Yankees rallied, began recruiting troops, and set such a watchdog vigilance on Johnston that he growled official protests back to General Scott and Floyd's successor, Joseph Holt. (Hon. Mr. Holt had been whistled over from postmaster general to secretary of war on Jan. 10. Interesting!)

When whispers filtered through that Secesh plans were well organized to assassinate Lincoln, either en route to Washington or in the Capitol itself, St. Louis and Kansas Republicans formed a lifeguard. More than one hundred of them rode to Washington, set up sentry duty around the Hotel Willard, then, after the inauguration, moved into the White House with the Lincolns. One of the lifeguards was William Gilpin, the daring Missourian who had fought for a transcontinental railroad since 1840.

Huffy Colonel E. V. "Bull" Sumner had been delegated Head of Escort and Chief Protector for Lincoln during the ride to Washington. Pinkerton detectives planned otherwise, gave "Bull" the slip in Harrisburg, and smuggled Lincoln on to the Capitol in a sleeping-car lower. Sumner huffed into town next day, stayed for a month, then suddenly raced west. Lincoln, in the midst of the bureaucratic chaos and with the Beauregard-Preston cannon finally slamming the walls of Fort Sumter to smithereens, had promoted "Bull" to Brigadier General and sent him on a mission deemed just as urgent as the call for "75,000 volunteers to put down Secession."

Sumner clattered into the Presidio dog tired on April 25,

adjusted his cravat and headed down the hall to Johnston's suite. "General Sumner reporting for duty." Albert Sidney Johnston packed his gear, rounded up a horse cavalcade of Secesh who "couldn't abide the California climate no more," and rode south toward El Paso. Major Pickett guessed he'd be moseying along, too.

The Pony had already delivered Lincoln's inaugural address, in another record-breaking run. The gangling Illinoisan had drawled:

I hold that in contemplation of universal law and of the Constitution, the union of these states is perpetual. . . . It is safe to assert that no government ever had a provision in its organic law for its own termination. . . . no state upon its own mere motion can lawfully get out of the Union . . . I therefore consider that . . . the Union is unbroken; and . . . shall take care . . . that the laws of the Union be faithfully executed in all the states.

"Yes, sir. Ol' Abe's got guts." The nods of approval spread from San Francisco out to the mother lode, into Virginia City, down the valley through the mission towns. "T' hell with this Confederacy stuff. Looks like they's a *man* in the White House again."

The basic law of co-operation is communication. The only means for that communication was the Pony Express.

William Russell came home to Leavenworth in April, met with the C. O. C. & P. P.'s board of directors. The news trailed out of the conference room that he had resigned and Ben Holladay's banker cousin, Bela M. Hughes, had been elected president in his place. Hughes promptly moved the C. O. C. & P. P.—and the Pony Express—headquarters to Denver.

Alexander Majors didn't bother to attend the meeting. He had sold all his properties months before, then quietly handed the funds over to Russell, Majors & Waddell's creditors. In later years, he was the only partner of the three whose name would be uttered without expletives by any of the firm's creditors. Now almost fifty, he started from scratch again in Nebraska City. About the matter of keeping the Pony running through the winter of 1860? Oh, that! Well, somebody had to, didn't he? Freedom is everybody's business.

11.
THE TALKING WIRES

The Pony Express was only a gallant makeshift. It pioneered, and maintained, the Central Route to California against superhuman odds not only of weather, wilderness, and Indians but the desperate plotting of Secretary of War Floyd, the Postmaster General, and their Secessionist confederates. Now, despite more stodgy bungling in Washington, the telegraph wires hurried along this transcontinental shortcut the Pony had blazed.

Even before the Pony, discerning men were thinking in terms of the telegraph. Another, thinking in terms of saving the Union, was Abraham Lincoln, who finally prodded Congress into appropriating four hundred thousand dollars to aid its completion. Quick communication was vital to Union victory. But the line had to be started by private capital. It took men of vision and courage to risk their money on it.

The main objection, of course, was that since the line would have to run across one thousand miles of Indian territory, the warriors and brash young bucks would destroy it as fast as it could be built. Then it would be impossible to provide enough soldiers for its protection. There was always great danger from the Sioux and other Plains Indians, and an even greater threat through the Paiute country of Utah and Nevada territories. Far easier for Indians to cut wires and pull down poles than to kill those Pony riders.

The best protection, the pioneer telegraph builders discovered, was an intangible called superstition. They used it to the utmost. They invoked the spirits, of whom all Indians stood in awe. The Indians called the telegraph "the talking wires."

Engineers and construction crews grabbed the phrase, and added embroidery. The talking wires, they said, carried messages from the spirits, as well as to the Great White Father in Washington. Any interference would bring a curse upon the intruder. Some braves tried anyway and became violently sick after drinking acid from the batteries. They became more cautious of spirit powers.

Edward Creighton, whose name is perpetuated in Creighton University in Omaha and the town of Creighton, Nebraska, was father of the first transcontinental telegraph. Hiram Sibley, president of Western Union, urged him on once it became clear that Creighton would complete the St. Louis–Omaha line in 1860. The Ohio-born builder was proving himself as dauntless as any native son of the Great Plains. By the fall of 1860, he had pushed a line west along the Platte as far as Fort Kearny.

In California, too, Virginia City's Comstock Lode had lured the talking wires across the Sierra. In November, 1860 —the month that Russell, Majors & Waddell's bankruptcy and the Floyd-Russell-Bailey Bond Scandal should have closed down the Pony Express—a fifteen-hundred-mile gap existed between the telegraph's Fort Kearny terminal on the east and its Carson City terminal on the west. While Sibley in New York and Ben Ficklin—and perhaps Majors—in Nebraska perfected the organization of the Pacific Telegraph Company, Edward Creighton took the Pony Trail to Salt Lake. There, either Majors or Ben Holladay, and maybe both, had arranged conferences with Brigham Young. Again, as he had when the Pony Express was launched, the Mormon leader pledged full co-operation, and offered both workmen and supplies.

In the dead of winter, Creighton followed the Pony Trail to Sacramento, stormed on to San Francisco, and organized the Overland Telegraph Company. West Coast stockholders agreed that James Gamble was the man to push the western line across "Paiute Hell" into Salt Lake. Gamble accepted the challenge. Creighton hurried back to Omaha. The Nebraskans had 1,150 miles of line to rig to Salt Lake, but Gamble's crew faced greater difficulties in the bleak 450 miles between Carson City and Tabernacle Square. It was a toss-up who would win. Reports of progress were carried from each line's end by the intrepid Pony Express riders. Now the youngsters were riding hard actually to put themselves out of business. Speed, speed, and more speed was the Wyoming-Nevada battle cry.

Gamble's men worked under extra handicaps. The wooden poles had to be brought out of the canyons; often the ground lay deep under snow. But Brigham Young came to the rescue. He contracted to build many miles of the line himself, then subcontracted it to able Mormon builders such as Adam Sharp, who built the line from Salt Lake to beyond Callao, far out in the desert.

Other Mormons contracted to deliver the poles. Under the rigorous conditions, some quit. Jim Street, Gamble's right-hand man, went forthrightly to Brigham Young. Young called the balky Mormons into his office and demanded to know if they had contracted to deliver the poles of their own free will. They answered that they had. "Then your word must be made good," Young told them. "The Mormons will not break a contract." To Street he said, "You shall have your poles, Mr. Street, even though it makes paupers of us all."

Young's word was law. The Mormons struggled out through the snowdrifts to cut the poles, snake them by horse and log chain to sleds.

Brigham Young as a contractor had a personal interest in its success. Yet from our knowledge of the kind of man he was, we may safely assume that he would have kept his bargain if he hadn't stood to make a penny of profit from it. All his life he was faithful to his agreements. He drove his people hard, but in so doing he held them together and so became the greatest colonizer this country has ever known. Legend has it that some Mormons were converting the poles to their own needs, or selling them to others. It is said that Brigham Young gave them the choice of bringing back the poles or dealing with Porter Rockwell and his men. The poles were returned.

Setting up the poles and stringing the wires were the least difficult part of the work. The men worked together, so were reasonably free from Indian attacks. Food and water could be hauled to them; they had shelter from the worst of the storms. It wasn't a life of ease and luxury, but it wasn't nearly so hard as that of the men struggling to bring the poles out of the canyons. Often these men had to wallow through snow up to their waists. Their horses and oxen were often down, and roads had to be broken. The poles had to be transported over long distances, and the companies were small. If attacked by Indians they couldn't run; they had to stand and fight. Few Americans have ever worked harder under more adverse conditions.

Meanwhile, Creighton's men were driving hard from the east, along the old Oregon Trail up the valley of the Platte and the Sweetwater and through South Pass, thence on across the Green River to Fort Bridger, and down Echo Canyon. There was always danger from the daring horse Indians of the Plains. Companies of soldiers from Utah were sent out to protect the workers. One writer tells of soldiers coming out from Fort Bridger in mule-drawn wagons to pursue Indians on horseback. Yet, somehow, Creighton's crews managed to string the wires and repair the cuts within reasonable time. The messages kept coming through; the route of the Pony Express slimmed.

There were far fewer battle casualties on the telegraph route than there were among the Pony Express riders and stationkeepers. Many workers suffered from frozen feet, hands, ears, and noses, but few from guns or arrows. The battle was won at last. The nation was united by a small strand of talking wire. The connection of the wires at Salt Lake was to remain the most important achievement of the West until two railroad locomotives, one from the East and one from the West, touched cowcatchers at Promontory Point, Utah, on May 10, 1869.

The eastern part of the telegraph line, though built over easier terrain, reached Salt Lake only two days ahead of the men from the west. They strung their poles right up Main Street of the city and connected wires to an instrument in the telegraph office building. On October 22, 1861, Brigham Young sent the first message to Jeptha H. Wade, a Western Union official at Cleveland, Ohio.

Young's message closed with a thunderous pledge: "Utah has not seceded, but is firm for the Constitution and the laws of our once happy country."

When, two days later, James Gamble and his toil-worn crew brought in the line from the West, the wires were connected. After the system was tested, this great historical message, the first transcontinental message ever sent, flashed a final answer to Floyd, the Johnstons, and all the plotters of Western confederacy:

To Abraham Lincoln, President of the United States: In the temporary absence of the governor of the state, I am requested to send you the first message which will be transmitted over the wires of the line which connects the Pacific with the Atlantic states. The people of California desire to congratulate you upon the completion of the great work. They believe it will be the means of strengthening the attachment which binds both the East and the West to the Union, and they desire in this—the first message across the continent—to express their loyalty to the Union and their determination to stand by its Government on this its day of trial. They regard the Government with affection, and will adhere to it under all fortunes.

STEPHEN J. FIELD, Chief Justice of California

Such was the triumphant conclusion of one of the greatest and most hazardous of early American enterprises. Its dangers were not over. Men had suffered and died to build it. Others were to die keeping it in operation. With the big crews gone, lonely operators had to defend themselves the best they could. The Sioux War was still to be fought, with the telegraph lines as prime objects of attack. And there were always marauding parties who defied the superstitions of the talking wires.

Some of the courageous operators built dugout forts in which they could defend themselves. Not all were successful. One man stuck to his post, clicking off his account of the attack, until a bullet put a period to the message. There are other stories of equal heroism which could be told.

So the telegraph succeeded the Pony Express. But its builders would never dim the glory of, or disdain, those epochal riders and the men who created the Central Route.

12.
GOLD FOR OLD ABE

Clark, Gruber and Company opened their newly built bank in Denver on July 25, 1860. In the smelter room and mint adjoining it, they began shaping the first coins made from Rocky Mountain gold. Now, with the opening of a coinage plant by a reputable banking firm, the world was assured that precious metals were being mined in the Pike's Peak country in considerable quantities. The importance of 'the States' maintaining quick contact with the Western gold fields was more urgent than ever.

Denver, by this time, was a mixture of Indians' rawhide lodges on the banks of Cherry Creek, tents and covered wagons teeming with gold-hunters, the crude log huts made by the first arrivals in 1858, and a conglomeration of frame houses and brick tenements still under construction. The old Trappers' Trail had become a bustling business street.

Coincident with the erection of the Clark, Gruber bank and mint, Alexander Majors erected a twenty-five-by-one-hundred-foot brick store, on Ferry Street, three stories high. That summer, too, the *Rocky Mountain News* began to publish as a daily instead of a weekly newspaper. In addition to news brought in by stagecoach and Pony Express, the *News* published letters from correspondents in the mining districts.

Congress had guaranteed an annual subsidy of forty thousand dollars for ten years to any company completing transcontinental communication by electric telegraph. Now, Edward Creighton rode in to sell twenty thousand dollars' worth of telegraph stock. This, he vowed, would justify the Overland Telegraph Company's extending its line to Denver at an early date. He failed and went back to Omaha in August, determined to build the telegraph line two hundred miles north of Denver, across what later became Wyoming.

Also soliciting funds along Cherry Creek that month was the burly Reverend John Chivington. He, too, had got the "Pike's Peak fever," had been sent out from Nebraska City to become presiding elder for his church in the Rocky Mountain district, and now hoped to build a Methodist Episcopal church in Denver.

Since a government mail contract had not yet been awarded to the Central Overland California & Pike's Peak Company, it was rumored that the Pony might be discontinued. On September 5, William H. Russell announced that the Pony Express would be continued until January 1, 1861; then, if Congress still refused to underwrite the route, it must be abandoned.

On November 3, the telegraph wires reached Fort Kearny, Nebraska. As they unrolled west, the Pony Express riders moved with them, covering the route only between east and west telegraph terminals.

Had the proposal to create Jefferson Territory from West Kansas been approved in Washington? Had South Carolina grumbled back into the Union, as she did in 1833? Deep snows blocked the Overland Trail. Stagecoach mail piled up at Julesburg for a month. The Pony was one of Denver's few contacts with the world while the Union snarled toward dissolution. The *News*, on January 24, 1861, reported that Captains Walker and Desseur had resigned their commissions at Fort Wise and would go home. "Their residence," commented the editor, "is in the chivalric South."

At last, word arrived that the Territory of Colorado came into existence on February 28, during President Buchanan's last week in office. The name Jefferson had been changed to Colorado, meaning "red earth." Report said that "Jefferson" smacked too much of the South and the Democrats—even for Buchanan!

Rumors that Fort Sumter had surrendered were announced in the *News* on April 18. Four days later, when a Pony clattered in with the details, the *News* sent a special courier back to mountain mining camps; he rode the twelve miles to Golden City in forty-eight minutes.

Now the paramount question was: Is Colorado for the Union, or will it declare for Secession? The Southern element was strong. On April 24, a Confederate flag creaked to the top of the Wallingford & Murphy store. Union sympathizers rallied, shouting demands that it be hauled down. Bela M. Hughes was one of them. He had been a Democrat. But now, like Majors and cousin Ben Holladay, he was a Union man.

The next night one thousand citizens of Denver gathered for a Unionist rally. There was a huge bonfire. A band played "Hail, Columbia" and "John Brown's Body." The resolutions, adopted with cheers, stated that "as for Colorado, she, with willing heart and ready feet, will follow the flag and keep step to the music of the Union." There were similar meetings in Boulder, Central City, and Golden.

But many stayed home. "Uncle Dick" Wootton did. A native Virginian, he had dispensed "Taos lightning" on Denver's first Christmas in 1858, then moved south to try ranching on Fountain Creek, nine miles above Pueblo. "It's a mean man," he boomed, "who has no feeling of loyalty for his native state, and no love for his birthplace." Friends warned him to "stay away from Denver."

William Gilpin turned his rifle over to the White House guards and reached Denver on May 27 to assume his new duties as Colorado's territorial governor. By June, 1861, he was reporting "a strong and malignant Secession-element, ably and secretly organized." He went to work at once to build up a strong pro-Union military organization.

Texas had seceded in February. It seemed likely that New Mexico would be drawn into the Confederacy. Many of the social and political leaders of California favored Secesh. Arizona leaned that way. And with Albert Sidney Johnston commanding the Army's Department of the Pacific, multiple treachery might be afoot. And the Mormons? Did they hate Johnston and slavery enough to turn down the lavish offers of the Western confederation's agents?

Colorado's first legislature met in September, 1861, created seventeen counties, chartered the city of Denver, enacted various laws, then resoundingly passed a resolution pledging loyalty to the Union.

But not so much as one Clark-Gruber five-dollar-piece was tacked on to that pledge. Either the Secesh victories at Bull Run and Wilson's Creek didn't bother them, or lobbying pressures were too great to extend loyalty beyond the heart to the pocketbook. Governor Gilpin wasn't to be deterred. He issued warrants on local merchants for $350,000 worth of military supplies, then established Camp Weld a mile and a half out of town; by October 1, the First Colorado Regiment of Volunteers was drilling there. John F. Slough, a pudgy attorney, was elected colonel.

Reverend John Chivington showed up at Camp Weld, too. He'd learned that his Secesh brother had signed on with Sterling Price in Missouri, been elevated to colonel, then died at Wilson's Creek. Colonel Slough offered Chivington the chaplaincy. The reverend shook his head and roared; he wanted a battle-line spot. Both Slough and Gilpin grinned approval. Within a week he was Major John Chivington.

Inevitably, some of Gilpin's warrant notes turned up in Washington for payment. The United States Treasury refused to honor them. Gilpin shrugged, blamed the confusions of Bull Run and the pauper aftermath of Buchanan's regime. Approval of his expenditures, he vowed, "comes from a high office in the Administration." Some of the merchants and bankers scowled and went into huddles; off to Washington went their petition for a new governor.

Then Brigadier General H. H. Sibley, C.S.A., formerly Captain Sibley of Fort Leavenworth, lulled their plaints. He was commanding the expeditionary force of Texas Rangers marching north into New Mexico. His spies and advance agents were already in Colorado, rallying "true Southerners and States'-righters" to the cause. After Santa Fe fell, the agents whispered Sibley would march to Denver, then west to conquer Utah, Nevada, and California.

Sibley and the Texans rode up the Rio Grande del Norte valley toward Albuquerque. Messengers skirted back trails past Fort Union and Santa Fe with dispatches from his Colorado spy network; more than a thousand Secesh fighting men wanted to join him, they reported, when he set the Lone Star standard atop Raton Pass. After that, the Mormons would be an easy victory because California Secesh brigades would be ready by that time to push in from the west. As for Union troops? General Sibley snickered. Why, wasn't his fussy, thumb-fumble brother-in-law Ed Canby in command at Fort Union? Anyway, hadn't Sibley himself supervised construction of those new gun—placements and powder rooms at Fort Union in 1859?

Colonel Edward Richard Sprigg Canby obliged the prediction by bobbling the Union strategy at the battle of Valverde. The Texans rode leisurely into Santa Fe, deployed among the courtesans and, for two delicious weeks, disrupted the Lenten season.

Meanwhile, following urgent appeals from Leavenworth, the First Colorado (soon to be immortalized in the state's history as "Gilpin's Pet Lambs") marched off toward Fort

Union. Crossing Raton Pass in bitter cold and through waist-high drifts, they reached the fort on March 10. Then, on March 22, despite countermanding orders from Canby's aides, Colonel Slough ordered his column south to attack Sibley at Santa Fe.

Major John Chivington and the advance column reached Glorieta Pass on the twenty-fifth. They captured a group of Sibley's scouts, including an ex-Denverite named Hall and a Lieutenant McIntyre, who had deserted to Sibley after Valverde. The prisoners admitted that Sibley's main column had left Santa Fe and would enter the south end of Glorieta next morning.

Chivington's troops engaged Sibley's advance patrols at Pigeon's Ranch on the twenty-sixth. Alexandre Valle, owner of the ranch, watched the battle from a bluff; describing the fighting preacher, he said: " 'E poot his 'ead down an' foight loike uh mahd bool." Both Slough and Sibley brought up their main forces that night. Then Slough decided to send Chivington, with a third of the First Colorado, over a mountain path to scout Sibley's rear.

On the afternoon of the twenty-seventh, while Slough and Sibley slugged it out in frontal attacks, Chivington's column discovered the Secesh wagon train and *remuda* parked at the base of cliffs near the south end of the pass. The Coloradans slipped and slid down a precipice, knocked out the small guard, burned the wagon train, then bayoneted six hundred horses and mules.

A messenger brought Sibley the news about dusk. Suddenly without supplies, ammunition, or horses, the invaders had but one course. Before dawn on the twenty-eighth, the Texans headed back toward Santa Fe.

Canby, meanwhile, had holed up in Fort Craig, south of Albuquerque. Slough sent messengers back to Fort Union to announce Chivington's feat and ask permission to "pursue and destroy" the fleeing Secesh. Canby, via semaphore from Craig, sent back a curt No. Colonel Slough promptly resigned his commission. Chivington was promoted on the spot to colonel of the First Colorado.

Yet he fared no better with Canby's regard for brother-in-law Sibley. One night in April, south of Santa Fe, Chivington's scouts saw Sibley and his officers frolicking at a ranch house dance while the Rangers engaged in industrious crap games and jug-squeezing on the grounds. Chivington drew up his cavalry, hurried over to Canby's command post and begged the privilege of capturing all the Secesh before dawn. Colonel Canby was downright annoyed. Night attacks, he squeaked, are always disastrous. General Sibley finished the evening's waltz in peace and "with love from Ed."

After a while, the Rangers buried their cannon outside Albuquerque and, with promises to return in a few months, limped home to Texas.

They didn't return. By May, a column of fifteen hundred Union troops from California showed across the desert, following a "display in force" at Yuma and Tucson. The C.S.A. dream of conquest of the West vanished; five regiments, hurriedly assembled at Fort Leavenworth to march to the relief of Fort Union and Colorado, could be rushed east to support Grant in the Tennessee campaign.

The battle of Glorieta Pass proved to be the "Gettysburg of the West." From Julesburg to the Golden Gate, the supporters of Secesh went underground. The C.S.A.'s agents dropped the campaign for a confederacy of the West and concentrated on stirring up insurrections among the Sioux, Comanche, Apache, and other Great Plains tribes.

Yet the fears persisted. On October 8, 1862, a Denver gunsmith named Morgan L. Rood wrote a letter about a friend who had fallen in with a "strong Secesh and, by pretending to be one himself, found out their whole plan in this Territory. They are holding private meetings and have large forces organized in by-places in the mountains and southern part of the Territory, and calculate to make a rise this Fall. . . . I never saw such a rush for repairing guns and pistols and enquiries for Colt's revolvers in my life. I have informed the Governor of it and he is making preparations for it but it may happen too soon, but if it does I am going to gif them a specimen of my shooting, if I don't get killed too soon. I am surrounded by traitors and would like to have this kept still for they would have revenge on me if they knew it."

While similar rumors circulated, William Green Russell and his brothers, whose discovery of gold on Little Dry Creek had precipitated the great gold rush of 1859, lit out for Georgia. On Fort Smith road in New Mexico, seventeen of the party came down with smallpox. A Lieutenant Shoup and his patrol herded them back to Fort Union, where they were committed as prisoners of war. Several months later, after taking an oath of allegiance to the United States, they were released and their property—including twenty-eight thousand dollars in gold—was restored. The Russells came back to Denver. Soon, however, two of the brothers rode east again. This time they reached Georgia. Their Colorado gold dust equipped a company of volunteers for the C.S.A.

But neither the Texas Rangers nor any other C.S.A. army

ever returned to Colorado. Down from the Virginia City and Pike's Peak mines, silver and gold ore streamed into the San Francisco and Denver mints to bolster Old Abe's credit for Union troops and ships. The C. S. A.'s agents concentrated on Indian rebellions. What changed the picture?

13.
THEY WON THE WEST

The leaders of the rebellion are hated in the North. The names of Jefferson Davis, of Cobb, Tombes, and Floyd are mentioned with execration by the very children. This has sprung from a true and noble feeling: from a patriotic love of national greatness and a hatred of those who, for small party purposes, have been willing to lessen the name of the United States.

ANTHONY TROLLOPE, *North America*

"Ta-da-da-ta-dadda-de-dit." He spattered Junction's call again, settled back on the stool and glowered out the window at the blue-backed sentry waddling down the platform; probably the same way he toed in across his potato patch back in Iowa. Clem shook his head. It'd be an even bet who got shot at first if that big Kraut ever got into a battle—his danged *Kameraden* or the Secesh. Depend on what he was looking at when the sergeant yelled the order!

The key hung there, deader than a January corn shuck. All day. Nary a clatter out of the westbound. Could mean a bad line storm. And it could mean guerrilla raiders again. He flipped the switch, began to pound another call. "W-e-s-t-p-o—" He stopped, shook his head and started over again. Things moved too fast. They'd gone high 'n mighty downstream these last two years. Now, big nosed and bumptious, it was K-a-n-s-a-s—C-i-t-y. Just went to show you what can happen in a war, if you play your cards slick. Not like poor Jeff Thompson. Gory glory, suppose it was old Jeff and some of his Swamp Foxes sneaking along out in the hills, snipping H. & St. J. telegraph wires. Jeff'd probably stand there crying while he gave the orders.

"K-a-n-s-a-s—C-i-t-y." He made the call again. Nary a whisper. Both lines cut off. Were Price and the C.S.A. roaring up from Arkansas again? A great day for it—July 4, 1863. Lee was halfway across Pennsylvania. Last thing the wire had said last night was about this General Pickett leading one helluva Secesh charge up some hill outside Gettysburg. Morgan, too, slashing around in Ohio and Indiana. Pemberton sat on that Vicksburg hilltop, thumbing his nose at Grant and the gunboats. So, why not Price, Thompson, Quantrill, and their drunken Indians howling back toward Springfield and St. Louis again? Everything was so upside-down crazy, a fellow didn't care much who won. Just stop it and come on home to see if we can patch up the pieces again—ever!

He frowned again at the receiver, twisted on the stool, and stared across the yards toward the flag drooping from the new staff on the post-office roof. July Fourth used to be Chinese firecrackers, dawn to midnight. No sleep for doctors for the next three nights, patching up the burns and wounds. A larruping, mile-long parade at noon; every fire-company man with his brass-'n'-leather helmet polished. Cannon banging away. Always some nitwit determined to bore a hole in an old anvil and shoot that off, too. Free barbecue that was worth sitting through the speeches to get at. And then, every Fourth of July night, go down along the riverbank to watch the rockets and Roman candles and set pieces throw rainbow curlecues across the sky and make those shadow patterns that little Lucy had always called "my river dragons."

And now? Clem snorted. One little firecracker pop and there'd be twenty bugles yawping and bawping and fifty-nine officers screaming out the door of the Patee House bar and three thousand Hunztlehaufs and Zimmermanns and Schluesserbergers in that Iowa and Illinois Cavalry blazing carbines at anything that wiggled, from a cat's whiskers up.

A shadow fell across the window. The station door creaked open. Clem didn't even bother to look up. Damn clodhoppers! His grandfather used to tell him about the Hessians in the Revolution and the way Generals Morgan and Arnold really smashed them in the big fight at Saratoga. But here they were again—in Union uniforms. Didn't know any more English than a jaybird—*ja, nein,* or a stupid headshake. This was it. July 4, 1863. Old Glory's day. *Ja! Nein!*

"Afternoon, Mister Huniker, sir."

Clem opened his mouth to grunt a "Hi," then straightened and turned slowly on the stool. That wasn't no low-down Iowa accent. It had a real twang to it. There was a red gleam through the wicket that he couldn't see very well against the light. It was a red shirt—a red flannel shirt. Couldn't be! The world was full of flannel shirts. Anyway, the Pony was dead; along with everything else worthwhile. Fellow had a mustache and long hair. He was grinning. Youngish looking.

"G'd afternoon to you, too." Clem came up to the wicket,

139

and squirreled his eyes. That hair and grin . . . "Billy!" He hollered it like a train whistle, swung the door wide, and threw his arms around the youngster. "Billy Cody. Man—a sight—a sight." He drew back, glowered toward the door. "It's all right fer you to be here?" he hissed. "You—you ain't with Jeff and—them?"

"Naw." Billy grinned and jerked a thumb down at his cavalry pants. "I'm Union. Ma's been pretty sick. I come back to Leavenworth a few months ago. Ridin' scout for the Red Legs before that. Somehow, I couldn't abide Secesh; not any more than Mr. Majors could. We've always been Free-Soilers, y'know."

"Wouldn't make a bit of difference, I guess." Clem stood with an arm grasped around the boy's shoulders. His hand clutched tight into the red shirt as though, somehow, through its contact the past just might return. "It's got so that's the first thing you ask somebody you haven't seen for a long time."

"Yes, sir. Guess it's that way all over. Fellows you used to rassle an' horse around with out shootin' at one another." He slid away from Clem's arm. "Guess—mebbe—that's why I asked for leave to come over and look around. I wanted to see how things are. You an' Mrs. Huniker's well, I hope?"

"Can see for yourself." Clem led the way back into the office. "You lay over with us tonight. Just—uh—one thing we don't mention. Lucy's husband took off with Jeff Thompson. Rest of the family's swung around real firm to the Union. We—we just don't talk war to home."

"Sure be a pleasure." Cody eased down in the corner chair. He'd grown a foot taller; shoulders and hips were filling out. "It makes you feel real old. Everybody's gone. I went down to the stables and didn't know a soul. Sign over on Canal Street says 'A. Majors Transportation Co.'; but it was closed up tight. I sure hoped you were still around. I kinda thought —well, with all this talk about startin' a Pacific railroad, mebbe there'd be some signs of it. I—I hoped they'd make you superintendent, I guess."

"Won't be any railroad out of St. Joe." Clem's eyes snapped. "Long as we live—St. Joe and me—guess we'll be sittin' right here on th' side switch. And poor Jeff's gonna take the blame for it."

"But, Mister Thompson—"

"I know. Jeff had the dreams. We all heard 'em—right down there where that clodhopper's pacin' sentry now. And every word he said was true—but not for St. Joe, not for St. Joe."

"Guess I don't understand."

"Flags and politics, boy." Clem pointed toward the post-office roof. "Pony was still running when it happened. Y'see . . ."

St. Joseph wasn't, for sure, any Republican-landslide town. There were more than two thousand slaves in the county the year the Pony Express began. That, as wealth was estimated in 1860, totaled to a cash value of almost $1,500,000. So, behind the bitterness and sudden death between Kansas and Missouri after 1855, consider that leering old despot, the $awbuck. It had much to do with local voting in November, 1860, when Bell, representing the Constitution Union party jerry-built from Whig and Know-Nothing arch-conservatives, took 1,287 votes. Senator Douglas' regular Democrats snuggled close with 1,226 votes. Breckenridge, the Secesh choice, wandered in with only 614 votes. The ballots for Lincoln were hardly worth counting, 100 or so.

That vote pretty much reflected public opinion along Missouri's frontier. It stood right up and said, "Home rule. Keep Federal government and your East-South fight away from us. Leave us alone." Nobody was the least bit surprised when, in the late spring of 1861, the mayor and Common Council called an emergency meeting to pass the resolution that neither the Union nor the Secesh could fly its flags within the city limits. Matters were just that bad in Missouri. It seemed the most logical thing to do.

When the South Carolinians took Fort Sumter and Lincoln called for volunteers, most of western Missouri put its foot down. Governor Claiborne Jackson refused to turn the state militia out to fight for the Federal Government. The St. Louis Republicans and Germans jawed back, then organized their own militia. Governor Jackson appointed ex-Governor Sterling Price his commander-in-chief; the down-staters appointed Nathaniel Lyons and Franz Sigel.

That was when St. Joseph's City Council passed the ordinance against raising either the Stars and Stripes or any of the Southern states' flags inside the city limits. But J. L. Bittinger had just moved in from St. Louis to become city postmaster, as the Lincoln appointee. Bittinger vowed that the city ordinance didn't apply to him. Up over the post office rose the Stars and Stripes, as usual.

Jeff Thompson had stepped out as mayor, and gone back to his law and real-estate practice. His office was across the street from the post office. When a crowd formed and began pointing up at the post-office roof, Jeff joined them. Some told that he pleaded with the crowd to go away, then went in and argued with Bittinger. Whatever the truth, quick-tempered Jeff finally led the way to the roof and personally hauled the flag down. He helped cut it into bits, stood by while the flagpole was chopped down, then led the parade down to the wharf to throw both flag shreds and pole into the Missouri.

It was probably the all-time high-water mark for home rule in Missouri. The Republic of St. Joseph, which logically describes Jeff's attitude for the day, lasted just long enough for Bittinger and the more sedate citizenry to get word to Leavenworth. The cavalry clattered in shortly after Jeff and a few followers had ridden off to join Jackson and Price at Springfield. St. Joseph went under martial law pronto.

The Pony Express was still running. Now, even in Washington eyes, the H. & St. J.'s run across Missouri became vitally important. General Lyons' death at the battle of Wilson's Creek turned a Union victory into shameful defeat. Jackson and Price marched back into Jefferson City and Springfield. The C.S.A. moved in reinforcements of Texas and Louisiana regiments in natty gray uniforms, hauling cannon Floyd had "arranged" for them. Jefferson Davis and the C.S.A. bade Missouri hearty welcome to the ranks, but denied both Price and Jeff Thompson commissions as commanding officers.

John C. Frémont strutted onstage in St. Louis as Lincoln's new commander-in-chief in the West. He lasted a hectic three months, was credited with passing out millions of dollars' worth of "boodle," issued an emancipation proclamation three years before the White House, then was bounced after Mrs. Frémont threatened Lincoln with a confederacy of the West in which "The Pathfinder" would be dictator.

Through it all, the H. & St. J. rattled desperately. Rail lines in south Missouri were changing hands every other month as battle lines swayed between Jefferson City and Lexington. (During the battle of Lexington, one of Waddell's sons was killed and the family mansion was fired. Waddell himself was forced to take the oath of allegiance to the Union.)

As the fastest Union supply line for Kansas and the Central Route, the H. & St. J. became a vital target for the C.S.A. Orders to put it out of commission came up from Alabama in the spring of 1861. Slashed telegraph lines and loosened rail joints during May and June signaled the troubles ahead. The Monroe station, plus seventeen passenger and freight cars, was burned by the Secesh on July 9. Three weeks later, a company of the Jackson-Price militia kidnaped Colonel Joshua Gentry, president of the H. & St. J., and demanded the line's shutdown as his ransom. Unionists retaliated by kidnaping the mayor of Hannibal and six other "known Secessionists," dumping them into a boxcar and announcing they would be shot unless Colonel Gentry was "promptly released." (Everybody got home safely after a few days. The H. & St. J. kept running.)

Potshooting at trains became so commonplace that barricades of boiler steel were built around the engineer cabs, and coach windows were boarded up save for narrow slits. When C.S.A. raiders burned one of the railroad's bridges, Union commanders sent troops out to levy repair costs—"cash or bayonet"—from planters and merchants in the neighborhood who were known to be Jackson-Price supporters. Special accounts of bridge repairs and levies were kept by the quartermaster of the Army of Missouri. Colonel U. S. Grant commanded some of the troops hustled in from Illinois and Iowa during the summer of 1861 to patrol H. & St. J.'s right of way, and assure the "green ball" for Central Route mail and Pony Express "tissues."

"That's the way it was—and that's the way it is." Clem finished his story of war on the H. & St. J., then leaned forward to flick on the telegraph switch again.

"Gee whiz." Billy Cody hunched on the edge of the chair, fists clenched. "And all the time we thought we were doin' th' real job out there on the run. Why, we'd never had no reason to ride atall if it hadn't been for you and Add Clark and the rest of you railroaders."

"It's teamwork." Clem tensed over the telegraph, hammered Junction's call again, and paused. The clacker hung mute. He tried again. "K-a-n-s-a-s—C-i-t-y." Nary a flicker. "Teamwork," he repeated with a sigh. "Just like this thing here. I can holler and hammer my arm off. It doesn't do the least durn bit of good unless th' line's all in one piece and there's somebody on the other end to work with you."

"I guess"—the youngster stared at the floor and spoke haltingly—"mebbe that's why I could never go along on this Secesh stuff. Out there runnin' that trail, you got to realize that you wouldn't get nowhere at all without teamwork. No Indians or holdup men ever work solo. They come at you in bunches. Th' way I figger it, th' same thing could happen to states and mebbe countries. You get one fellow won't play straight—well, say like that Floyd—and bang, what good are you alone? With everybody, it's Union or bust."

Clem stared at the boy. "Got a head in among them muscles, ain't you?" he said. "Fellow could even get a mite religious about it all, same way Mr. Majors did. 'Justice is mine.' Floyd got his. Ran out of the top Secesh command at

Fort Donelson like a rat when Grant closed in. So high an' mighty, he couldn't afford to get mixed up in a surrender; passed the job on to Buckner. That was too much even for Jeff Davis. He yanked Floyd's commission."

Billy nodded. "Kinda does good down inside to hear that. I'll bet he's still pussyfootin', though."

"Well, might be." Clem's jaw jutted. "He's up against shrewder competition than Russell—or even Grant—this time. The devil knows a lot more tricks than John Buchanan Floyd. Yup. Virginia politicians put Floyd right back in business after Davis fired him. Made him a major general in the state militia—right in there with his buddy Joe Johnston. Guess th' Lord decided enough was enough. Floyd's dead, they say. Anyway, he disappeared right after Albert Sidney Johnston got killed at the Corinth battle."

Billy's hands clenched again. "Them two dead, nobody will ever find out the truth about that Mormon War an' the mess Russell got into. Somebody's got a pretty good idea, though. About the time word got out to us fellows on the Wyoming division that Russell was in jail, the Utah boys passed on the story about a big holler against Floyd in Salt Lake. Said there was a ceremony and speeches, an' then, no more Camp Floyd. They renamed it for Senator Crittenden."

"Heh." Clem sniffed. " 'Let-us-have-peace' Crittenden. More politicians runnin' around with the 'only pure snake oil.' Crittenden was going to patch up everything real dandy. What happened? One of his sons is a Union general. Another one's a Secesh general. And equally bad.

"Nope, it ain't the patch-up boys who get the job done. It's th' dreamers and th' daredevils. And, most of the time, all they ever get out of it is the satisfaction. Look at 'em. Russell stony broke. Fellow said he saw him over in New York a few months ago, lookin' as though he couldn't afford a shave. Jeff Thompson hiding out in Arkansas; a price on his head and people calling him 'that sneaky, damn Swamp Fox.' Majors up in Nebraska City, runnin' a piddly little freighter business."

"But she worked!" Billy's hands tensed. "The Pony proved the route! Now the telegraph's using it. And that Collis Huntington out in San Francisco—th' lawyer that used to send so much stuff on the Pony—is fixin' up with some fellow named Stanford out there to build a Pacific railroad right along our trail. But, golly, now the whole Overland belongs to Ben Holladay, lookin' as all-fired important as the devil himself—and actin' it. And—and Mister Majors whackin' a broken-down ox train outuv Nebraska City. I just don't—"

"There ain't no logic in a lot of things in this life, son." Clem sighed. "Preachers been sayin' for a long time now how you get full justice in heaven. Every oncet awhile, somethin' like what happened to Floyd comes along to make us think mebbe they're right. Anyway, I suspect that someday somehow th' truth will be told about what you fellows—"

"Us," Billy said sharply. "You railroaders was as much a part of it as any of us."

"Thanks. Thanks, son, more than you'll realize yet awhile. Day's going to come in this country when a man'll be prouder to have his name linked with the Pony Express than he would be to be a general or—yes—even a Ben Holladay. We dreamed big on the railroad an' here in St. Joe, like everybody else. But I betcha we're just as gone as Russell and Majors and Waddell. Jeff did it, dang him, with that bad temper. Sure they'll build a railroad to the Pacific. But no senator's going to locate the east terminal at a town that tore th' flag off th' post office. No, siree. They'll move her up alongside the telegraph. Them Hickenloopers an' Schraftheimers an' th' rest of them Iowa and Illinois foreigners will see t' that. They was loyal to the party. Us Missourians was a lot of damn Democrats. All we did was open th' Central Route, prove it with the Pony, an' hold it open so's Abe could get enough gold and silver out to keep his paper money afloat."

Clem gave the telegraph desk a kick and stared out the window. "You wait," he gloomed. "The Union wins this war, they'll move everything we did up into Iowa. Nebraska City or Omaha will be what St. Joe dreamed t'be—the gateway to the West. Them big trains Jeff talked about, th' warehouses! Yes, and they'll swipe that other thing Jeff or Russell or somebody used to talk about. You heard about young Mr. Davis and his railway-mail car?"

"Mail car?" Bill shook his head.

"Well, this Davis—William A. is his full moniker—got appointed assistant to Bittinger over at the post office. Crazy damn war. He's a Virginian, like Jeff Thompson. Got transferred up here from Richmond. Only, like a lot of folks down there, too, this Davis preferred the Union to Secesh. So, when the Pony got goin', he went as daffy as some of the rest of us and stayed up nights worryin' how it could be improved. Really wasn't any affair of his first along, because Floyd and Holt and th' Secesh, of course, held th' mail contract to the Ox-bow. But just the same, he figgered, there should be some way, some— Hullo, Betsy! Listen!" He held a hand up, swung around and stared away to the hills. "It's

145

her," he howled, and pointed away toward the wall of smoke jutting up behind the Patee House cut. "By golly, something's got through. Come on. Mebbe you can see for yourself."

They rushed out the door, almost colliding with the sentry, musket in hand, who was also glowering up the high iron. Again the sound rolled in. *"Boooo—hoooo. Booo—hooo."*

"That's her. That's her." Clem's grin even included the soldier. "You can see it for yourself, Billy."

"Dos voz logomotifs, yaah?" The sentry frowned at them, musket wavering. "Should callink korporal?"

"Sure." Clem beamed. "Go ahead. Call him. It's a fine train. He should see it, too."

"Korporal uf d' gu-uard." The bellow echoed across the yard. "Korporal uf d' gu-uard." A finger brushed against the trigger. The explosion kicked the gun from his hands. He reached down, picked it up, pulled to attention, and stared stiffly away toward the Patee House. A bugle blared. Down the Patee House steps clattered a corporal and a half-dozen men, on the double, guns cocked.

"Good exercise." Clem beamed and beckoned Billy up the platform. "Only way they get to sweat out th' beer. Like I was saying, Mr. Davis figured time could be saved if you were to have a separate railroad car for the mail, with clerks ridin' in there sortin' letters out for each station. You see, it used to take hours sometimes, when Pony finally did get to the part of the U. S. Mail, to sort Pony tissues out from the rest of St. Joe's letters. He drew up plans for th' car. Washington finally approved it last year and two of 'em was built down at the Hannibal yards. They work real good. Well, look for yourself. There it is—America's first railway-mail car!"

The engine, grim and blunt as a Mississippi gunboat in its steel barricade, chuffed through the cut. Behind it swayed a bright-yellow car sheathed solid as a freighter van except for a barricaded window at one end and a high center door. Beneath the window, in tall black letters, stood the insignia U.S. MAIL.

Billy gulped, thought again of Majors with his shabby ox train, Russell needing a shave, proud, gruff Waddell signing an oath of allegiance at gunpoint.

"Don't look like she's shot up at all," Clem mused, then grinned back down the platform. The corporal and patrol had arrived, panting, had taken in the situation, and were howling at the sentry phrases of such ancient Saxon lineage that no translation was necessary from San Francisco saloons to Hammerfest *Bierhäuser*.

The engineer creaked his steel door open, ran a kerchief across his face. "You know that Pershing, section foreman over at Laclede?"

Clem nodded. "He hold you up at gunpoint and make you two hours late?"

"Held us up, nothin'. If it hadn't been for him we wouldn't be here. Twister through there last night. Knocked a half-mile of track out of line. He rounded up his crew right afterward, worked all night. They finally got us through."

"Really a most refreshing layoveh." The voice echoed crisply from the railway-mail-car door. Billy stared up at the tall youngster lolling there. He was wearing high black shoes and a checked suit under his canvas work apron. Sounded English. "This Pershing chap has a wife who can really cook. But, love us, one little tyke of theirs—Johnny, I believe they call him—had never heard of taffy. I've a mind, y'know, to get my hand back in and make them a batch. After all, we're heah because of them, eh?"

"Paste some taffy on th' telegraph lines, too, Fred." Clem grinned. "Darn wires been out all day. I want you to meet one of your granddaddies."

"Granddaddy? Oh, no. He's too young. Furthermore—"

Clem hooted. "Granddaddy to your mail car, anyway. This here is Billy Cody, one of the Pony Express riders. He was right here the day she started. Billy, that frustrated cook up there is Fred Harvey, America's first railway-mail clerk."

"Nothing frustrated at all." Harvey beamed. "I mean to get back to it, too, soon as this blinking war's over. Delighted to meet one of your noble corps, Mr. Cody. You know, you fellows are as famous already as this Daniel Boone. I almost said 'as famous as Grant,' but after yesterday, I rather doubt it, eh?"

"After yesterday, what?" Clem straightened. "We been cut off here all day like we was atop Pike's Peak. What's happened?"

"Oh, I say. I'm sorry. Everyone's very excited. Secesh finally got a comeuppance, it seems. Lincoln's announced a great victory over Lee at some Pennsylvania hamlet—umm—Gettysburg. Yes, that's the place. And bless me if old Grant didn't answer right back from Vicksburg with the news that Pemberton has surrendered."

Billy put his hand on Clem's shoulder. The fingers squeezed tight. "That means," he shouted, "Union's got th' whole Mississippi clear down past New Orleans."

"Precisely." Harvey beamed. "Exactly what General Scott urged them to do in 1861. Bottle up C.S.A. behind the Ohio and Old Miss, then proceed to throttle 'em. They're on the defensive now, for the first time."

"Yup." Clem nodded back. Then, for a reason he couldn't explain, he felt himself turning and his eyes focusing out toward the sunset glory of Kansas across the swirling brown river. He knew that Billy had turned with him and, somehow, that Fred Harvey was staring off there, too.

"Well," he said for all of them after a minute, "I guess you're Union now. I guess mebbe pretty soon we can team up on you again—together." He squeezed Billy's arm. "Gonna talk future at home tonight. Even Lucy will want to hear about this."

14.
EXPRESSLY ABOUT PONIES

by Frank C. Robertson

Much has been written about the Pony Express riders, little about their horses. These unsung and unwilling heroes are worthy of notice. Probably without exception they objected to being broken to ride. Yet, once under the saddle, they gave their all. Many a rider owed his life to their speed, endurance, and gallantry.

In 1860, Russell, Majors & Waddell brought in fine Eastern horses that had blood lines, and were tractable and gentle. They didn't fill the bill; they lacked the toughness to cope with the dreary desert sand of summer and the heavy snow of winter. Ficklin, Egan, and Roberts discarded them and turned to what were generally known as "native" horses. These came from many parts of the West, and were called by many names. They had one thing in common: they were bred up from Indian cayuse or mustang ponies and were used to desert or mountain conditions.

Many of the horses used on the west end of the line came from California, descendants of the hardy ponies, often with Arabian blood, that had been used by the Mexican dons. Since the West was full of horse-traders, it is possible some of them came from the Northwest, where blooded animals had been bred with the tough, intelligent cayuses developed by those superb horsemen the Nez Percé and Cayuse Indians. These horses were so good that efforts were made to establish distinct breeds. The Oregon George horse was such a one. In other places and times they were called Steeldust, for the famous Texas racer. No horses were ever better fitted for the desert and mountains of the West. They resembled the modern quarter horse, but had harder hoofs and greater endurance. Although Westerners called them simply cayuses, they were larger than the typical Indian cayuse.

Porter Rockwell is said to have imported Kentucky mares and stallions. Some escaped to the desert and bred with mustangs. Their offspring were being caught on the Nevada desert as late as 1900. No better horses ever wore a saddle.

Even blooded animals have a way of adapting themselves to their environment, but not in a single generation. In the early days, the Mormon Church invested thousands of dollars in stallions and brood mares. They were turned loose on Antelope Island, in the middle of Salt Lake. Here, reports tell, they became "nimble, wiry, and sure-footed by continually traveling over the rough trails of the island from the time they were foaled until they were grown. It became second nature for them to jump up and down precipitous places four or five feet high. . . . They neither stumbled nor fell, no matter how rough the country or how fast they went. . . . In many ways they seemed to be as intelligent as human beings." Possibly some of these horses were used by the Pony Express. But we are told they would escape their riders and go back to the island whenever they could.

No horse has ever surpassed the native cayuse or mustang in intelligence or hardihood. And the spirit of the devil was born in most of them. They would favor a rider all day while they waited the opportunity to catch him off guard, then buck him off in a pile of rocks. The mixed breeds were larger and more dependable, but they, too, had to be unkinked on a frosty morning, and would buck at the drop of a rider's hat.

None were easy to ride. Unlike the "locked-in" saddles of today's rodeo riders, the Express rider's saddle was a mere hull, consisting of a wooden tree covered with thin leather, over which hung the four-pocketed *mochila,* held together by a leather rigging on which the rider sat. The best riders rode by balance; the others stayed aboard by main strength and awkwardness. Since a man's life might depend on his pony at any hour, the boys had to learn to ride. So, most of the pony boys were bronco-busters.

Nick Wilson tells of his first job breaking horses for Doc Faust. He was only sixteen, but as a test he was asked to ride a horse that had thrown the best riders in Faust's employ. Nick rode the horse.

Horses wore out, were killed or stolen, and constantly had to be replaced. The job of breaking them was usually assigned to the stationkeepers, who had time on their hands. One of the best of these was Pete Neece, keeper of the Willow Creek Station. Neece considered a horse broken "when a rider could lead it out of the stable without getting his head kicked off."

Characteristic of these horses were their flint-hard hoofs. For generations they had run at top speed over the rockiest ground in the country. If they threw a shoe, it did not matter. In winter they were seldom shod because snowballs forming inside the shoes made traveling difficult. Bucking snow is a natural, seldom an acquired, art. The heavier, more domesticated breeds seldom acquire it. They try to lunge through a snowdrift and quickly give themselves out. The mustang or cayuse worked his way through, pawing when necessary. And there were plenty of snowdrifts to buck along the Pony Express route in the wintertime. Besides, these animals had an instinct for finding a trail that kept many a rider from getting lost in darkness.

The Express ponies did not weigh over a thousand pounds, a tremendous advantage when plodding through the deep, hot sand in the summertime, when the heat and sand and alkali dust were unbearable.

In winter, snow lay deep in the passes, and blizzards raged. At times even these hardy ponies gave out after hours of bucking snow up to their bellies. Frozen ears and noses were common. There were no airplanes or helicopters to spot them when they were marooned without food or shelter. Only skill, native intelligence, and resourcefulness brought them through.

The horses endured as much privation as the riders. At least one rider has gone on record as stating that he preferred the mountains, with all their hazards, to the heat and sand of the desert. It is likely that he was thinking of his horse more than himself. There is a unique companionship between horse and man, where the life of each depends on the other, that the city dweller can never understand.

15.
WELDED IN STEEL

Promontory Point, Utah, six miles west of Ogden, was clear and cold on May 10, 1869. Biting winds off the Wasatch had slicked ice on the streets. The Californians slithered, sploshed, cussed in the block's journey from their sidetracked Pullmans to the village's five saloons.

Ponderous Leland Stanford, president of the Central Pacific, and his partner, Mark Hopkins, held aloof in their private car until a delegation of Mormon bishops filed out of carriages, past the coolie gangs screaming to get shoulders under these final rails and crossties for the transcontinental railroad. Stanford welcomed the Mormons aboard, grunted regrets that Brigham Young could not attend in person, and offered alibis for Collis Huntington's "urgent business trip" to New York and fat Charles Crocker's "unfortunate confinement" in bawdy, gourmandizing Sacramento.

Stiff as the car's damask drapes, the conversation rasped until the coolies started to cheer, the lesser California nabobs roared back out of the saloons, and the locomotive whistle echoing in from the east drowned anything less than a shout. Glumly, Stanford lifted the lid of a little chest on the table beside him, allowed the Mormons a peek at the gold spike. He sighed, tucked the chest under his arm, and waddled out.

The Union Pacific locomotive ten yards down the track gleamed like a steel-driver's hammer and had a new yellow Pullman in tow. Groaning like a lovesick monster, a Central Pacific "hog" moved out on the high iron and headed toward it. Cameramen jostled with newspaper correspondents, bullwhackers, Chinese and Irish work gangs for a clear view. Dapper Thomas C. Durant hopped down from the yellow Pullman and hurried, grinning, to pump hands with Stanford and Hopkins. A Mormon spoke brusquely. Heads were bowed. The voice that intoned was drowned in the asthmatic hiss and groan of the monsters. A telegrapher, watching from the station window, tapped to the waiting world: "We have got done praying, and the spike is about to be presented."

Several other spikes appeared; Leland Stanford gave each a hammer pat. The United States of America was welded, from the Atlantic to the Pacific, by steel along the Pony Trail. Within ten minutes, factory whistles in San Francisco and New York yelled the astonishing news. Poet Bret Harte in San Francisco inquired: "What was it the engines said, pilots touching,—head to head . . ."

Not mentioned among the "prominent people present" in the newspaper stories next day was a passenger from Durant's Pullman. Alexander Majors had come to witness this final ceremony of his lifelong dream. He had no official part. Since the dissolution of Russell, Majors & Waddell, he and his son Benjamin had worked as supply contractors on the Union Pacific's construction from Omaha to the Promontory junction.

"It was regarded at that time," he would recall in *Seventy Years on the Frontier*, "as the greatest feat in railroad enterprise that had ever been accomplished in this or any other country, and it was a day that will be remembered during the lifetime of all that were present to witness this great iron link between the oceans, Atlantic and Pacific. My calling as a freighter and overland stager having been deposed by the building of telegraph lines and the completion of a continental railway, I was compelled to look after a new industry, and as the silver mining at that time was just beginning to develop in Utah, I chose that as my next occupation."

Of the leading participants in the Pony Express, Majors was the only one to witness this victory for the Central Route —a victory considered so meaningful at the time that the westbound construction was named *Union* Pacific, and the eastbound was called *Central* Pacific. Russell was still in New York, fallen now to peddling a patent-medicine "cure" for neuralgia. Waddell, broken in health, was at his home in Lexington, Missouri. John Buchanan Floyd, spurned even by the Confederacy after his skulking treachery at Fort Donelson, finally died in August, 1863 (the records graciously say, "of the fevers"). Jacob Thompson, Buchanan's secretary of the interior, had directed Copperhead and Knights of the Golden Circle plots from Canada during the last years of the war, and was finally arrested in Portland, Maine, but pardoned by Lincoln. He was now in hiding in Europe, since evidence pointed to him as one of the group that had plotted Lincoln's assassination. General Joseph Johnston, currently in seclusion, was finally developing such an interest in rapid transportation that President Cleveland would appoint him Federal Commissioner of Railroads in 1885.

Of all the "great builders" and new millionaires staring at the gold spike that day, none knew this full story as Majors did, or realized the debt they owed Russell, Majors & Waddell and the red-and-blue-clad youngsters who proved the Central Route in 1860/61. If the United States Government had subsidized the Pony Express in 1860, Russell and Majors and Waddell might now have been the ones posing those shiny new hammers for the photographers.

It wasn't a fool's dream. Ben Holladay had sold Central Overland to Wells Fargo for millions and stalked off to new conquests in the Pacific Northwest. Edward Creighton had sold part of his stock in Pacific Telegraph for $850,000; the two hundred thousand dollars worth he still held would doubtlessly earn him millions more in a few years. The Union Pacific and Central Pacific promoters—Crocker, Hopkins, Durant, and the rest—had, without expenditure of a single dollar of their own, built their stock capitalization to $139,000,000.

Inspired by the engineering imagination of Theodore Dehone Judah in Sacramento, in 1859—the year when Majors' trucking business was most lucrative—a small group organized: Leland Stanford, lawyer and grocery clerk; Charles Crocker, dry-goods seller; Mark Hopkins, accountant for a hardware store; and Collis P. Huntington, who ran that store. Infected with Judah's vision of a railroad across the Sierra Nevada, they had all become millionaires. The Union Pacific group had done the same thing. Majors at the same time in 1858 had greater financial resources. He, too, could have organized a railroad.

At that time, Russell had done his best to raise money, fighting, without fully realizing it, an implacable enemy in John B. Floyd. When more was known about him, Floyd had been denounced for transferring Federal war materials from Northern arsenals to the South. Best known were the arms he sent to South Carolina and Texas in 1859–60. Majors had never trusted him. He had simply hoped that Russell could do something in Washington. However, Buchanan's Cabinet had met that July 10 of 1860, and had done nothing about the mail route.

Later, a congressional investigation had indicated that Floyd had personally profited from the Russell, Majors & Waddell contracts. But no direct, conclusive evidence was ever made public. Russell had admitted having secured and disposed of the Indian Trust Fund bonds—but he could not locate them. He, Godard Bailey, and Floyd had been indicted. Floyd had refused to come back to Washington from Virginia. Bailey, too, had slunk south.

Thomas P. Akers, from Lexington, former pastor of the Methodist Episcopal Church, member of the Thirty-fourth

Congress and attorney for Russell, had declared: "It is firmly believed that Floyd sent Bailey to Mr. Russell.... It is sufficient to say that this act of flagrant injustice has been traced to the President who seeks to screen the deformities of a rotten and fallen administration by offering up Mr. Russell as a victim of popular clamor. . . . In a word, if it were possible to drag to light the doings of the administration, the evidence would be as clear as noonday that the President and his Cabinet ministers have deliberately spread their meshes to victimize and entangle Mr. Russell."

The historian H. H. Bancroft believed Russell had been lured into a trap by Floyd. He said, in his *Chronicles of the Builders*: "Russell . . . fell into difficulty—if, indeed, it were not a trap set for him by the friends of the Southern Route . . . he was induced to take $830,000 in bonds of the Interior Department, as a loan, and giving as security acceptances on the War Department furnished him by Secretary Floyd, a part of which were not yet due."

Meanwhile, Russell, on March 28, 1861, added up what the government owed Russell, Majors & Waddell, as follows:

For freights withheld in 1857	$ 655,550
For interest, three years, 12% paid by firm	235,998
For losses in 1857 train	300,000
For interest on same, three years	108,000
For freights withheld by Government for 1860-61	50,000
Total:	$ 1,349,548

Waddell and Majors had stripped themselves of their possessions. Majors lost more in other deeds of trust. Thus he ended his career as government freighter, stagecoach operator, and financier. He never criticized his partners publicly. His own account shows much self-restraint. Under more favorable conditions, with the right associates, he might have established a railroad. He had all the know-how. His memoirs show that he had been thinking about the problem a good part of his life. In chapter XXXV of *Seventy Years on the Frontier*, entitled "How English Capitalists Got a Foothold," he draws conclusions that are not for the English alone and that indicate that his Pony Express might easily have grown into the first and one of the most successful of the transcontinental railroads.

Majors saw how the government gave away land to the railroads for the purpose of building roads, whose promoters offered bonds of all kinds, using the money to build roads. The railroads made vast fortunes out of watered stock, then collected hundreds of millions from the sale of the grant lands awarded them by the government, lands that had not cost one cent, not even for taxes. These rails would run through virgin land for thousands of miles. Wherever a railroad company thought proper it could lay out towns and cities, and sell the lots at fancy prices. This was the destiny of the lands, the wilderness that the Pony Express had opened first for the "talking wires" and now for the steel rails.

Such quick fortunes are almost impossible to believe, even today. The trifle that the Pony Express cost was minute in comparison. These were the events Majors had watched. He had seen the opportunities in railroading. Now it was too late. Floyd and the Secesh plotters had seen to that.

The locomotives belched great, steamy sighs of content, whistled their spent love, and backed away. Mr. Stanford bowed to the Mormon bishops and waddled back toward his car. The pianos clanked in the saloons again. Alexander Majors crinkled his eyes toward the Wasatch peaks. Perhaps somewhere up there a silver lode waited for him, as it had for Ben Holladay in the Ophir Mine. Whatever . . . His hand touched the shabby Pony Express Bible in his coat pocket.

"Thy will be done," said Alexander Majors, and strode back toward the train.

16.
THE KID GROWS UP

Of all the four hundred or more youngsters who carried the mail for the Pony Express, the one whose name became known around the world was William F. Cody, "Buffalo Bill."

Youngest of the riders, Billy Cody set a record with his nonstop ride of 322 miles. And in the world at large he went the farthest on the road to fame. But the fame was not achieved through accident. It came because Cody was able by superb showmanship to portray through his Wild West Show the real Old West, abounding in life and color.

Some believe that the Buffalo Bill who was hero-worshiped by the masses was only a creation of the pens of Buntline, Ingraham, and Burke. It is true that he was lionized in dime novels and through extravagant publicity, in which he was credited with outlandish feats that he did not perform. But those who knew Buffalo Bill intimately assert that he did not boast. He was a real frontiersman. He was the Great Showman, who rode and shot and roped with the best of 'em before the crowned heads and presidents of two continents. He gripped and held the public's imagination.

Folks saw him riding at the head of his dashing Congress of Rough Riders of the World. They were charmed by his fine physique, his superb horsemanship and marksmanship. Cody was always accepted as an equal, on scout duty or elsewhere. He was a natural gentleman, able to adjust himself to a hunting camp, a ranch bunkhouse, a New York club or an English lord's castle. His audiences knew that the men and women in his Wild West Show, especially during its early years, were cowboys, marksmen, Indians, and riders who were acting the experiences they had known on the Western frontier.

After Cody quit riding the Pony Express, he took part, it is said, in some border jayhawking into Missouri. Then, for a time, he carried messages to wagon trains, and worked as a teamster and scout. After his mother's death, he enlisted, in 1864, in the Seventh Kansas Cavalry and was put on scout duty. Next he served as chief of scouts for the Fifth Cavalry under General Eugene Carr.

Cody married Louisa Frederici, promising to settle down and become an innkeeper. He soon found that he could not stand to be confined by a town business, and returned to the plains to work. The Kansas Pacific Railroad hired him to supply meat for construction crews. According to his count, Cody shot 4,280 bison on this contract, thus earning the nickname of Buffalo Bill.

Because of his great skill as a hunter, Buffalo Bill was asked to guide many parties that came West to hunt. In 1872, he guided Grand Duke Alexis of Russia, lending him his pet buffalo gun, Lucretia Borgia, and his expert hunting horse, Buckskin Joe. The flattered Grand Duke gave Buffalo Bill a fur coat, and cuff links and a scarf pin studded with diamonds and rubies.

During another hunting party, James Gordon Bennett, editor of the *New York Herald,* became so impressed with Cody's skill and personality that he titled him the "beau ideal of the plains," then invited him to New York, all expenses paid. Cody went, but when he was offered a salary of five hundred dollars a week to play the part of Buffalo Bill in one of Ned "Know-Nothing" Buntline's adaptations, he refused.

Back in Nebraska, Cody went on an Indian campaign in the vicinity of Fort McPherson, and performed so remarkably as a guide that he was awarded the Congressional Medal of Honor on May 22, 1872. (Years later, Congress recalled the medal on the ground that Cody was of civilian, not military, standing, at the time he performed such noteworthy service!)

Buntline kept begging him to go on the stage. Finally, Cody took "Texas Jack" Omohundro to Chicago to take part in a play called *The Scouts of the Prairie*. The acting in the rough-and-tumble melodrama was said to be terrible, but Cody's naturalness won the audiences. So, despite the critics' continued "pans," eager thousands went to see Buffalo Bill. The play went on from Chicago to St. Louis and New York. When it closed in June, 1873, Cody had cleared six thousand dollars.

He decided then to leave Buntline and organize his own theatrical company. For eight years he continued on the stage. Probably no other actor ever switched back and forth so rapidly from play-acting to the real thing—at the close of each theater season he would rush to the West as a hunting guide, or would scout for the Army.

In July, 1876, following Custer's catastrophe at the battle of the Little Big Horn, Buffalo Bill scouted for General Merritt near War Bonnet Creek. There he met Chief Yellow Hand in a hand-to-hand fight, then killed and scalped him. The struggle made headlines across the country.

In 1877, Cody and his old friend Major Frank North, of the Pawnee Scouts, bought two large cattle ranches on Dismal River in Nebraska. Cody established his headquarters on an acreage at North Platte, and named it Scout's Rest. There, after staging an outdoor show for a Fourth of July celebration in North Platte in 1882, he decided to launch a big outdoor traveling show. Hence, the "Wild West, Rocky Mountain and Prairie Exhibition" opened at the fair grounds in Omaha on May 17, 1883. At the climax, a Pony Express rider dashed through the grounds, followed by a Deadwood coach being pursued by Indians. Close behind were galloping scouts.

The next year Cody teamed up with the actor Nate Salsbury, with whom he had discussed an outdoor show some years earlier. Salsbury was just the person Cody needed as manager. Various experts, well-known horsemen and plainsmen, and one hundred Indians were added to the cast immediately. The show played to overflow audiences.

At this time, the Western-range cattle boom was reaching its peak. Newspapers, books, and prospectuses published in America, Great Britain, and France kept the public in a fever of excitement over profits to be made on range cattle. Young men and old dreamed of life on the Great Plains. No wonder that Buffalo Bill's cowboys and cowgirls straight from Western ranches were greeted with admiration. They were from the land of adventure where heroes were made overnight!

According to Julia Cody Goodman, Mark Twain saw the show twice and wrote Cody as follows: "It brought vividly back the breezy wild life of the plains and the Rocky Mountains. . . . Your Pony Express-man was as tremendous an interest to me yesterday as he was twenty-three years ago when he used to come whizzing by from over the desert with his war news; and your bucking horses were even painfully real to me as I rode one of those outrages once for nearly a quarter of a minute. . . ."

That winter, the same "dangerous gallop of a Pony Express rider" thrilled audiences at Madison Square Garden in New York. In March, 1887, the Wild West Show sailed for Great Britain, where Buffalo Bill became "the lion of the London social season." The tall, handsome frontiersman attended garden parties, dinners, festivals, athletic performances, and many other events. Early visitors to his camp included Prime Minister Gladstone, the Prince and Princess of Wales, and other court members.

When Queen Victoria requested a special performance, Buffalo Bill obliged at once. The Queen brought with her to the grounds many of Europe's royalty, then in London, for her jubilee. Cody took these visitors for rides in the old Concord coach, while he himself handled the ribbons. He later claimed that his Deadwood coach had had the distinction of carrying more notables than any other vehicle in the world. His passengers included the Prince and Princess of Wales, President Carnot of France, young Emperor Wilhelm II of Germany, the Kings of Sweden and Italy, the King and Queen of Belgium, the Marquis of Butte, the Kings of Greece and Denmark, the Marquis of Lorne, and the Duke of York.

It was estimated that by the end of summer, 2,500,000 persons had visited the show. After a tour of the principal cities in the Midlands, the show returned to Hull in May,

1888, then took ship for America. During the rest of the year, it toured such cities as Philadelphia, Washington, Baltimore, and Richmond.

Buffalo Bill and Nate Salsbury always scheduled the Wild West Show, when possible, for long stands on the fringe of some big celebration or exposition, such as the Queen's Jubilee in England; the Jubilee for Pope Leo XIII in Rome; the Paris Universal Exposition; the North German Exposition and the Bremen Industrial Fair in Germany; the Venice Fetes in Italy; the Trans-Mississippi Exposition in Omaha.

The European tour, which began in Paris in 1889, lasted for three and one half years and included performances at most of the cities on the Continent. The cast spent the winter of 1890 in a Strasbourg castle.

Then, in 1892, the troupe landed back in New York. The Indians paced along Broadway for a day or two, stared unbelievingly at the new electric lights gleaming across Brooklyn Bridge, then vanished into the maw of Grand Central Terminal. Cody felt the same longing. He held to the routine of gallant showmanship during stopovers in Buffalo and Chicago. There were flecks of silver now in his goatee and shoulder-length hair. He bowed to the right gentlemen along Chicago's Gold Coast and kissed the hands of the right ladies, while he made plans for the Wild West Show to reopen at the Columbian Exposition. But his eyes didn't light up until the morning a slow, hollow clank of the train wheels indicated a long bridge, and suddenly the unmistakable earthy odor of the Missouri River flooded his stateroom. Omaha! Home again in the West.

The itch to see more of it came after a week or two in North Platte. They said he wouldn't know Denver these days. The mud alleys and slab-side cabins were about gone. Damn few people even remembered who Governor Denver was; some of the mansions and hotels matched Chicago's.

Colonel Cody and entourage took an overnight train. Overnight train—lordy, lordy. Probably the engineer didn't even carry a Colt. No Sioux; no grizzlies; no half-drunk, murderous Jack Slade sneering at an adobe station door. Denver really was a city, and almost as dull as Philadelphia or Liverpool or Turin.

There were receptions and parties and bows and more flabby white hands to kiss. One afternoon, when he was thoroughly bored, a portly banker pattered across a drawing room toward him. "Colonel," he said, after a moment of chitchat, "I recently met an old fellow you may know.

Possibly not, though. He's very close mouthed. Poor as a church mouse and—uh—really quite stuffy."

"Oh?" Cody smiled. "Some of them have reason to be proud." He twirled his glass absently. "Recall his name?"

"Oh, goodness, yes." The puffy little man beamed. "Very simple name to remember. It's—uh—oh, dear me—some Army rank. Captains. No. That couldn't be it. Mr. Colonels. Oh, now, really. Mr.—Mr.—"

Bill Cody carefully set the glass down. His hand trembled as he took a flabby chunk of the banker's shoulder between two fingers and squeezed. "Is it Majors?" he gritted.

"Why, yes. That's right. Heh. Good grief, Colonel. You have a grip like a wrestler. Please. Yes, thank you. Majors. That's the old fellow's name. Alexander Majors."

The suavity crumbled. Cody made abrupt apologies to the hostess and dashed down the stairs for a brougham, the banker puffing along behind like a rheumy Boston pug. The cabby recognized Buffalo Bill and whipped the nags all the way out Sherman Street. The pavement ended in slimy clay; the mansions gave way to cottages and the cottages to shacks. Finally, the banker wheezed and pointed.

Cody climbed slowly from the carriage. Suddenly his legs were water. The cabby stared, grimacing. He pulled himself erect and walked to the sagging, paintless gate. The door was creaking open. The figure that loomed quietly in it was as erect and proud as it had been forty years before, even though the black trousers were stained and patched and the shirt was frayed and gray. The flowing beard was snowy white, the eyes hawk keen.

The great showman leaned on the gatepost and tried to smile. Then he heard himself saying, "Mr. Majors, sir. It's Billy. May I come in?"

17.
HALLELUJAH!

On July 7, 1893, the *Nina*, *Pinta*, and *Santa Maria*, seeming no larger than fishing smacks alongside the tooting, beflagged escort of gunboats and whaleback steamers, swayed toward the south shore of Lake Michigan. Three days late after a seven-thousand-mile journey, they sped in tug tow past Chicago's Loop, the black-iron maze of railroad yards, the gaunt brownstone memorial to Stephen A. Douglas, on toward the most spectacular dream city ever built in the United States—the shimmering, mile-long Columbian Exposition.

Among the million people crowding the piers and beaches that morning, two dapper oldsters may have swirled Malacca canes with the deftness of Chauncey Depew. One, towering above the crowd, flourished a white beard so long and dazzling that small boys tugged mothers' skirts, pointed after him, and asked if "Sandy Claus has comed down, too." His perky escort, who came barely to his shoulder, wore a gray fedora tilted down over his right eye. Now and then he twirled his mustache with a flourish that shouted cavalry to any denizen of the High Plains gawking after them.

No reporter interviewed the pair. No photographs were taken of their solemn inspection of this replica of Columbus' fleet that Spain had built for the United States' four-hundredth-anniversary tribute to the New World's discoverer. Yet, in all the wonders of the White City and the glories of its six months, that was perhaps its most historic moment.

When Alexander Majors and Pony Bob Haslam stared out at the three caravels, Dame History turned again to "them Fate sisters" and smiled. The Columbus of the Old World and a Columbus of the New West were finally well met. And in the right place, because much of the glory of Chicago depended on the trade route she dominated—the Central Route that had been blazed thirty-three years before by the Pony Express.

Surely, then, in appropriate "coincidence," History would have arranged a triumphant salute for the little ships warped to moorings in front of the Agricultural Hall. The bands played, in massed dazzle, on the Midway. Now, with trumpets ahoist and drummers poised, they would burst into the "Glory" refrain of "The Battle Hymn of the Republic." "Ta-ta-te-da-da-da"—the drums whispered it. Soft as the beat of hoofs on a prairie trail, the bugles echoed. The drums again, higher, urgent, until the bugles, with the shrill impertinence of "Little Boo Hoo," called fifes, trombones, cymbals and French horns into the roar of the chorus.

"Glory, glory, hallelujah." The crowd chanted with them. "Glory, glory, hallelujah." Haslam swept off the fedora, stood as rigorously at attention as he did for "The Star-Spangled Banner." Alexander Majors squared his shoulders, gripped the Malacca's gold handle so tightly that his right-hand knuckles stood in brown ridges.

It was, in History's subtle way, a benediction. The tune had marched through his lifetime as a prophetic chant. It went west with him as a boy—a roaring camp-meeting hymn for Southerners building their promised land beyond the Mississippi. Then, too, for Methodist, Baptist, Campbellite, and Disciple, the refrain had pledged, "Glory, glory, hallelujah."

But, in bloody omen, the struggle for the West had changed the words. Historians said that "John Brown's Body" sprang from the gaunt, wild Yankee's attack on Harper's Ferry, his capture by Lee and Stuart, his hanging at the insistence of John Buchanan Floyd's successor—and protégé—as governor of Virginia. Yet these patient ferrets of Yesterday overlooked the fact that there could not have been a Harper's Ferry without a Kansas. John Brown rode east from Lawrence to rouse the slaves to rebellion, whip the Abolitionists to frenzy—and save the West for human freedom. With an omnipotence that shone brighter than any mosaic of subjective fact a historian could assemble, the 1860 transition from Southern camp-meeting chant to Abolitionist war song signaled *crisis* for the West.

The Pony Express had answered that signal, proved the worth of the tortuous Central Route for year-round communication, then held it as the Union's "thread of destiny" to Colorado, Wyoming, Utah, Nevada and California during the tense months between the Floyd-Johnston-Secesh treacheries and the completion of the telegraph line. Back over the same route, between 1862 and 1865, streamed raw gold and silver to support the Union's staggering expenditures on the war.

(The $150,000,000 in gold lent the Federal Government by New York, Boston, and Philadelphia banks during the summer and fall of 1861 just about exhausted the national supply, E. G. Spaulding, Chairman of the House Ways and Means Committee, reported in his 1869 financial history of the war. Northern banks were in danger of suspending specie payments after December, 1861. Yet, despite a final war debt of $2,500,000,000, the Union's dollar never fell below a specie value of fifty cents. Meanwhile, the C.S.A.'s dollar dropped to a twenty-cent specie value in 1862, then slid on to shin-plaster worthlessness, despite the brilliance of its armies and the tremendous toll of the *Shenandoah*—commanded by a North Carolina Waddell—*Alabama*, and other sea wolves. The South had lost the West and its treasures. Central Route gold and silver made the vital difference between U.S.A. credit and C.S.A. credit, and led Lincoln himself to say, "I would rather have Nevada in the Union than another million men." This was Pony Express riding to the challenge of "Glory, glory, hallelujah's" rebirth.)

Now, across three thousand miles, the song hurled its final triumph. The new words, composed in Maryland by a New York banker's daughter and first published in Boston (the Yankee editor shelled out four dollars for them!), were a Northern grafting on the Old South dream—with one miraculous exception. The chanting crescendo of the refrain remained intact. Camp meeting, Abolitionist, Grand Army of the Republic—all used the "Glory, glory, hallelujah." In unconscious symbolism, each repeated the phrase three times, changing the last line from 1859's "On Jordan's golden shore" to 1860's "But his soul goes marching on" to 1862's "His truth is marching on." And the three words of that refrain—had they always foreshadowed the truth of "Glory," Southern pioneers, and "Glory," Kansas-Missouri martyrs, to this 1893 "Hallelujah" of the New West?

Perhaps. That, at any rate, is the way it had happened. The first transcontinental railroad followed the Pony Trail and the telegraph across the Central Route after 1865—but from Council Bluffs and Omaha. St. Joseph's gloom about Jeff Thompson's desecration of the post-office flag had proved accurate. Iowa and Nebraska senators used the incident as the political fulcrum to lever the eastern terminal upstream. Omaha, on that meaningful west bank of the Missouri, grew to greatness; east-bank St. Joseph became "another historic river town." Now Nebraska's new state capital, Lincoln, loomed above the plateau midway between Nebraska City and the Platte. Cities and rich farms sat, like great pearls spawned from the gritty intrusion of youngsters "willing to risk death daily," along the Pony Trail. Denver, the "mile-high city," was queen of the Rockies. In all, nine great areas adjoining the Central Route had "bust their pioneer britches" and whooped from territory knickers to statehood long pants since 1861. The trains roaring daily up the Platte and across Wyoming did bear the names of Overland Limited and Pacific Express. And, as Jeff Thompson had foretold, they were not the fastest runs into California. The fast-mail trains screamed ahead of them. Now you could post a letter to California friends an hour before your train left Chicago, and have them carriage down to the Oakland Ferry Building to meet you the day after they received it. "Glory, glory, hallelujah!" This was phase three of a dream song. This was the hallelujah.

The band brassed to the last paean note. The two old men reclaimed their poise, and tapped away to explore the Exposition's wonders. Sometime during the day, they may have sauntered into Transportation Hall, and come up to the alcove where, between a display of Army mule wagons and the Studebaker brothers' shining new Tally-ho Coach, stood a shabby *mochila,* a worn desk, a handful of franked envelopes beneath a placard reading: MEMENTOS OF THE PONY EXPRESS. Again, there is no record that they paused there long enough to make the young attendant wonder "what those old coots are fixin' to do." Yet, a glance at their old gear, a quiet snicker, and a sprint back across the Hall to revisit the shiny magic of the "motor-driven carriage" would have been in harmony with a Majors-Haslam frolic to the Exposition.

And there is proof-nigh-on-positive that the two were Exposition-bent the week that Columbus' caravels moored in the shelter of the new South Pier. Indeed, the visit would explain the mystery of a hastily scrawled note, on the letterhead "P. E. Studebaker, Michigan Ave., Chicago, Ill.," still in the files of Rand McNally & Company at their Skokie, Illinois, headquarters. The note says: "July 5/93. Messrs Rand & McNally. Gentlemen: If you will advance the bearer Mr. Alex Majors one hundred dollars and he does not pay you— I will. Yrs truly, P. E. Studebaker."

The sequence leading to that acceptance from Peter E. Studebaker, vice-president of Studebaker Brothers Manufacturing Company, to Alexander Majors' publishers traces back to the 1892 afternoon when Bill Cody found the old patriarch living in a shack on Denver's outskirts. Ever the pioneer, Majors had sold the remnants of his freighting business to Edward Creighton, builder of the transcontinental telegraph. Majors had been in Salt Lake City soon after the war, first as a wagon contractor on the transcontinental railroad's construction, then as a silver prospector in the Wasatch. He provided well for his family. One of his sons became a prominent municipal judge in California. Doubtlessly, he would have been welcome there, or with other relatives in Kansas City. But Alex Majors walked alone. Denver beckoned him back, as it beckoned Colonel John Chivington in 1883.

When Cody rediscovered him, Majors was scribbling day and night to record everything he could recall about the West and the changes it had seen in his seventy years.

Cody called in Prentiss Ingraham, the bumptious preacher's son from Natchez, Mississippi, who was excelling even Ned Buntline in ghosting chiller-diller novels about, and supposedly by, Buffalo Bill. Ingraham agreed that Majors' manuscript had promise. Cody assured Majors that he would underwrite its publication, and agreed with Ingraham that it would be a "smash" to peddle during the intermissions of the Wild West Show. Then, the record runs, Cody moved Majors into better quarters, placed a substantial sum to his account in a Denver bank, and took to the road.

He kept his word. In the Rand McNally files, alongside the Peter Studebaker note, is another, reading:

CHICAGO, MARCH 30, 1893

TO MESSRS. RAND, MCNALLY & CO., PUBLISHERS, Chicago

Gentlemen:

In consideration of your agreeing, at my request, to publish the manuscript at present entitled "On Mountain and Plain," written by my old friend Mr. Alexander Majors, and now in your possession, but subject to a change of title if such be deemed advisable by you, I hereby agree and undertake to guarantee the payment of the cost of the composition, electrotyping and engravings of the said publication, not exceeding the sum of $750, this price contemplating a book of not more than 288 pages with 16 illustrations.

Very truly yours,

(signed) W. F. CODY

The book was published that spring or summer under the title *Seventy Years on the Frontier*. And, like the Pony Express itself, it not only pioneered, but created turmoils that have never been explained and a mystery that still has bibliophiles and historians searching for what could be a priceless treasure trove of Western Americana.

Published in both paperback and hard-cover form, *Seventy Years on the Frontier* was the first book to give even a summary account of the Pony Express. Most of the hundreds of Pony books written since, including Arthur Chapman's authoritative *The Pony Express* and the Settles' *Empire on Wheels*, quote liberally from it. Coincidentally, it signaled an era of wider sales, and prestige, for the paperback. As the self-effacing account of a pioneer who had played a critical role in shaping the West, the book found favor as a lively sales item for the "butchers" who hawked everything from sandwiches to "authentic Indian kerchiefs" through the transcontinental trains. Books by Kipling, Dickens, Henty and other popular authors joined the "butchers' library" to lift the paperback up from the dime novel and "yellow-back" slough of the Buntline and Ingraham word mills.

Yet the sparsity of detail and stubborn reluctance of *Seventy Years on the Frontier* made it an object of wonderment to successive biographers of the Pony Express—and set off the search for the "rest of the manuscript." A clue to a clash between Majors and Ingraham and the existence in 1892 of far more voluminous data appeared in Majors' obituary published by the *Kansas City Star* on January 15, 1900.

"When he [Cody] returned," the *Star* said, "he found Majors had written enough for several books. So he hired an editor and the manuscript was trimmed and published. Prentiss Ingraham, Buffalo Bill's Boswell, was the editor."

" 'The only fault I find with Col. Ingraham,' " the *Star* quoted Majors as saying, " 'is that he will stray away from facts despite my most earnest entreaties. If I say three Indians, he sticks in five and where I see 200 buffalo, he finds 2,000. I know he merely wishes to be picturesque, but I am dictating history and as a truthful historian, I cannot countenance gross exaggeration, even if the book does not sell a copy.' "

" 'The trouble with Col. Majors,' " the *Star*'s reporter quoted Ingraham as retorting, " 'is his extreme modesty. He is so far from being a boaster that he hugs the other shore altogether too closely and will never let me give his narration the benefit of a doubt. Fortunately, I have an understanding with his publishers and am enabled to correct proofs after they leave Col. Majors' hands.' "

The product of the tiff was sadly summed up by the Settles when, in 1949, they wrote of *Seventy Years on the Frontier*: "The major portion of it is devoted to dull, uninteresting chapters on Missouri, the Mormons, etc. . . . with only minor attention to himself, his family, his partners, the freighting and staging business and other matters of vital importance."

Again, Majors' insistence on "dictating history" and his known devotion to meticulous detail do not jibe with the scanty account of the Pony Express, Russell, Majors & Waddell, and the Central Overland California & Pike's Peak Company that finally appeared in *Seventy Years on the Frontier*. No mention is made of Floyd or the Secesh plotters or the 1860 Bond Scandal and other vital details that the Settles, Chapman, and others would screen bit by bit from Federal archives and local records. No effort is made to explain the great mystery about the Pony's relentless deliveries during the winter of 1860–61, with Russell in jail or before congressional hearings in Washington, and Waddell in frantic bankruptcy proceedings.

Who ran the Pony in those crucial five months before Holladay and Wells Fargo took over? Who teamed it with Creighton's telegraph lines unrolling across Nebraska and the Sierra? Did these answers go on Prentiss Ingraham's "cutting-room" floor, together with masses of fact and conviction about Floyd, the Johnstons, Bailey, Russell, and even Ben Holladay?

They may well have, and for reasons that must have seemed logical. After all, the Buffalo Bill Wild West Show was a commercial enterprise. It toured the South as well as the North. Consequently, it dared not hawk a book that would simmer old wraths about Secesh plotting and the reasons for the Civil War. This could be the basic reason for the dullness of Alexander Majors' account of his vital lifeline for the Union across the West. Add to this probability the fact that Prentiss Ingraham was from Natchez, a fiery soldier of fortune who needed little incentive to edit out material that put the finger of blame on such Southland heroes as Jefferson Davis and Joe Johnston. (Johnston was still living when the book was published; Davis had died only four years before.)

Whatever the reasons, the book was published sometime in 1893 as Ingraham edited it. The mysterious one-hundred-dollar pledge from Studebaker to Rand McNally proves that Majors was in Chicago during the first week in July that year. And a prim "mug-shot" photo labeled "Copyright, 1893 by Grabill" proves that Majors, Pony Bob Haslam, Cody, and Ingraham were in the Loop together for at least one day. The portrait, reproduced in *Seventy Years on the Frontier,* shows Majors, in a satin-edged dark suit, wing collar and dashing cravat, seated between graying "W. F. Cody" and Colonel John B. Colton. Behind them, in poses worthy of Booth or Barrymore, balding Pony Bob stands with right hand tucked between the first and second buttons of his four-button waistcoat, while Ingraham mugs straight into the camera with arms in a declamation-by-Antony fold across his chest, and white walrus mustache swirling almost to coat lapels.

The background of fact leading to the Haslam-Majors reunion that summer is as vague as the reasons for the Studebaker note. Majors' book states that " 'Pony Bob' is now a resident of Chicago, where he is engaged in business." This doesn't jibe with the biography given by the Chicago newspapers after Pony Bob's death. They report that he served for many years under General Nelson A. Miles on the frontier, was appointed an Army veterinary by Miles and so "saw service in Cuba and the Philippines." The Spanish-American War began five years after *Seventy Years on the Frontier* was published. Thus, Haslam must have served with the cavalry until 1901 or later. But General Miles and various cavalry units were in Chicago for the Exposition. And, obviously, Haslam was in town, too, either as a veterinary assigned to cavalry units at the Exposition or on leave.

Haslam's presence in Chicago through the Fourth of July week that year would offer the most logical reason for Majors' carrying a note from Studebaker to Rand McNally for a hundred-dollar advance. Again, a study of backgrounds lends logic. Some authors have contended that Majors was a "good Methodist" and "a lay Methodist preacher." But Majors never stated his church affiliation in his book. He reported that his mother was a Baptist and that he was as prone to a good sermon by an Episcopal rector or a Mormon bishop as he was to one by a ripsnorting Methodist circuit-rider. Peter Studebaker, like his brothers, was a staunch Methodist and a contributor to such Methodist institutions as DePauw University. But—dig deeper. In 1870, Peter Studebaker went to St. Joseph, Missouri, to open the first branch house of Studebaker Brothers. He lived there for years, selling the firm's wagons to freighters and immigrant families bound for Kansas, Nebraska, and Colorado.

Fellow Methodists, old friends, or both, Majors and Peter Studebaker met on July 5. If they chatted in the old-neighbor pattern, Studebaker could have told Majors that the marvelous chain of restaurants along the Santa Fe Railway's high iron and the amazing décor of Santa Fe dining cars were twin creations of Fred Harvey, the H. & St. J.'s first railway-mail clerk. Majors could have replied with the news that the son of the H. & St. J.'s section foreman at Laclede was now Major John J. Pershing, director of military instruction at the University of Nebraska, and showing promise of even greater achievement. Together, then, they could nod agreement with Colonel McCoy's contention that it was the H. & St. J.'s willingness to accept cattle shipments out of Dodge City in 1867—after the president of the Missouri Pacific had shooed him off—that veered the rush of Texas longhorns from St. Louis to Chicago, and assured Chicago's dominance as queen city of the meat industry.

They reminisced, perhaps, about sundry happenstances. The slinky station helper named "Duck Bill" who shot down Secesh Dave McCanles and two cronies at the Rock Creek Station door one day in 1861, won the name of Wild Bill because of it and swaggered on to become Marshal James "Wild Bill" Hickok of Dodge City. The youngster Samuel Clemens who, fleeing West away from a Secesh uniform in 1861, gained such deep admiration for Pony Express riders that he would extol them again and again in books and letters. Sam and Jim Gilson, the Pony-rider brothers who turned prospectors in 1862 and became millionaires through gilsonite, the new mineral they exploited. The grandeur of aged, bankrupt Ben Holladay when, after Congress gave his Sioux Uprising damage claims the same sniffling runaround it had given Chorpenning, Gilpin, and Russell, the old fellow drew himself up, roared, "If the United States cannot pay its just bills, I hereby cancel them!" and stormed home to Oregon to die.

Somehow, that afternoon, Majors' interest in a bit of spending money came to light. Cody, from all reports, had provided amply for his needs. It seems illogical that he would storm at Ingraham about the book, stalk off the Rand McNally premises, then show up a day later with a note for a hundred-dollar advance signed by Studebaker. The most logical reason focuses on the Columbian Exposition. The Studebaker Brothers' wagon exhibit and the mementos of the Pony Express were in the same section of Transportation Hall. Possibly Studebaker heard of Majors through Rand McNally, asked him to give a lecture at the Studebaker display, and the old man—refusing any honorarium—accepted the note for Rand McNally so that he could bring Pony Bob along and they could "do" the Exposition together.

The 1893 meeting seems to have been the last between the Pony Express' founder-manager and its "greatest rider." Cody took Majors firmly under his wing, calmed his tiffs with Ingraham and appointed him a supervisor of his ranching operations.

What became of the unpublished bulk of Majors' memoirs? Did he carefully retrieve them and pack them off to Nebraska? Are they still there, somewhere, stacked away in a trunk or—like Boswell's manuscript originals—in an attic croquet box? Did wily, plot-wise Ingraham "latch on to them" but never get around to reworking them? Did a Rand McNally cleaning woman sweep them up, sniff, and toss them into a waste bin?

Neither Majors nor Ingraham ever uttered a clue in public. Majors paraded on convention and exposition platforms with Cody in 1895, 1896, 1898. Chivington died, forgotten by his church, and was quietly buried in Denver. Gilpin died a few months later. Russell had lain in an unmarked grave at Palmyra, Missouri, since 1872. Waddell had preceded him by six months to a stately plot in Machpelah Cemetery, near Lexington, Missouri.

In December, 1899, Alexander Majors strode off a train at Chicago's Union Station, toured State Street and Michigan

Boulevard to greet old friends, then headed for the home of J. Craig at 40th and Drexel to spend the Christmas holidays. During the next week, he developed a head cold and chest pains. A physician ordered him to bed. The fever mounted. The doctor pronounced pneumonia. Some accounts say Cody dropped all engagements and hurried to the old man's bedside. Relatives did come in from Kansas City. The nineteenth century died. The towering patriarch gasped on, then, suddenly, on the night of January 13, 1900, went limp. He was eighty-six years old. Chicago newspapers didn't bother to run a death notice. After all, he didn't live in Cook County.

But Bill Cody proved that week that his devotion to Alexander Majors was not, as some biographers have insinuated, "another publicity stunt." The *New York Herald* for January 20, 1900, said:

William F. Cody (Buffalo Bill) speaks thus of Alexander Majors, the originator of The Pony Express, who died in Chicago the other day: "The man who could, in the face of all dangers and obstacles, carry to success a line of freighter wagons, a mail route from the Atlantic to the Pacific, and a pony express flying at the utmost speed of a hare through the land was no ordinary individual. Although severe in discipline, Mr. Majors was never profane or harsh. He was a Christian temperance man through all. He governed his men kindly and was wont to say that he would have no one under his control who would not obey an order unless it was accompanied with an oath. In fact, he had a contract with his men in which they pledged themselves not to use profanity, get drunk, gamble or be cruel to animals, under pain of dismissal, while good behavior was rewarded. Every man, from wagon-boss and teamster down to rustlers and messengers, seemed anxious to earn the goodwill of Colonel Majors, and to hold it, and he had more friends than any man I know who had to deal with such men as he had to deal with."

Now, too, as the ranks of the Pony Express thinned, "Billy" became their patron, sometimes with anonymous gifts, sometimes with letters and visits. Pony Bob came back to Chicago in 1905 or 1906 and took a job as a clerk, or steward, at the Hotel Auditorium. Cody kept track of him. Then, when he failed to find Haslam at the hotel in 1911, he trailed him down to a shabby rooming house on Wabash Avenue. The little horseman had suffered a stroke, was a hopeless paralytic, and destitute. Cody called a meeting, launched a funds-raising campaign, with Will J. Davis, manager of the Illinois Theater, as treasurer, and led off with a substantial personal check.

In March, 1912, when Pony Bob died, Cody wired Cy de Vry, animal keeper at the Lincoln Park Zoo and a mutual friend, that he wished to share the costs for Haslam's funeral expenses and tombstone.

Five years later in Denver, the "Great Scout" began the last journey, too.

Today, like prophets surveying their Land of Promise, these three immortals of the Pony Express lie in Denver, Kansas City, and Chicago. Cody's grave, a world-famous shrine, looks out on the looming Transcontinental Divide the Pony conquered in 1860. Alex Majors rests, with historic justice, in Union Cemetery, Kansas City.

But, in the event you don't believe in History's justice, in the inevitability of her carefully arranging the meeting of Columbus' caravels and the Columbuses of the Central Route on July 7, 1893—if, indeed, you doubt the whole shabby tale of Secesh intrigue and the fact that the Pony's hoofbeats of destiny held the West for the Union through 1860 and 1861—concede a believer's whim.

Follow Sacramento Street down through Chicago's mighty heart. Far south, skirt the fifty-acre intrusion of the Wabash Railroad yards—the line that carried Pony Express mail from Detroit to the H. & St. J. junction at Quincy. Pick Sacramento up again at 79th Street, follow it beyond the city limits until it dead-ends at the fence of Mount Greenwood Cemetery. From the cemetery gate on 111th Street, walk north and west two blocks until, beside railroad tracks, dead in line with Francisco Street, you face Lot 15. Walk down to the lone grave sheltered by the tallest, oldest tree in sight. Lean over and read the inscription: ROBERT H. HASLAM, "PONY BOB." 1840 ... 1912.

Ask yourself: Why?

18.
THE TRAIL TODAY
by Roy E. Coy

There are probably more "expert" opinions and fewer recorded cold facts about the Pony Express than there are about any critical hour in the entire saga of the United States of America. Another century of patient analysis and research may be necessary to reclaim the records and other bits of evidence that were destroyed—some of it carelessly, much deliberately—during the crisis of Secession and the frenzied years of Civil War.

Nature, despite the savage cruelties she still imposes on her High Plains and shimmering mountain domain in the great West, has proved a more faithful guardian than man of the Pony's lifeline for the Union. Many of the relay and swing stations are still standing. Friendly ranchers will point out grooves and ruts made a century ago by wagon trains and Pony Express hoofs, or lead you out to a windmill built from the 1861-62 telegraph poles that followed the Pony's pioneership. Adventure pairs with clearer history awareness in a Pony-Trail journey across those two thousand miles—or almost any portion of it. We did it in the spring of 1959. So can any careful motorist.

Using my new station wagon, equipped with overload springs and carrier rack, we drove 6,372 miles between St. Joseph and San Francisco, searching out Pony Express sites and determining the accessibility of the route for vacationers as well as for sincere students of Western history. The cost of the entire trip was just a little less than one thousand dollars. Desert rocks dented our fenders; the only other casualty was the theft of a taillight in Nevada.

The trip, as we took it, is not advisable for a family with young children. If you do take the pigtail set on a Pony-Trail adventure, stay on—or close to—the main highways. Be sure to carry an extra five-gallon tin of gasoline, a gallon jug of water, some tinned or nonspoilable food, a good tool kit and a tire-patch kit. Obviously, too, you'll want a copy of this book for day-by-day reference, as well as one of the illustrated Pony Express Route maps by W. H. Jackson or Harry E. Wright.

Bring along cameras and plenty of color film; the entire route just stands up and begs to be photographed. Don L. Reynolds, staff photographer for the St. Joseph and Pony Express Stables Museums, was my relay companion on the trip. We shot three thousand feet of 16-mm. movie film, plus four hundred color slides and more than two hundred black-and-whites. The travelogue we fashioned from the movie film and titled "On the Trail of the Pony Express" was immediately purchased by the National Broadcasting Company for use on NBC-TV networks, as well as for lectures and group rentals. I report this merely as an illustration of the photogenic potentials along the Pony Trail for any semicompetent lensman.

Our trip began at the Patee House and the Pony Express

Stables Museum in St. Joseph. With two grand museums operating in our city of eighty thousand, we should be satisfied, I suppose. Yet I couldn't help but look up again that morning at the Patee House and dream that one day a philatelic society—or perhaps the Federal Government—will realize its virtues as a national postal museum. There isn't a museum anywhere in the fifty states that tells the amazing story of that splendid fellow the mailman and the travails he has known in the two centuries since Benjamin Franklin, as postmaster general of His Majesty's Colonies in America, designed the symbol of a rider on horseback, "with saddlebags well filled." No building or site on the continent would be more appropriate for a national postal museum than the Patee House, the place where the Pony Express was literally born.

KANSAS

The Pony rider was ferried across the Missouri River from St. Joseph. We drove over the Pony Express Bridge. On the Kansas side we found a town of Elwood, but not the same one. The original town had been destroyed by a flood many years ago. From Elwood, we drove to Troy, Kansas, thirty-five miles from which, on a dirt road, is the site of the Kennekuk Station. Although we passed by the Kickapoo, Granada, and Log Chain station sites, we were unable to locate them exactly. Here in the fertile northeastern part of Kansas, time and industry have erased all trace of the Pony stations.

At Seneca, Kansas, the Pony Express station still stands, though, unfortunately, it has been moved from its original location, and the former all-wood structure has been covered with asphalt tile. Nevertheless, it would lend itself well to being a Pony Express museum. The spring where the riders watered their horses is flowing just outside town, but it is now a part of the public water supply, and has a concrete house covering it.

We were able to locate the site of Guittard's Station, north of Highway 36, by a fine monument on the gravel road near where the station was. The old Guittard Cemetery is in ruins on a nearby hillside, and, not far away, the tracks of the Emigrant Trail can still be seen. Medium-size elm trees grow in the trail itself. We were there late in the afternoon. Its loneliness, with the long shadows of the trees falling across the tumble-down grave markers, added to the feeling that we were now for the first time among those who blazed the early history of the West.

Marysville, Kansas, is now a city of four thousand. Here the Oregon Trail from Independence, Missouri, joined with the old St. Joe Road to wind west up the fertile valley of Little Blue River. Before we drove into Marysville, we stopped at the home of Roy Lewis at Home, Kansas, six miles east. We knew that Mr. Lewis has a private museum of Western items and is well informed on Pony Express history. He gave us a warm welcome and showed us his collection of everything from firearms to Pony shoes. Otto Wulleschleger, also a Kansas historian, was visiting him, too. They gave us much helpful information on the Pony Express in Kansas. The Marysville station is still standing, but it has been stuccoed and so changed throughout the years that it does not look anything like the original building.

Hollenberg, Kansas, the next Pony stop and the last Kansas station, is a delight to the eyes of anyone interested in history because it is intact and on the original site. The building is oblong in design, of wood construction and with a wood-shingle roof. The interior was being restored properly.

After leaving Hollenberg, we proved to be tenderfeet in Pony-Express Trail adventuring. We ran out of gas. I managed to flag a ride with a local newspaperman to a gas station over the hill. We had extra gas cans in the car but had not filled them as yet!

NEBRASKA

Still following the Little Blue River on the northeast side of its banks, we crossed the Nebraska line to the town of Endicott. There, with the wonderful help of the local postmaster, we located Rock Creek and the site of the infamous Rock Creek Station, where young James Butler Hickok, then an assistant at the station, won the nickname of Wild Bill by shooting David C. McCanles and two companions. A large granite boulder marks the alleged grave of McCanles. We also located, nearby, the large outcropping of dolomite limestone rock where Kit Carson and General Frémont carved their names in the 1840's. Efforts at marksmanship seem to persist here. An enamel Pony Express marker at the site had been so badly shot up that we couldn't read it. A few trees are growing where the Pony Express station stood. Here, too, you can see the Emigrant Trail as it cut across the creek.

We tried to follow the Little Blue River on up to Fort Kearny, but we were unable to locate the sites of the Big Sandy, Thompson's, Kiowa, Liberty Farm, Thirty-Two Mile,

Lone Tree, Summit, or Hocks' stations. Local historians told us nothing is left on any of these sites. We did venture off the route to visit the Pioneer Village at Minden, Nebraska, where there is one of the most complete collections of Nebraska historical items—over seventeen thousand of them trace American progress for the past 120 years. There are twelve buildings in a two-block area.

Nearby, we visited another famous Nebraska museum, called the House of Yesterday, at Hastings. This is not only a splendid historical museum, but outstanding in its natural-history displays. W. E. Eigsti, the director, routed us to the grave of Susan Hail. Legend has it that Susan and her husband left St. Joseph as newlyweds on a wagon train in the 1840's. Some three hundred miles west, just outside of present Hastings, Susan died from "the fever." Mr. Hail rode back to St. Joseph, then sold his horse to buy a monument for her lonely grave. Being unable to "hitch" a ride, he is alleged to have trundled the gravestone in a wheelbarrow all the way back to Hastings. The grave today has a new marker. Nobody knows what became of Mr. Hail's memorial—or of Mr. Hail.

At Fort Kearny State Park, a granite monument marks the site of the old fort. The outlines of the buildings are still visible as banks of foundation earth, one to two feet high. But these, and a grove of cottonwood trees planted by the men under General Kearny, are all that remain today.

In Gothenburg, Nebraska, we visited Harry Williams and his son, Bob, on their ranches, the Lower 96 and the Upper 96. The Lower 96 Ranch has a well-preserved Pony Express station, listed on the map as Midway. To preserve it, Mr. Williams has covered the sod roof with wood. The original cedar beams came from trees much larger than any growing in the area today.

At Gothenburg, too, we met the Oregon Centennial Wagon Train that had left Independence, Missouri, several weeks before. The wagon train rode out to Midway Station and posed for pictures. Then, on May 14, Gothenburg held a parade to honor this Oregon Trail cavalcade. Appropriately, it passed the Sam Mattache's Station, which Mr. Williams had moved from his Upper 96 Ranch and presented to the Gottenburg city park. The blacksmith shop that was part of the station still stands on the original site back on the Upper 96. That night, we drove out to the Oregon Wagon Train camp, where the wagons were placed in the traditional protective circle. We all sat around the campfire and sang "Acres of Clams," "Betsy from Pike," and other lovely Old West folk songs. At seven o'clock the next morning, we were back to watch the wagon train hitch up. They would be in Independence, Oregon, by mid-August, they told us.

The rest of that day, we hunted down sod houses of the type used by the early Nebraska and Wyoming settlers. In one of the ruins a prairie rattlesnake, the nemesis of all sod-house folks, buzzed warning that some of the pioneer inhabitants are still around. These houses were built from grass sod, stacked up like bricks, usually plastered on the interior, then finished off with a cedar-branch roof. Cedar branches were used for reinforcement throughout. The floor was usually dirt, packed hard enough to sweep. Nebraska has a State Sod House Society, some of whose members we were privileged to meet at Lexington.

Our next station was Cottonwood, located near the site of Fort McPherson. Cottonwood is marked by a red sandstone marker beside a plowed field; the site of Fort McPherson is commemorated by a stone marker depicting a soldier of the plains. The cemetery, a mile away, is now a national shrine and park.

Following the Pony Trail just south of the city of North Platte, we noticed a high sand hill with a large rock or marker atop it. It was steep, and covered with clumps of broom sedge. I judged it to be about one quarter of a mile to the top. What we thought was a rock or marker proved to be a stone statue of a Sioux Indian, beautifully executed in life-size figure, but—again!—disfigured by vandals. This is the famous Sioux Lookout—a scouting and signal point for the Sioux, and a trail marker for travelers along Emigrant Road.

Cold Springs was not as easy to locate as some of the previous stations. There is a marker about a quarter-mile from the site, but nothing is left of the station but a few mounds in a pasture on the Doolittle Ranch. On station sites in this area we found remnants of the cedar poles used in the 1861–62 telegraph line. Some fences and windmills have these historic poles as part of their structure, but it is difficult to tell the originals unless an old-timer is present to point them out.

We visited William Cody's Scout's Rest Ranch just out of North Platte, Nebraska, and wondered if this was the property Alexander Majors "managed" for his former messenger boy between 1893 and 1900. Only sixty years ago—and a mystery already!

Next, we hunted down Art Anderson, a former blacksmith at Brulé, Nebraska, and found him fishing for carp, with a bow and arrow, at Lake McConaughy, north of Ogallala. Mr.

Anderson immediately quit fishing, even though he was doing very well, and took us to the Diamond Springs Station site. Like many others, this site is in a pasture; only variations in the vegetation, and its color, betray the location of former buildings. He showed us a collection of horse, mule, burrow, and ox shoes he had picked up there.

To find South Platte, Lodge Pole, and Midway—all of which are only weed-covered ground—we asked the help of Mr. Emil Kopac of Oshkosh, Nebraska. He proved to be an excellent historian and student of Western Americana, and his help was invaluable in locating many of the stations, locally and farther west.

COLORADO–NEBRASKA

We located the Julesburg site in Colorado with the help of Mrs. J. G. Cavendar, and visited the location of the town of old Julesburg. Again, there is nothing left.

Mud Springs was easy to find. There are two markers on the road beside a beautiful little spring and pond in a quiet valley. A granite-boulder monument supports a bronze plaque with a Pony rider on it, but there is no sign of the exact station location or any other buildings.

The next station locations are well known to everyone interested in the geology or history of the West. They are the outstanding Jail House and Court House Rock landmarks, south of Bridgeport, Nebraska off U.S. Highway 26. Chimney Rock, the second station site west, can be seen some twenty miles away.

WYOMING

Horse Creek, Spring Ranch, and Badeau's are the stations between Scott's Bluffs Station and Fort Laramie. The fort is now a national monument, maintained by the National Park Service, and well worth the time for a visit. Some of the old buildings are still standing, including the Sutler's Store, used by the Pony Express.

We took a back road along the old trail out of the fort to Register Cliff to find Rocks Station site at Star Ranch. The roads were wet and full of mud puddles. But no complaints. After all, we had not yet seen a hostile Indian, or a single case of cholera. Register Cliff is sandstone, buff in color. Here many early emigrants camped and carved their names before moving into the Black Hills. Hundreds of the names can still be seen. Some are crude; others were executed with fancy Spencerian flourishes. No effort has been made to preserve and protect them.

The city park in Guernsey, Wyoming, just north across the river from Register Cliff, has one of the most spectacular items to be seen along the Trail—a sandstone ledge where the pioneer wagons and Pony Express Trail came through. Due to the many wagons passing over this point through the years, a groove, some four feet deep, was cut into the stone. The trail where the bullwhackers walked along the side of the wagons is still visible, too. Yet no markers have been placed to tell the visitors about this remarkable spectacle, nor is there anything to protect it.

West of this spot, a few miles into a beautiful canyon, is Warm Springs, where the pioneers stopped their wagons for water and a family wash-up. We got a little misplaced (not lost, you understand), and it took about three hours of wandering to get located again and head for Wendover, the site of Cottonwood Station. There is nothing there except some very large cottonwood trees. And the beaver have been trying to cut these down.

The station site of Horseshoe is outside Douglas, Wyoming, on the ranch of J. R. Lancaster. Only the old well is left, and it won't be there much longer. In Douglas, we were guests of Albert Sims, local historian and sheep rancher. Here again we received invaluable guidance: his friends, the Lyle Hildegard family, acted as our guides and took us to La Bonte, La Prele, Deer Creek, and Platte Bridge stations, then gave us some good advice regarding the South Pass crossing. The hospitality of Mr. Sims and the Hildegards is in full keeping with the tradition of Western hospitality.

Between Douglas and Casper, the Pony Trail crossed the great oil fields. Beyond Mountain View, it crossed through Emigrant Gap past Red Butte and Willow Springs to Rock Avenue. The latter is lined on either side by jagged rock outcroppings. We saw hundreds of antelope along this trail, red-ant hills by the thousands, and a golden-eagle's nest in the only tree visible for miles. The old trail is still very plain, and it is possible to follow it closely.

The first awe-inspiring sight as one comes out of Emigrant Trail and along Highway 220 is the sudden appearance of that large granite monolith called Independence Rock, with Devil's Gate on the western horizon. Soon, the journey became a rough one. We finally arrived at the famous South Pass Crossing of the Continental Divide. Here the Oregon Trail veered northwest, and the Overland and Pony Express Trails southwest. It was raining when we attempted this crossing. After visiting South Pass City, the Pacific Springs site, we were happy to pass through Green River Station site and reach the little town of Granger, where we saw the almost complete remains of a rock house called Granger Station. Apparently some effort has been made to save it; it is well marked by a very good monument.

Nothing is left of the Church Buttes Station on the old Highway 30 between Granger and Lyman. But Fort Bridger has been preserved and restored by the state of Wyoming. There is a museum there.

UTAH

We took another gravel road out of Fort Bridger on an abandoned Union Pacific Railroad bed to the Muddy Station site. It was well named. Don Reynolds said he would be glad to drive. I told him I would rather worry him. There were more-than-300-foot drops on either side; staying in the ruts was imperative. And it was slick clay. All we found after this toboggan run was a ghost town. Four charcoal kilns sat in a beautiful valley, sentinels for a little cemetery and a dozen log buildings.

Aspen Springs is still flowing, but that is all there is to tell of the Pony station. It is listed as Quaking Asp on some maps. Echo Station is now a town in beautiful Echo Canyon. We did not locate Hanging Rock. Henefer is a nice little town today. By taking Highway 65, you can locate the sites of Dixie and Snyders (now called Bauchmanns); there is still a building on the Bauchmanns site. Finally, on to Mountain Dell and out on the spot where Brigham Young said, "This is the place."

In Salt Lake City, the Pioneer Village is an excellent museum, and living replica, of an early-day village complete with oxen, covered wagons, and handcarts. It is a wonderful preservation project of early Utah history.

Crossing the Great Salt Desert, we used the Dugway Road to Ibapah to see the site and rock ruins of Simpson's Springs, the great black rock where Black Rock Station once stood and the frame building covering the log structure of Fish Springs Station. At Boyd's there is a rock ruin. Across a dry, hot desert is the Bagley Ranch, where the Willow Springs Station, now painted red, still stands. From here to Ibapah there are more sites. But it was getting dark. We saw no more stations or station sites until we reached the Shell Creek site in Nevada next day. We drove half of that night trying to find a place to stay, and finally discovered we were roaming in circles through the Gosiute Indian Reservation.

NEVADA

At Shell Creek, there is intact not only the adobe building that was used as a Pony Express and stage station, but also the log blacksmith cabin with bellows and workbench. Like a timeless giant, the stone walls and cast-iron doors of Fort Schellbourne are here to greet you. We were shown around by Mrs. Ruth Russell, owner of the ranch, who told us that she and Mr. Russell are proud of these historic items and intend to preserve them. We picked up horseshoes and other relics of the Pony days. It seemed as though the Gosiute Indians might come riding over the nearest ridge at any instant.

With a retired cowboy, Ralph Franks, as guide, we were able to follow the Pony Trail from Cherry Creek to the sites of Fort Egan, Butte, and Mountain Springs, where a rock chimney remains. Ruby Valley is visible, with remains of a stone fort similar to Fort Schellbourne. From here across Nevada, it was hit and miss. We found Simpson's Park and Reese River (better known as Jacksonville). The Nevada dessert has most of the Pony station sites hidden. All we found was hot sand, volcanic rock, sagebrush, dust devils, and lizards. How the early pioneers and Pony Express riders ever made it will always be a source of amazement and admiration to us!

Fort Churchill is in ruins. One of the buildings used to have a marker in front of it designating it as the Pony Express station, but, apparently, it has been stolen even though it is in a state park. The only thing we found in Carson City is a marker on the lawn of the capitol building. The state museum, in the old Federal mint building, is excellent but has nothing about the Pony Express.

CALIFORNIA

At Genoa we found another almost hidden marker. Through the steep drive called Kingsberry Pass, one can see the trail almost all the way. This is a beautiful scenic ride and comes out on U.S. Highway 50, with Lake Tahoe glimmering ahead. The Pony Trail did not go to Emerald Bay, but we did—and so will most cameramen. On into Sacramento the station sites are well marked. Today, near the Strawberry site, there is a fine modern inn. Placerville still has the appearance and air of an old Western town. At Folsom, the Pony station still stands.

There were two Pony Express offices in Sacramento. Both buildings are still standing, but in a shabby district of the city. Russell, Majors & Waddell used a corner building as their office; Wells Fargo moved the Pony near the center of the same block to a more ornate building, which still has some of the original iron grillwork on it. (The State Historical Society and local historians hope to save these buildings and eventually develop them into museums.)

While Sacramento is the official western terminus of the Pony Express, the first rider and horse to arrive from the east was ferried across the bay to San Francisco. We, too, went to San Francisco, but by bridge. Even in 1959, the end of the Pony Express trail called for a weekend of snoozing. We could better appreciate the herculean job the men of the Pony Express had to face, as well as the hardships of the early wagon trains and stage travelers. We had had some idea of all this beforehand, but only a trip of this kind can make one realize its greatness and rugged reality. It is no wonder the Pony Express will live forever in the hearts of men.

19.
HERE THEY RIDE ON

From Chicago west, you can relive the excitements of *Hoofbeats of Destiny*, recapture the stark daring of its heroes, see the equipment they used, and live it up during a two-thousand-mile bliss of Western cooking, zestful fresh air, and some of the world's choicest scenery. Here, east to west, and city by city, are the shrines of the Pony Express.

CHICAGO, ILLINOIS

ROOSEVELT UNIVERSITY, Michigan Avenue and Congress Street, occupies the Auditorium Hotel building where Pony Bob Haslam worked as an impoverished steward between 1905 and 1910.

MOUNT GREENWOOD CEMETERY, West 11th Street and South California Avenue. The grave of Pony Bob Haslam is in Lot 15. The small headstone, paid for in part by Buffalo Bill, reads:

>Famed Pony Express Rider
>Robert H. Haslam
>"Pony Bob"
>1840 . . . 1912

4003 DREXEL BOULEVARD, at 40th Street, is the former J. Craig residence, where Alexander Majors died on January 14, 1900.

SKOKIE, ILLINOIS

RAND MCNALLY & COMPANY, 8255 North Central Park. Here the stories of the Pony Express were first published. The first-floor library contains one of the most complete collections of early paperback books, printed between 1870 and 1910, for peddling by "train butchers" on Western railroads. The correspondence on Alexander Majors' *Seventy Years on the Frontier* is also on display.

AURORA, ILLINOIS

BURLINGTON RAILROAD YARDS has on permanent display a replica of the first railway-mail car, where mail clerk Fred Harvey ducked Secesh bullets.

HANNIBAL, MISSOURI

JOHN M. CLEMENS' LAW OFFICE, is on Hill Street. Here, one evening in 1846, perhaps while his son Sam slid down a drain pipe and prowled off on a moonlight hunt for "real spooks," Justice of the Peace Clemens held the initial meeting to discuss the advisability of building the Hannibal & St. Joseph Railroad.

KANSAS CITY, MISSOURI

UNION CEMETERY, 28th and Warwick streets. The simple granite shaft of Alexander Majors' last resting place can be seen here.

ST. JOSEPH, MISSOURI

PONY EXPRESS STABLES MUSEUM, 908 Penn Street. The building was restored in 1958–59 and opened as a museum May 3, 1959. Pony stalls plus dioramas and exhibits recreate the exciting atmosphere of St. Joseph and the West in 1860.

PONY EXPRESS STATUE, 9th Street and Frederick Avenue.

ST. JOSEPH MUSEUM, 11th and Charles streets. Here are splendid dioramas of early St. Joseph and of Missouri Valley animals, birds, etc. The museum building is a former mansion. (Don't miss the exquisite mosaic inlays in the director's office. These were installed by artists from Tiffany and Company, New York, and are reputed to be the first art assignment Tiffany undertook in the "Wild West.")

JESSE JAMES HOME, southeast of city on U.S. 59-71. On

April 3, 1882, the thirty-second anniversary of the Pony Express' first run, Jesse James was assassinated here. The James boys began their deadly careers in the Missouri-Kansas Civil War, went on to serve as Quantrill's favorite gunmen through 1865. Jesse James's death marked the close of Missouri's frontier years.

NEBRASKA CITY, NEBRASKA

J. STERLING MORTON STATE PARK contains relics from the days when Morton—long before he thought up Arbor Day—worked with his neighbors Alexander Majors and Reverend John Chivington to build Nebraska City into a river metropolis that would rival St. Joe and Omaha.

HOLLENBERG, KANSAS

ORIGINAL PONY EXPRESS STATION. Take Highway 15E from Highway 36 at Marysville, or Highway 6 from Hastings, Nebraska.

HASTINGS, NEBRASKA

HOUSE OF YESTERDAY MUSEUM

MINDEN, NEBRASKA

HAROLD WARP PIONEER VILLAGE

GOTHENBURG, NEBRASKA

PONY EXPRESS STATION, with museum, U.S. 30. This was formerly Midway Station on the Upper 96 Ranch. (Another station still stands on the Lower 96 Ranch, but is not easily accessible.)

NORTH PLATTE, NEBRASKA

BUFFALO BILL MUSEUM was still being run in 1959 by Major Boal, grandson of Colonel Cody.

JULESBURG, COLORADO

Bronze plaque reads:

> TO THE BRAVE MEN WHO
> RODE THE
> PONY EXPRESS 1860-1861

DENVER, COLORADO

STATE CAPITOL DOME contains portrait windows of Alexander Majors and Bela M. Hughes.

STATE MUSEUM has the flag of Gilpin's "Pet Lambs" a bronze bust of Bela M. Hughes and a life-size portrait of

Buffalo Bill. On display in the library is a Pony Express Bible carried by Jay G. Kelley. (During 1960 there will be a special Pony Express exhibition on the main floor.)

MAIN POST OFFICE, 18th and Stout streets. Carved high on the stone walls of the main lobby are the names of ten Pony Express riders: Rand, Cody, Kelley, Keetley, Beatley, Haslam, James, Rising, Boulton, and Baughn.

CROWN HILL CEMETERY, West 29th and Wadsworth avenues. Has the grave of Joseph Donovan, Pony Express rider.

SITE OF CAMP WELD, West 8th Avenue and Vallejo Street. Right of the west end of the viaduct is a granite marker with a plaque reading:

> This is the Southwest corner of Camp Weld, established September 1861 for Civil War Volunteers. Named for Lewis L. Weld, first secretary of Colorado Territory. Troops leaving here Feb. 22, 1862, won victory over Confederate forces at La Glorieta, New Mexico, saved the Southwest for the Union. Headquarters against Indians 1864-65. Camp abandoned 1865.

PUBLIC LIBRARY, Broadway and 14th Avenue. The Western History Department has a large collection of photographs, programs, etc., of Buffalo Bill's Wild West Show.

LOOKOUT MOUNTAIN, COLORADO

BUFFALO BILL MUSEUM, twelve miles west of Denver on U.S. 6. Here are graves of William F. "Buffalo Bill" Cody and Louisa F. Cody.

CHEYENNE, WYOMING

LAKEVIEW CEMETERY. The grave of James Moore, Pony Express rider, who died in 1873, is here.

CASPER, WYOMING

A monument in the center of town, near the site of Old Platte Bridge, reads:

> SITE OF
> OLD PLATTE BRIDGE
> BUILT BY
> LOUIS GUINARD
> 1858-59
>
> Immediately South and
> West Are the Sites of
> Platte Bridge Station.
> First Overland Telegraph,

Stage, and Pony Express
Stations on The Old Oregon
Trail

FORT LARAMIE, WYOMING

FORT LARAMIE NATIONAL MONUMENT contains the Old Sutler's Store, where Pony Express riders delivered mail.

CODY, WYOMING

CODY was named for William F. Cody. Irma Hotel was named for his daughter. There is a huge bronze equestrian statue of Buffalo Bill scouting trail.

BUFFALO BILL MUSEUM is designed like Cody's old TE ranch house near Meeteetse, Wyoming. In the museum are many Cody relics, and a large oil painting by Robert Lindneux of the Cody-Yellow Hand Duel. The old Cody home near Leclaire, Iowa, was moved here several years ago.

PAHASKA TEPEE, once Cody's hunting lodge, is on Yellowstone Park Road, near Sylvan Pass.

FORT BRIDGER, WYOMING

FORT BRIDGER STATE PARK. Here still stands the old Pony Express stable.

SALT LAKE CITY, UTAH

PIONEER VILLAGE, Highway 65 or 40. This completely restored village includes a Pony Express station.

FAIRFIELD, UTAH

CAMP FLOYD, the second largest community in Utah, with seven thousand soldiers and civilians, bristled here after 1858. Fairfield, in 1960, had only one hundred or so inhabitants, with no reminders of former glory except a Pony Express monument and a fenced-in cemetery where a single stone honors the seventy members of Johnston's army buried there. The surface of the cemetery is flat; not a single grave can be discerned. The plot has grown up to thistles. No names are given. They are truly forgotten men.

Nearby is an old pit where Mormons dug the clay and made the 'dobes that built the barracks for the Army of Utah, which gave work to hundreds of the thrifty, industrious churchmen they had crossed the Rockies to conquer. When the Army post was abandoned, the Mormons profited still more. Goods worth about five million dollars are said to have been sold to the Mormons for around one hundred thousand dollars. Some of the wealthiest people in Utah founded their fortunes on Camp Floyd's bargain sales.

Nor were the Mormons the only beneficiaries. Alex Toponce, a stableman at the camp, told about a sale of mules. There were about one hundred little scrub mules, and a lot of big, valuable ones. The wagon boss gave Alex some matched tags and told him to put them on the headstalls of the little mules, which were then brought out to be auctioned off at from thirty to forty dollars a span. The chief buyer was Ben Holladay.

Toponce noticed that after the sale, the tags of the little mules were removed and fastened on big mules. But only the little mules were auctioned. Deciding to get in on a good thing himself, Alex bid on twelve of the little mules. When they were turned back into the corral, nobody changed his tags to the big mules. So he went in and changed them himself, to the best riding mules he could find. "Nobody made any objection," he said years later. "They did not dare to. I knew too much."

OLD FORT CHURCHILL, NEVADA
RUINS AND MUSEUM

CARSON CITY, NEVADA
STATE MUSEUM

SACRAMENTO, CALIFORNIA
SUTTER'S FORT

SAN FRANCISCO, CALIFORNIA
WELLS FARGO MUSEUM, Wells Fargo Bank & Union Trust Company, Market and Grant Streets. An excitingly authentic array of Pony Express, Wells Fargo and "Old West" Americana.

20.
THE RECORDERS

BOOKS

BAKER, JAMES H., and HAFEN, LEROY R. *History of Colorado*, Vols. I and II. Denver: Linderman Co., Inc., 1927.

BANCROFT, HUBERT HOWE. *History of Nevada, Colorado and Wyoming*. San Francisco, 1890.

BILLINGS, FREDERICK. *Letters from Mexico, 1859*. Woodstock, Vt.: The Elm Tree Press, 1936.

BOND, ISABELLA BACON. *The Memoirs of Isabella Bacon Bond*. Edited by Mrs. Edith Bond Stearns. Boston: Privately printed, 1934.

BRADLEY, GLENN D. *The Story of the Pony Express*. Chicago: A. C. McClurg & Co., 1913.

BROWNLEE, RICHARD S. *Gray Ghosts of the Confederacy*. Baton Rouge: Louisiana State Press, 1958.

BURTON, SIR RICHARD F. *The City of the Saints*. New York: Harper & Brothers, 1862.

CHAPMAN, ARTHUR. *The Pony Express*. New York: J. P. Putnam's Sons, 1932

DRIGGS, HOWARD R. *The Pony Express Goes Through*. New York: Frederick A. Stokes Company, 1935.

FREDERICK, J. V. *Ben Holladay, the Stagecoach King*. Glendale, Calif.: The Arthur H. Clark Company, 1940.

HAFEN, LEROY R. *The Overland Mail, 1849–1869*. Cleveland: The Arthur H. Clark Company, 1926.

HEITMAN, FRANCIS B. *Historical Register and Dictionary of the United States Army*, Vol. I. Washington: Government Printing Office, 1903.

HUNGERFORD, EDWARD. *Wells Fargo*. New York: Random House 1949.

INMAN, HENRY. *The Great Salt Lake Trail*. Topeka, Kansas: Crane & Co., 1914

KNAPP, EDWARD S. *Pony Express* (A description of Pony Express stamps and covers). New York: Scott Stamp & Coin Company, 1936.

MABEY, CHARLES RENDELL. *The Pony Express*. Salt Lake City: The Beverly Craftsmen, 1940.

MAJORS, ALEXANDER. *Seventy Years on the Frontier*. Columbus, Ohio: Long's College Book Company, 1950.

MONAGHAN, JAY. *Civil War on the Western Border, 1854–1865*. Boston: Little, Brown & Co., 1955.

———. *Swamp Fox of the Confederacy*. ("Confederate Centennial Series.") Tuscaloosa, Ala.: Confederate Publishing Co., 1956.

MOODY, RALPH. *Riders of the Pony Express*. Boston: Houghton Mifflin Co., 1958.

MORGAN, GENE. *"Westward the Course of Empire . . ."* Chicago: The Lakeside Press, 1945.

PERKIN, ROBERT L. *The First Hundred Years; An Informal History of Denver and the Rocky Mountain News*. New York: Doubleday and Company, 1959.

RICHARDSON, ALBERT D. *Beyond the Mississippi*. Hartford, Conn.: American Publishing Company; New York: Bliss & Company, 1867.

ROOT, FRANK ALBERT, and CONNELLEY, WILLIAM E. *The Overland Stage to California*. Topeka, Kansas: Crane & Co., 1901.

SETTLE, RAYMOND W., and SETTLE, MARY LUND. *Empire on Wheels*. Stanford, Calif.: Stanford University Press, 1949.
——. *Saddles and Spurs*. Harrisburg, Pa.: Stackpole Co., 1955.
SMILEY, JEROME C. *History of Denver*. Denver: Denver Times, 1901.
SMITH, HENRY NASH. *Virgin Lands: The American West as Symbol and Myth*. Cambridge, Mass.: Harvard University Press, 1950.
SPRING, AGNES WRIGHT. *Caspar Collins*. New York: Columbia University Press, 1927.
VISSCHER, WILLIAM LIGHTFOOT. *A Thrilling and Truthful History of the Pony Express; or, Blazing the Westward Way*. Chicago: The G. T. Powner Co., 1946.
WHITFORD, WILLIAM CLARKE. *Colorado Volunteers in the Civil War; The New Mexico Campaign in 1862*. Denver: The State Historical and Natural History Society, 1906.
WILKINS, JAMES H. (ed.) *The Great Diamond Hoax and Other Stirring Incidents in the Life of Asbury Harpending*. Norman: University of Oklahoma Press, 1958.

MAGAZINES, PAMPHLETS, UNPUBLISHED MANUSCRIPTS

BARKER, EMERSON N. "Early Colorado Mails." Denver, undated.
BODER, BARTLETT. Numerous carefully researched articles on the Pony Express and its personnel in issues of *Museum Graphic*, St. Joseph Museum, II–XI (1950–60).
FISHER, DR. RAY H. "The Pony Express," *Improvement Era* (February, 1949).
PACK, MARY. "The Romance of the Pony Express," *Union Pacific Magazine* (August, 1923).
REMSBURG, GEORGE J. "Pony Express Riders I Have Known," *Pony Express* (Placerville, Calif., 1934–36.)
ROOT, GEORGE A., and HICKMAN, R. K. "Pike's Peak Express Companies," *Kansas Historical Collections* (Topeka), XIII, XIV.
SANFORD, A. B. "The Story of Bob Spottswood." Unpublished manuscript, State Historical Society of Colorado Library.
SANGOIOVANIN, CLEVE, KING, CAMPBELL, etc. Numerous unpublished memoirs of Pony Express riders, collected for periodic publication in *Museum Graphic* by St. Joseph Museum during the 1920's.
SETTLE, RAYMOND W. "The Pony Express: Heroic Effort—Tragic End," *Historical Society Quarterly* (Salt Lake City), XXVII (April, 1959).
SMITH, XENOPHON. Letter to Agnes W. Spring from Librarian, United States Post Office Department, Washington, D.C., October 16, 1959.

THOMAS, CHAUNCEY. "Buffalo Bill's Grave," *Outdoor Life* (New York, January, 1922).
UNITED STATES DEPARTMENT OF THE INTERIOR. "Fort Laramie National Monument," *Guide Series, USGPO* (1942).

NEWSPAPERS

Chicago Record-Herald. Obituary of Robert H. "Pony Bob" Haslam (March 2, 1912).
Christian Science Monitor. The Pony Express Centennial (October 21, 1959).
Dawson Scrapbook. Newspaper clippings. State Historical Society of Colorado Library (Denver), XIV.
Denver Republican. The Pony Express Riders (August 19, 1894).
Kansas City Star (Mo.). Obituary of Alexander Majors (January 15, 1900).
New York Herald. Colonel William F. Cody Tribute to Alexander Majors (January 20, 1900).
Rocky Mountain News. Numerous references in 1859–61 files.
Sacramento Union (Calif.). Numerous references in 1860–61 files, beginning April 2, 1860.
Summit County Journal (Colo.). Pony Express (June 9, 1923).

APPENDIX

Records indicate that a total of 400 men and boys "rode The Pony" during its 18 epochal months. But a complete roster of these riders has never been assembled. Perhaps it never can be. Here is a listing of the names we now know to have been Riders for The Pony Express . . . some for only a day or two; the majority for only a few weeks or months. A.W.S.

ALCOTT, JACK
AVIS, HENRY

BALL, L. W.
BARNETT, JAMES
BAUGHN, JAMES
BAUGHN, MELVILLE (MEL)
BEATLEY, JAMES (JIM)
BECKER, CHARLES
BLACK, THOMAS
"BLACK TOM"
"BOSTON," JIM
BOULTON, WILLIAM
BRANDENBURGER, JOHN
BRINK, JAMES W. (DOC)
BROWN, HUGH
BUCKTON, JIMMY
BUCKLIN, JAMES (JIMMY)
BURNETT, JOHN
BUSH, ED

CAMPBELL, WILLIAM
CARLYLE, ALEXANDER
CARR, WILLIAM (BILL)
CARRIGAN, WILLIAM
CATES, WILLIAM A. (BILL)
CLARK, JAMES (JIMMY)
CLERK, JIM
CLEVE, RICHARD
CLIFF, CHARLEY
CLIFF, GUSTAVAS (GUS)
CODY, WILLIAM F. (BUFFALO BILL)
CUMBO, JAMES (SAW-OFF-JIM)

DANLEY, JAMES
DEAN, LOUIS
DENNIS, WILLIAM (BILL)
DERRICK, FRANK W.
DOBSON, THOMAS
DONOVAN, JOSEPH (JOE)
DORRINGTON, W. E.
DOWNS, CALVIN
DUNLAP, JAMES E.

EGAN, HOWARD R.
EGAN, RICHARD R. (RAS)
ELLIOTT, THOMAS J.
ELLIS, J. K.

FAUST, H. J.
FISHER, JOHN
FISHER, WILLIAM (BILLY)
FLYNN, THOMAS
FREY, JOHNNY (or FRYE)

GARDNER, GEORGE
GENTRY, JAMES (JIM)
GILSON, JAMES (JIM)
GILSON, SAMUEL (SAM)
GLEASON, JAMES
GOULD, FRANK

HASLAM, ROBERT (PONY BOB)
HAMILTON, SAMUEL (SAM)
HAMILTON, WILLIAM
HARDER, GEORGE
HAWKINS, THEODORE (THEE)
HELVEY, FRANK

HENSEL, LEVI
HIGGINBOTHAM, CHARLES
HOGAN, MARTIN
HUNTINGTON, LESTER (LET)

"IRISH JIM"

JAMES, WILLIAM (BILL)
JAY, DAVID R.
JENKINS, WILLIAM D. (WILL)
JOBE, SAMUEL S. (SAM)
JONES, WILLIAM

KEETLEY, J. H. (JACK)
KELLY, HI
KELLY, MIKE
KELLEY, JAY G.
KING, THOMAS O.
KOERNER, JOHN PHILLIP

LAWSON, WILLIAM
LITTLE, GEORGE EDWIN
"LITTLE YANK"
LITTLETON, "TOUGH"

MACANLAS, SYE (MACAULAS)
MARTIN, ROBERT (BOB)
MAXFIELD, ELIJAH H.
MCCAIN, EMMETT
MCCALL, J. G.
MCCALL, PAT
MCDONALD, JAMES (JIM)
MCEARNEY, PAT (PAT MCENEAMNY)
MCNAUGHTON, JAMES (JIM)
MCNAUGHTON, WILLIAM (BILL)
MAZE, MONTGOMERY
MILLER, CHARLES B. (BRONCHO CHARLEY)
MOORE, JAMES (JIM)
MURPHY, JEREMIAH H.

PAGE, WILLIAM
PARSHALL, ZACHARY TAYLOR
PERKINS, JOSH
PRIDHAM, WILLIAM (BILL)

RANAHAN, THOMAS ("IRISH TOM")
RAND, THEODORE (YANK)
RANDALL, JAMES
REYNOLDS, THOMAS J.
RICHARDSON, JOHNSON WILLIAM
RILES, BART
RISING, DONALD C. (DON)
ROFF, HARRY L.
RUSH, EDWARD

SANGIOVANNI, G. G.
SEERBECK, JOHN
SERISH, JOSEPH
SHARP, JAMES TAYLOR
SINCLAIR, JOHN
SLADE, JACK JOSEPH
SPURR, GEORGE
STREEPER, WILLIAM H. (BILLY)
STRICKLAND, ROBERT C.
STROHM, WILLIAM
SUGGET, JOHN W.

THATCHER, GEORGE
THOMPSON, CHARLES
THOMPSON, JAMES M.
TOPENCE, ALEXANDER
TOUGH, W. S.
TOWNE, GEORGE
TUCKETT, HENRY

UPSON, WARREN

VAN BLARISON, WILLIAM E.

WALLACE, HENRY
WESCOTT, DANIEL (DAN) GEORGE-DAN
WHELAN, MICHAEL M.
"WHIPSAW"
WIGGINS, O. P. (?)
WILLIS, H. C.
WILSON, ELIJAH N.
WILSON, NICHOLAS (NICK)
WINTLE, JOSEPH E.
WORLEY, HENRY
WRIGHT, MOSE

ZOWGALTZ, JOSE

NEW WESTERNS FROM BALLANTINE BOOKS

THE LANDSEEKERS, Fred Grove	$.95
COMANCHE CAPTIVES, Fred Grove	$.95
NO BUGLES, NO GLORY, Fred Grove	$.95
THE HIGRADERS, John Hunter	$.95
DEATH IN THE MOUNTAIN, John Hunter	$.95
MANHUNTERS, Elmer Kelton	$.95
AFTER THE BUGLES, Elmer Kelton	$.95
GREENHORN MARSHAL, Lee Leighton	$.95
HOMBRE, Elmore Leonard	$.95
COLORADO GOLD, Chad Merriman & Lee Leighton	$.95
APACHE GOLD AND YAQUI SILVER, J. Frank Dobie	$1.25
THE WHEEL AND THE HEARTH, Lucia Moore	$1.25

To order by mail send price per book(s) plus 25¢ per order for handling to Ballantine Cash Sales, P.O. Box 505, Westminster, Maryland 21157. Please allow three weeks for delivery.